Shattered Jewels
Tales of Wonder and Terror

Brian S. Converse

All Stories Copyright 2025 by Brian S. Converse

This is a work of fiction. All characters in this publication
are fictitious and any resemblance to real persons, living
or dead, is purely coincidental.

ISBN: 978-1-7339334-7-6

For LAZDE
Always

Thank you to King, Koontz, McCammon, Straub, Jackson, Lee, Barker, Rice and so many others for their inspiration.

Stories

Zerkers

"Hey, it's Matt. Matt Wilson from Castle Rock, Colorado. I know I'm the age when I should be getting into trouble with my friends at the mall or scoping out girls at the movie theater or sitting in my basement playing video games until all hours of the night. Instead, I'm holding a shotgun while sitting in the bed of a broken-down F-150 and hoping that nothing happens while I'm on guard duty."

"I ask myself often, how did this happen? One minute I'm flunking Mr. Finkle's tenth grade biology class, and the next, the president is calling a national emergency and imposing martial law. The rest of the world wasn't doing much better back then, from what I've heard, and it wasn't too long after that when the power went out for good. At least school was canceled."

"It was something that affected both the living and the dead. Corpses began walking around, doing the 'eat your brains' shuffle and being a general nuisance. I call them 'ramblers' because they don't seem to know where they're going or how to get there. The ramblers are easy enough to avoid on their own, and easy enough to kill for those with weapons, such as my afore-mentioned shotgun. We learned early to always go for the head."

"It's the people who were bitten while still alive and then turned who are the real problem. They get real sick, and real hungry, and suddenly they're running around biting others. I call them berserkers, or zerkers for short. My mom, dad, and sister all became zerkers. I don't know if they're dead now or still running around eating people and making more zerkers."

"When I had the chance, I packed as much stable food and supplies as I could into my backpack and headed south to Colorado Springs. The city was a real mess, so I headed west into the mountains, though thankfully I didn't get far before I found other people. Now when I'm on guard duty, I spend most of my time sitting in this improvised crow's nest talking on this short-wave radio. The others said it would be easier for survivors to find us if someone was talking on the radio all the time—just in case they were flipping through the channels and hearing me. And I never saw Mr. Finkle again, so I don't know if I did flunk biology class, but I hope he's safe out there somewhere, and maybe someday he'll hear me talking on the radio, too."

"To be honest, though, I think I've run out of words for the night, so I'm going to sign off now. If you're out there, be smart. Be safe. Head west. We'll be here in Woodland Park, Colorado. I'm on channel 6."

I.

The young man sat in the bed of a truck that at some point had been hoisted into the top of a large oak tree—whether to be used as a makeshift tree house or in response to the zombie apocalypse, Matt didn't know for sure. He thought some well-meaning father who was too lazy to build an actual tree house had put it up there for his kids, because there were still mementos of an easier time in the truck bed—part of plastic tea pot, a Lego piece, a gum wrapper. It was sad to think what may have happened to the kids who left them behind.

After a few minutes, he slowly stood, collapsed the telescoping antenna on the small long-range radio transmitter and attached it to his belt, then looked below to see his friend Jay the Rapper walking towards the tree for his guard duty shift. His real name was Jason Abramovich, but his stage name was what he wanted to be called, so Matt obliged. They all had coping mechanisms, and who was Matt to say which ones worked better than others? Besides, Jay seemed talented enough in a "Dollar Store Beastie Boy" sort of way to merit the name.

Matt's first response to the apocalyptic events had been to close off from others. He'd witnessed the deaths of his family, for all practical purposes. It was months before he spoke after walking to the town of Woodland Park and finding a small group of other survivors. Over time that group had grown to almost thirty people—all of them with stories of their own. Tragedies and triumphs, as Matt called them. Some were lucky to be alive. Some, like Matt and Jay, had lost everyone they knew and loved.

One of the people that had helped him come out of his shell was Jay, and Matt was grateful to have him as a friend, even if he didn't care much for hip hop. "Didn't see anything, and didn't get any replies back on the radio, either," he said when he got to the bottom of the rope ladder and handed the rifle over to Jay. Jay strapped it over his back, then took the handheld radio from Matt.

"Going to try some new rhymes tonight," Jay said, smiling.

Matt rolled his eyes. "We're supposed to be encouraging people to come, not scaring them away."

"Ha ha," Jay said, but then laughed. "Be careful, Sheila's on another rampage."

"Great," Matt said and sighed. "Night, bro."

"Night, man."

◊

The next morning dawned bright and cold. Summer was turning into autumn, and in the Rockies, that could mean snow at any time, especially at eighty-five hundred feet above sea level.

Matt woke up hungry, as usual. He had gone to bed hungry as well. He was a seventeen-year-old and could never get enough to eat in the best of times, but now, he was lucky to eat two meals in the same day. Currently he was living in a small ranch-style house with Jay and a man and woman from Manitou Springs who were together, but Matt didn't think they were married or had even known each other just a few months before.

It was like that—people coming together, even though most had lost at least one loved one. It was a community of sorrow, held together by pain and loss, if nothing else.

But they were surviving.

After he got dressed in the same clothes he had worn the day before, he left the bedroom he shared with Jay. They had bunk beds, which he presumed belonged to the kids with the lazy father. He relieved himself in the bathroom and then went out to the kitchen and found David. David's skin was the same color as his coffee, Matt noticed. Sheila, (who was ghostly white on the best of days), was probably still in bed.

"Morning," David said, sipping his coffee—light on the cream, no sugar.

"Morning," Matt replied. He didn't like coffee, no matter how much sugar or milk he added, so he got a glass out of the cupboard and poured carefully from a large plastic jug of water that sat on the floor next to the fridge. He checked another cupboard and found there were a few Sugar Flakes left, so he ate straight from the box, knowing there was no milk to pour over them.

"We need to take a trip to the store to replenish some of our supplies," David said, nodding towards the box of sweetened cereal. "Later on today, depending on what Derick thinks." Derick was living in a house two doors down from them. He was the de facto leader of their group, mostly because no one else wanted to be, and he was a type A asshole who liked to order people around.

Matt liked David, though. The man had been the owner of an art gallery before, and he was friendly and down to earth and smart. He even knew how to play the piano, which he did sometimes on the electronic keyboard they had found in the kids' room, as long as they kept the volume turned down.

Which was why it was such a mystery to Matt and Jay both that David had hooked up with a bitch like Sheila. She acted like they were guests in her house, when in actuality, Jay had been there first before the two of them had straggled into town—cold, hungry, and in Sheila's case, half hysterical. Derick had told them that there was room in Jay's place. Shortly after, Matt arrived in town and had been told to stay there as well.

Matt had thought of moving to a different house along the street, but he felt bad about leaving Jay there with her. He assumed that Jay felt the same, because he complained about Sheila as well. But who knew what Derick would say if they asked him if they could move—when he was just as likely to turn them down.

"Who finished off the Sugar Flakes?" Sheila's voice brought Matt back to reality. Uh oh. He turned and raised his hand like he was in class again. "There weren't that many left."

"Dammit, Matty," Sheila said. He hated the nickname she had picked for him. "You need to at least throw the bag away and break down the box when you eat it all."

"I'm sure the garbage man will appreciate it," Matt said.

"I'm sure he will, smartass," she said. "Take care of it. Now."

Matt sighed. "Fine."

"And you might as well take out all of the trash while you're at it."

"Be sure to take your gun if you're going out to the garbage drop," David said, not looking up from the book he was reading. It was something on French art, and Matt looked forward to David explaining it to him later. He liked it when David would change into teacher mode and explain things like that to him and Jay. His voice was calm and soothing—just the opposite of Sheila's.

"I will," Matt said. He pulled the plastic bag out of the cereal box and scrunched it up before throwing it in the can next to the sink, which was almost full. He left them and went back into his bedroom to pick up the black handgun that sat on the table next to his bed. It had been his dad's and was the only thing he had left from that former life. He popped out the magazine and checked the number of rounds. Four left. He'd have to look for more when he went to the store later with David. The problem with having a handgun that used a popular size ammunition was that now it was difficult to find because most stores had already been looted.

He made sure the safety was on before putting the gun in his jeans pocket—no need to chance things—he might need his junk if they wanted to repopulate the planet sometime in the near future.

He stepped out the front door of the house, a white garbage bag slung over his shoulder, and began walking to the dumping area, which was a large culvert two streets over from their house. There wasn't anyone living in the houses over there, as far as he knew, or if there were, they were too scared to show themselves.

The day had started cool but it was warming up quickly. The sun at that altitude beat down unmercifully, and Matt knew if he wasn't careful, he'd be sporting a nice sunburn if he stayed outside for too long without sunscreen. But for now, it was pleasant to just walk in the sunshine and listen to the birds.

It wasn't long before he arrived at the culvert, which already had a small mountain of garbage bags lying in it. He could have just dropped the bag from his shoulder and watched as it lazily rolled to rest next to the pile, but he was still angry at Sheila, so did not think clearly. He grabbed the plastic strings at the top and turned around quickly, whipping the bags around like some old Greek Olympian and after three twirls, let the bag loose and watched it sail out over the pile.

He smiled, watching it fly, then the bag hit the top of the pile and made a loud crashing sound and the smile disappeared. Too loud. "Damn," he said quietly. He quickly looked around but couldn't see anything moving. Then he heard a rustling from the trash below. He quickly pulled his gun out and pointed towards the culvert. Suddenly a large, black shape came roaring from around the other side of the pile. Except it wasn't a zerker.

The word "bear!" echoed in his head as Matt turned and ran, unable to think of the proper thing to do when confronted by an angry black bear in the wild. He ran for the nearest house and jumped up the cement steps to the front door. "Shit, shit, shit," he said breathlessly as he fumbled at the handle. Locked.

He turned and saw that the bear was still coming. He looked around and wondered if he should try to run for the next house over when suddenly the door opened and a strong hand pulled him through the doorway, closing the door behind him.

Matt lost his balance and fell to the floor, painfully mashing his fingers under the gun as he put his hands out to catch himself. He cursed again and pulled his hand back and shook it, then looked up to see a large gun barrel pointed directly at his face. He froze. "Uh," was all he could think of to say.

"Leave the gun where it is," a deep, growly voice said. He looked over the top of the gun barrel into an intense man's face.

"Yeah, no problem," he said.

"Who are you?"

"I'm Matt," he replied. "I live a couple of streets over."

"Matt Wilson?" a much higher voice said from behind him. He turned to look. He caught a brief glimpse of long brown hair, an oval face, and large brown eyes.

"Look at me, not her," the gruff voice said. "I'm the one holding the gun."

"You have a good point," Matt said, turning back.

"Dad, he's not a robber," the female voice said.

"No, no, not a robber," Matt said quickly, forcing a smile.

"No, he's just the idiot that made enough noise to wake the entire neighborhood. I saw you throw that bag."

"Impressive height," the female voice said.

"Nora," the man said. "Go check on Henry."

"Dad..."

"Go. Now."

Matt heard her sigh and then her footsteps as she walked away. "Can I lower my arms?"

The man waited a moment, then backed up. "Fine. Slowly."

Matt lowered his arms and took a better look at the man. He appeared to be around his mid-forties, with a thinning hairline and grey showing in his dark beard. "I am sorry. I didn't mean to disturb you, but you know, bear."

"You can't dump that much trash and think it won't attract bears up here," the man said. He lowered the pistol, which must have been a .45 or something—Matt wasn't much into guns, but the barrel on the man's gun was considerably larger than the one on his own.

He slowly stood and found himself to be about the same height as the man. "How did your daughter know my name?"

"Because we've been hearing you talk just about every day on our way here," a new voice said behind him. He began to turn, then thought better of it and looked at the man. He nodded, and Matt slowly turned to see the girl and a younger boy, who looked about ten and shared his sister's features and coloring.

"You heard my radio commentary?" Matt said, feeling excitement—he wasn't sure if anyone had ever heard him.

"Yes," the man said. "We arrived here last night. Came from down south in Pueblo."

"You're different than your voice sounds," the boy said. "You look like a scarecrow."

"Henry!" the girl said, a look of shock on her face.

"Well, food is pretty scarce around here, I guess," Matt said, looking down at himself. He was getting awfully skinny, he decided.

"Sorry about him," the girl said. "He was born with no class and hasn't improved."

"Nora, don't talk bad about your brother like that," the man said.

Without missing a beat, she continued talking. "By the way, this is my dad, Todd. He's a bit severe at times, but he means well."

"Mr. Cooper," the man said, looking at Matt to make sure he got the point.

"Mr. Cooper," Matt said. "Nora. Henry. Welcome to..." THUMP!

The front door shook as something hit it from the other side. Matt walked over to the window next to the door and looked out, not thinking about how Mr. Cooper would take his sudden movement.

The bear was being attacked by two zerkers. It was putting up a brave fight, biting and clawing large chunks out of his attackers, but it was clear that he was losing. The zerkers, both men dressed in garbage company overalls, were also biting at the bear and tearing at it with clawed hands, and it was slowing down with the loss of blood. "Holy sh..." he began to say before catching himself. He looked over his shoulder at the other three. He had a queasy feeling in his stomach and a bad taste in his mouth. "You're not going to believe this."

"I want to see!" Nora said excitedly.

"No, no you don't," Matt said, looking over at Mr. Cooper.

"Nora, don't," Todd said before walking over himself and looking out the window. "Well shit."

Matt almost began to giggle, but stopped himself just in time, not knowing how they would take it. He looked out the window again. "Hey guys, the box is broken down for you," he said, and this time, he did giggle, though it sounded more like he was about to cry.

◊

The zerkers had left once they'd gotten their fill from the bear, leaving a half-devoured carcass on the front porch of the house. When Matt thought it was safe to come out, he slowly opened the front door, looking around as he did just in case the zerkers were nearby. He motioned Nora to follow, and she did the same to Henry, with their father bringing up the rear.

"Just follow me and I'll get you over to a safer part of the neighborhood," he said to her. She nodded. "Hold on a minute," he said. He stood over the bear's body a moment. He wished he had a knife on him so that he could stab the bear through its skull and make sure it would stay dead. No need to take chances. But he didn't, so he made a mental note to check back again after their trip to the store.

Matt left his pistol in his pocket but kept his hand on the grip. "Okay, follow me," he said to them. He noticed that Henry was still looking down at the bear. "Don't worry, Henry. Its dead."

They walked through the empty streets, past the wreck of two cars who couldn't get out of each other's way, and finally arrived on Matt's street without sight of any zerkers or ramblers. He would have to report the garbage men to Derick.

"That's where I live," Matt said, breaking the silence. The tree house is where we broadcast from, as well as serving as a lookout post when we're on guard duty."

Nora nodded and smiled. Henry was looking around as if he'd expected more, while Mr. Cooper looked like he was appraising the property for a loan.

"I'll take you to meet Derick," Matt said. "He's kind of the leader here."

"I would appreciate that," Mr. Cooper said.

Matt walked past the house next to his and then up the

walkway to the next house. He knocked softly on the front door. It opened and Matt saw Derick standing there, shirtless and chewing something. He swallowed before speaking. "Well?"

"Found some new people," Matt said, turning to show them.

Derick looked past him at the new arrivals. "Welcome to Woodland Park."

"Thank you," Todd said. "I'm Todd. This is my daughter, Nora, and my son Henry."

"Just the three of you?"

"Yes."

"We have people in about eight houses along this street," Derick said, pointing down the street to his right. We figure it's safer to be close together. I think Matt knows the ones that are empty. Usually if people come in, it's in one and twos and we just put them in a house that has room, but since you're a family, I'll assume that you want to have your own."

"I would appreciate it, yes," Todd said, looking over at Matt.

"Derick, there's something else," Matt said. "Ran into two zerkers while I was at the dump."

"How many times have I told you to stop using those stupid names?" Derick said. Matt grinned and shrugged.

"Did you kill them?" Derick continued.

"Didn't have the chance," Matt responded.

"They ate a bear!" Henry said.

"What?" Derick asked looking confused.

"There was a bear in the dump, and it chased me," Matt said, hoping it didn't sound as stupid as it felt. "I ran to a house, and it just happened that the Coopers were in there. The zerk...I mean, the zombies attacked the bear right on the front porch."

Derick looked perplexed for a moment. "Well, we'll talk about it at the meeting tonight." He looked at Todd. "We're having a community meeting tonight. You're welcome to come."

"Thank you, I will," said Todd.

"Until then," Derick continued, "like I said, Matt knows where the empty houses are. We've cleared them all and closed the doors so there aren't any nasty surprises when you go in. We'll see you all tonight."

"Thank you," Todd said. Derick nodded and then closed the door.

Todd turned to Matt. "I noticed you left the part out where you aggravated the bear."

"Didn't seem important," Matt said sheepishly.

"So which houses are empty?" Nora asked, changing the subject. Matt was grateful.

"Let's see," Matt said, rubbing his chin as he thought and feeling the stubble there. Sheila would ask him to shave soon. "There's the one on the other side of my house. There's that gray one over across the street. That one that's two houses down from Derick is empty, I think. I wouldn't go too far beyond that. Those two over there across the street are empty, but the one had a fire and is a mess inside. The other one is a mess for another reason." He looked at Henry, unsure of how much he should say.

"We understand," Todd said.

"I like the one next to Matt's," Nora said. "It's pretty."

"I like the gray one," Todd said, pointing to the one across the street from Derick's. "Can you show it to us?"

"Oh, sure," Matt replied, noticing the scowl on Nora's face. She looked at him and he smiled and shrugged.

They walked over to the house, which was a one-story Cape Cod style. "I haven't been in all of these yet," Matt said while opening the front door. He was relieved that there weren't any strange smells emanating from inside. He'd walked into the house two houses down and had immediately smelled death. It had taken all of his courage to walk in and see that the occupants of the home had decided that eating a bullet was better than the alternative. He hadn't returned.

"How many people total live around here?" Nora asked him.

"Probably near twenty-five or thirty or so, not counting you."

"I wouldn't count us," Todd said. "We're hoping to head up closer to Denver to see if there's anything left up there."

"I'm not sure that's a good idea," Matt said.

"Why?"

"You may have heard that I came from Castle Rock," Matt said. "The reason I came south was that I heard what had happened in Denver. Let's just say that it's not there anymore."

"What does that mean?"

"I mean the government spent a lot of money destroying it because it was one of the epicenters of all this, and it didn't work. I heard its crawling with zombies and most of the buildings are leveled."

"It's gone?" Nora asked. She looked like she was going to cry.

"I'm afraid so," Matt said. "Sorry. But don't take my word for it," he added, seeing the skeptical look from Todd. "You can ask around. You're not the first person who has wanted to go to Denver, or come from there."

"I will," Todd said, sounding defiant. Matthew didn't blame him, but he'd learn. Matt had no reason to lie. He stepped back so that they could enter the house.

"Thank you," Todd said, walking past him.

"Yes, thank you for everything," Nora said, smiling at him. He guessed that she hadn't seen many people her own age in a while, which is why she was being extra nice to him. Or maybe that was just the way she was, which would be surprising, given how everyone seemed to be caught in some type of depressive state over what had happened to them. He smiled back and nodded, then nodded again at Henry, who didn't say a word. He was too busy looking at the inside of the house.

"If you don't need me for anything else, I'll leave you to get settled in," he said. He saw Todd give him a half-hearted wave and took that for a dismissal. He closed the door silently and began walking away. He had the distinct feeling that Todd didn't like him, so he was happy to get away.

◊

Matt walked into his house just in time to see David strapping on his pistol belt. The man looked up at him and smiled. "Getting ready to go to the store. Derick wants you and Jay to come along. Make sure your gun is loaded." Matt had asked before where he'd found a pistol and gun belt to go along with it, but David had shrugged and mentioned picking things up along the way.

"Okay," Matt said. "Can I have a snack first?" There usually wasn't enough food to have a full lunch, but he knew he needed something to tide him over until dinner.

"Sure, but you'll have to eat on the way. I'm staying here to guard the houses while you're all gone."

Matt nodded, then searched for something. There wasn't much left. He finally settled on a granola bar that must have been old even before the disaster, based on how hard it was. Matt checked his gun to make sure it still had four rounds and that the safety was still on.

"How many rounds do you have left?" David asked him.

"Four."

David winced. "It will have to do, I guess."

He and David walked out to find a group of men waiting, including Derick and Jay. Jay smiled when he saw Matt and winked. Matt wasn't sure, but he suspected that Jay was gay, which didn't bother him at all. Jay was just...Jay. He saw that Jay had the rifle slung on his back.

Then he noticed that Todd was amongst the group as well. He didn't see Nora or Henry and assumed that they were staying behind. Todd walked over to him when he noticed Matt.

"Mr. Cooper," Matt said.

"I want to apologize for my skepticism earlier," Todd said. "The house is nice, and it seems like your Denver information was true, as disappointing as that is to hear."

"Glad you like the house," Matt said. It wasn't like he had sold it to him, but Matt kept the snark from his voice. He always seemed to be biting his tongue, so he didn't offend anyone. He guessed it was like that for most teenagers.

II.

There was little speaking as the group walked southwards down the street towards the large "superstore" at the other end of town. They passed by houses, parks, and small shops, all of which looked as barren as their conversations. The shops that sold food had all been depleted of their wares long before. It occurred to Matt that he would probably need to replace some clothes soon, but that could wait. The houses that were this close to their neighborhood had been gone through as well.

They were getting desperate which meant they were willing to walk in the open for the five miles to the store during the day. The zombies didn't seem to have any more ability to see in the dark than the living, but no one wanted to travel in the dark. Matt hoped that the trip wouldn't be for nothing. There were no guarantees there would be any supplies left in the superstore. They had gone to the supermarket two miles north of their neighborhood and cleared it out more than a month earlier. It hadn't been difficult—there wasn't much left that was shelf stable, and all the refrigerated and frozen food was either gone or spoiled.

Jay had suggested at one point to take the rifle and go hunting. There were plenty of deer, squirrel, and other possible edible animals to be found, especially since there were few people left. A small group had gone out and managed to kill a deer, and that's when the nightmare began. The sound of the gunshot had attracted both zerkers and ramblers from miles around. To make matters worse, it turned out that whatever was infecting the zombies wasn't exclusive to humans.

The members of the party spent three days in a large pine tree while a multitude of zombies, and one undead, sluggish, and confused-looking deer milled about below them. That had been the end of hunting for their own food.

It was too late in the season to plant anything, so they would have to wait until spring. First, though, they needed to find some seeds. There were also plans in motion to build a greenhouse due to Colorado's notoriously short growing season. Otherwise, they wouldn't be able to plant seeds in the ground until almost May. Matt didn't know the first thing about growing food, but some of the adults agreed on this point, so he assumed they knew better.

Just then, Matt could see Keith, one of the men who had gone ahead to scout, was coming back along the road towards them at a fast trot. That couldn't be good, he thought. Keith stopped when he was about ten feet away and walked the rest of the way, trying to catch his breath. Derick caught up to where he was and Keith turned and walked along with him, speaking softly but urgently the entire time.

"Well, shit, man," Jay said, walking up to be even with Matt. "Now what?"

Matt looked at him and shrugged. "Could be anything. Could be aliens and it wouldn't surprise me."

"If they tried to lure us into their spaceship with food, I'd be the first in line," Jay said, laughing softly.

"I'd sell my soul for a cheeseburger," Matt said. "No, a steak. Medium rare and smothered in mushrooms and onions."

"Oh man," Jay said. "I was off the red meat before this, but I think I'd have to agree with you."

Derick stopped and turned around towards them. He motioned with his hand for everyone to come in nearer to him, all the while scowling. Once most of them were gathered around, he started speaking in a low, urgent voice. "Seems we're not the only ones taking a trip to the store today. Keith says there's a group of men camped outside the store entrance, and they have a working pickup that they're using to fill up with supplies."

"Look like a bunch of preppers," Keith added. "Truck has a 'don't tread on me' flag sticking out the back."

There was a muttering amongst the men. Derick held his hands up for them to quiet down. "Now this changes our plans but doesn't change our goals. We're still going to get supplies at that store, whether they like it or not.

"Any idea how many there are? How well armed?" Todd asked.

"Keith?" Derick said.

"Maybe eight men. Looked like they all had guns. One guy looked like he was carrying an AK-47."

"So, we outnumber them, but they might be better armed than us," Derick said.

"We outnumber them by two people," Todd said. "Not great odds here."

"True," Derick said. "Keith, why don't you head on back home and round up some more volunteers. We should be able to bolster our forces up a bit."

"Forces?" Todd said. "We're not an army."

"I know that you're new here," Derick said, stepping up in front of Todd. "But this has to happen sometimes. It's inevitable. Now I'm hoping that a show of force from us will be enough to scare them off, but if it comes down to it, we may need to fight. I'm willing to fight if it means feeding our people. Are you?"

Todd looked at him for a moment before slowly nodding.

"Good," Derick said, nodding back. He backed up a step and raised his voice a little. "We'll wait here to allow Keith to get there and back with more people. I need you all to create a perimeter and keep out of sight. You know the drill—no loud noises, and no smoking. Damn zombies will be breathing down our necks."

◊

The boy couldn't have been older than six when he died. Matt could see the bite marks on his neck and face and knew that more than likely this was a zerker by the condition of the boy's body. The boy moved slowly now, walking unsteadily towards where Matt and Jay had squatted down behind an overgrown hedge, about six feet apart. Matt tried to signal quietly to Jay, but the other was looking down at his lap.

If the boy saw any of them, it would let out a loud, aggressive growl before attacking at full speed. Matt had seen it before, and besides being terrifying, it could alert the other group to their presence. He looked around for something to throw at Jay to get his attention and finally settled on a pebble. He threw the small stone and hit Jay in the arm. He saw that Jay was nodding off before the pebble impacted with him.

He looked up blearily and saw Matt waving at him frantically. Matt pointed at the boy, and finally Jay woke up enough to see the danger. He looked back at Matt and nodded, but shrugged, unsure what to do. Their silent communication was interrupted by the shriek of the boy as he saw another of their party and began to run towards them. Matt stood up and looked and saw that it was a man named Xander, who was in his early twenties and had told Matt that he had worked as a cashier at tool store.

Right now, he was looking around, confused about what he should do. If he shot at the boy, it would certainly end any hope for surprise, if the other group wasn't already aware of their presence. Finally, the choice was taken out of his hands as the boy reached his position and jumped at him. Xander held out his left hand to ward off the child and pointed his gun—what looked to Matt to be an old-fashioned .38 caliber pistol—at the boy and pulled the trigger.

The boy reached his hand before the bullet reached the boy. He bit down hard on Xander's hand between the thumb and forefinger just as the bullet ripped into his forehead and he was thrown backwards, taking a large flap of Xander's skin with him in his mouth. Xander began screaming immediately, clutching his wounded hand to his chest.

Neither Matt nor Jay had any type of large knife or ax on them to cut off Xander's hand, which they knew would need to happen quickly if they didn't want another zerker in their area soon. Matt stood behind the hedge and watched as Xander flailed about, bleeding profusely from his hand. Suddenly Derick appeared behind him, looking as though he had just sprinted the length of a football field—which he may have done. Derick put a hand on Xander's shoulder and turned him around so he could see that Derick had a small hatchet in his other hand.

Xander stared at it a moment before nodding and laying down in the middle of the street with his arm outstretched. Derick didn't hesitate and brought the hatchet down once; twice; and finally, a third time, with Xander screaming in pain the entire time. Others from the group were now appearing, and Derick shouted for someone to put a tourniquet on the stump.

Meanwhile, Jay was putting his rifle up to his shoulder and sighting down the barrel. Matt followed the direction he was aiming and saw that a group of men were walking slowly down the street towards them from the direction of the store. The other group had heard and were coming to investigate. Matt saw four men in the group and remembered that Keith had said there were at least eight total. The other four were either still at the store or were somewhere where he couldn't easily see them.

"Don't shoot yet," he told Jay, who nodded. "We may still be able to get out of this without a firefight."

Suddenly a shot rang out, and Matt turned to look in the direction it came from, only to see another zerker writhing on the front yard of a modest ranch-style house. Todd stepped out into the open from the side of the house and shot the dead man in the head. Gunfire erupted from the other side as the group of other men thought they were taking fire, and Matt knew that the situation had just become deadlier than it already was.

He turned to see that Derick was down on the ground in the middle of the street, and Matt could see a large, spreading stain on his shirt just above his belt buckle. "Oh, damn," he breathed, not even sure if he said it loud enough for Jay to hear. This was bad. "Jay," he said much louder this time. "Open fire!"

A shot rang out before Matt was even done speaking, and the sound made his left ear begin to ring. He looked over the hedge to see one of the other men fall on his face, unmoving. "Where are the others?" Jay shouted. Matt looked around for them and saw someone peeking out from behind the fender of a sedan that was parked on the street.

"Two o'clock," Matt yelled. "Behind the white Honda." He saw Jay change his aim towards the car. He looked around to see if anyone else was firing. He saw to his horror that there were now both ramblers and zerkers moving around the area, with their people trying to fight them off, with no mind to the group of men attacking from their front.

"You keep an eye on the men, and I'll guard your rear," he yelled at Jay. Jay nodded and then fired off a shot that hit the back windshield of the Honda. Matt nodded to himself and then turned to make sure there weren't any zombies near them. He held his pistol out before him, conscious that he wasn't a very good shot with it, so would have to wait until a zombie was close to their position to make sure he hit it in the head.

Another shot rang out from Jay's rifle, and he had to stop himself from turning and looking to see if the rapper had hit anyone. He couldn't lose focus on his own duties, or they could both die. He suddenly heard a whizzing noise past his right ear and realized that it was a bullet.

"Get down!" Jay yelled back at him. Matt dropped to the ground, still holding out his pistol. The other group of men had pinpointed where the shots were coming from, and they were returning fire.

He turned to his right to see a decrepit-looking older lady

shambling towards them along the row of the hedge. When she was within ten feet, he fired the pistol and watched her fall forward. He kept his eye on her for a moment, making sure there was no other movement from her, then turned back to his left. Derick had taught him that he had to keep his head on a swivel when outside the protective boundaries of their secure neighborhood.

Jay shot again, and Matt heard a loud scream coming from somewhere. He wasn't sure if Jay had hit someone or if it was coming from someone else. It was chaos now. He got up onto his knees and then was suddenly bowled over as Jay fell back on top of him, then rolled over and off his back. He was clutching his throat, and there was blood gushing over his fingers.

"Oh God," Matt said, dropping his gun and trying to help put pressure on the wound. "Oh God, Oh God," he kept repeating. He could see that there was blood coming not only from the wound in his throat, but from the back of his neck as well. He knew that Jay was going to die. If he didn't shoot him in the head, he'd turn into a rambler.

Jay's thrashing was lessening as Matt turned and picked up the pistol once more and held the barrel to his friend's head. "I'm sorry, I'm sorry," he whispered, and then pulled the trigger. Jay's movements stopped, and Matt could feel a scream trapped in his own throat. He knew he couldn't do anything to change it, so he swallowed it down and picked up the rifle, which Jay had dropped when he'd been hit.

He put it to his shoulder and rose slowly above the hedge, looking right to left and back again, trying to find a target. He was finally rewarded when he saw a man he didn't know make a break for the side of a house from behind a minivan that was parked askew in the street, as if the driver had stopped quickly and left his vehicle where it was. Matt tried to calm himself as he tracked the man's progress. Luckily, the man looked portly and out of shape, as if he hadn't run much in this life or his past one, before the outbreak.

Finally, Matt put his finger on the trigger and squeezed. He was rewarded with the sight of the man falling forward, his momentum causing him to fall on his face and roll a few times before coming to a rest, belly up. He didn't move.

A zombie walked up to where the man was lying, attracted by the movement. Matt was just about to shoot him when he saw that it was Derick. His mouth fell open when he realized that Derick must have died from the gunshot. Derick looked around, confused that there was no other movement from the dead man lying at his feet. Matt aimed at Derick's head but couldn't bring himself to pull the trigger.

A shot rang out, and Matt saw Derick fall down on top of the dead man. Matt looked in the direction the shot had come from and saw another man he didn't know. Someone from the other party, who was on one knee beside a large blue USPS mailbox on the corner of the road. He quickly aimed at him and pulled the trigger. He missed, and the other man changed his own aim to point in Matt's direction.

Matt shot again and saw a gout of blood exit the back of the man's head as the bullet went through his forehead. Matt felt nothing. He was numb. First Jay's death, then Derick's transformation, had left him on manual. His brain was foggy and all he could do was look for more targets. There was at least one more from the other group out there, if he hadn't already retreated.

He heard it before his mind cleared enough to understand it. A noise close behind him. He turned, knowing he was probably already too late to defend himself, and was met with the sight of Keith and a small group of reinforcements walking slowly towards his position. He sat down heavily and put down the rifle next to him and began to cry.

◊

"Where's Derick?" Keith was asking him. He looked up and saw that Keith was kneeling before him. "Matt, Where's Derick?"

"Gone," he replied while wiping the tears from his eyes. "He's gone. He got shot. He got shot and turned into a rambler...I mean, a zombie."

"Damn it!" Keith said, standing up.

"No! Get down," Matt said, pulling on the man's leg. Keith knelt again. "There's at least one more guy out there from the other group. I don't know where he went. Jay and I killed three of them before...before..."

"I understand," Keith said, placing a reassuring hand on Matt's shoulder. "I need your help now, Matt."

Matt nodded, wiping his nose on his sleeve.

"I need you to go up somewhere high. High, like a second story window in one of these houses. Take the rifle and keep an eye out for zombies and those men for me. Do you understand?"

Matt looked up at him. "Yes."

"Good. Take the rifle and gun with you. You might need the gun when you go into the house."

"Yes," Matt said, knowing there might be a zombie in any residence he went into, trapped and hungry.

Keith reached a hand down to him and Matt took it. They both got to their feet but stayed low just in case. "I'm counting on you, Matt. Watch our backs for us. We're going to check out the store and hopefully they'll be gone, or we can overpower them. We need this win. We've already sacrificed enough as it is. Go on, now."

Matt nodded again, feeling a little more like he could think again. He stooped down and picked up his pistol, then slung the rifle over his shoulder. He looked around and saw a nice two-story house with windows looking out onto the street. There was even a window up higher that may be a crawlspace where he could lie down even higher and have a view of everything. He began walking slowly towards it.

Luckily the house was on the same side of the street as he was, so he didn't have to cross over the open pavement. He came to the edge of the overgrown hedge and saw that the yard between him and the house he was heading for didn't have any type of fence, trees, or privacy hedge to provide shelter. He waited a moment and looked towards the back of the house. There was no telling if there was a better route going that way.

He decided that he would have to risk running through the front yard and getting to the yard of the other house, which had a high white picket fence, at least. He held his pistol in his left hand and then grabbed the rifle to steady it on his shoulder. One. Two. Three! He ran across the weedy lawn of the first house but didn't hear any shots.

He got to the fence and looked for an entrance, because the fence went right up to the house. Instead, he saw that there was a side door in the garage and decided to try that first. He ran down the side of the house until he reached the garage and tried the door, which he found to be unlocked. He quickly opened it, scooted through, and closed the door behind him.

The air in the garage was stale and humid, which wasn't surprising, as it probably had not been opened in a while. There wasn't a car, which was promising—perhaps the inhabitants had fled—which meant that the house might be empty. He hoped so.

He turned and saw that there was a lock on the knob of the outside door and turned it so that it was locked this time.

No reason not to be safe. If someone saw him entering the house, he didn't want them easily following him. He looked around and saw that it was a standard garage, with some racks of tools and storage boxes. Nothing unusual, or helpful.

He walked over to the door leading inside the house and found this one locked. "Damn," he said aloud. He turned back and went to the tools to see if there was something helpful to use to jimmy the lock. He decided on a long chisel and hammer. He put the handgun in his pocket, making sure the safety was on. If his count was correct, he only had one round left in it, and he didn't want that ending up in his leg.

He tried first wedging the chisel between the door and the jamb. That wasn't working particularly well. He had never tried breaking into someone's house before. The houses along the street where he now lived had either been unlocked or forcefully opened before he'd arrived in town.

He decided what he was trying wasn't working and put the chisel to the knob itself and hit it with the hammer a few times. The knob fell of with a low clunk. He pushed through the hole with the chisel, and the knob on the other side fell to the floor as well. He bent and put his eye to the hole and looked inside the house to make sure there weren't any surprises waiting for him, then put his nose to the hole to take a deep breath.

There was no death smell, so he put down the hammer and chisel on the floor and pulled his handgun back out of his pocket before pushing open the door. He held the gun out before him with both hands, and found himself in a small laundry room, which was open to the kitchen. He walked through and saw that there was a living room and then the stairway leading up to the second story. He walked slowly to the stairs, ears straining for any type of noise, but all was quiet.

He walked up the stairs, holding the gun pointing up towards the top. At the top of the stairs, he saw that there was a door for the bathroom between two bedrooms that were either way along a carpeted hallway. He turned right and went down to check what seemed to be the master bathroom, which was at the back of the house. It was empty, with clothing items strewn over the bed and floor. They had packed a bag hurriedly to leave, he surmised, and had not stayed to clean up first.

He turned back and headed towards the front bedroom. He saw that it was decorated as a child's room, with a small bed, bookcase filled with colorful books, and a dresser that was white with pink flowers. The closet doors were closed, and he put down the rifle and checked them just in case, but they were only filled with drawers of toys—mostly dolls and doll clothing and accessories—and clothing. Definitely a little girl's room.

He walked over to the window, which had white blinds that were made to look like wooden slats, as well as curtains that somewhat matched the dresser. He peeked through two of the slats and saw that he was correct in his initial assessment. The window looked out on the street, and if he looked from one side of the window or the other, he could pretty much see the entire street laid out.

He knelt and slowly raised the blinds, using the pull string to the left side of the window. Then he stood to the side and attempted to open the window but couldn't because it was locked. He carefully unlocked it and then knelt back down. He waited a few minutes, afraid that he had caused too much motion with the blind. If someone outside saw it moving, they would know he was in there.

He looked out again at the street and didn't see any movement. He pushed the window up about a foot. He cursed when he realized that there was a screen on the outside. He sat down to think. Either he would have to remove the screen or shoot through it if he had to. They sure made it look easier on TV, he thought. He finally made the decision to remove the screen. It was difficult enough to shoot at a target without a metal grid in his line of sight.

He sighed and got back to his knees, looking at the side of the screen to find the latch that would allow him to take it out. He found it on both sides and pushed them up, then saw that it was also latched at the top. "Damn it, he said, feeling anger building within him. He should have been ready by now in case they needed him. He looked out and caught movement to his right. He stopped what he was doing to get a better look.

It was David. He hadn't seen him when Keith had approached earlier. They must have brought more people than he realized. It was smart, he supposed. They needed to outnumber and overwhelm the other group at the store. He knelt there and watched as David turned to speak to someone and then saw Todd walk up to him. At least the new guy was still alive, he thought. Soon he saw Keith walk to where the two men were standing. They stood and talked together for a few minutes.

Matt thought it was safe now to stand and take out the screen. If they felt safe enough to stand and speak together, then it was safe enough for him to show himself. He stood up and pulled up the blinds so that he could easily reach the top tabs on the screen. He had finally pushed the screen out, letting it hit the roof and slide down, when he heard a shot. He saw the group drop to their knees and look around. Another shot, and he realized that it had hit the outside of the house he was in.

It must be the man from the other group, he thought

as he got to his knees. He looked around in the room and realized that the rifle was leaning against the wall next to the closet. He duck-walked over and grabbed it, then returned to the window and looked out. Keith and the group were nowhere to be seen, having taken cover somewhere out of sight.

He looked around at other houses, hoping to see if the man had the same idea and taken up residence on the second floor of a house. He couldn't see anything—no open windows or even blinds. He put the rifle up to his shoulder and began scanning the ground around the houses. He wished Jay was with him. As much as he hated to admit it, Jay was a better shot with the rifle, though he himself wasn't too bad.

He scanned to the left and then slowly back to the right before seeing motion. There, next to another ranch style house, was the man, kneeling down and holding what looked like an AR-15 or similar rifle. He wasn't looking up at Matt. Shots rang out and he ducked back behind the corner. Keith and his group had pinpointed his location. He saw the man lean out and fire off a few shots then duck back again. Again, return fire issued from somewhere, but didn't find their target.

Matt pointed the rifle at his location and tried to calm himself so that he could take a shot. All he could think about was Jay writhing on the ground, holding his throat. He fought back tears, knowing they wouldn't help him see any better. He sighted down the barrel of the rifle and waited for the man to show himself again. It was only a minute or so before he did. Matt was ready as the head leaned out again and the man began to fire. He slowly pulled the trigger of the rifle until it fired and saw with grim satisfaction the man fall backward as the bullet struck him.

Matt wasn't sure where he had hit him. He had been

aiming at the man's head but wasn't sure if he hit there or lower on his body. He watched a moment, and the man didn't move again. As he watched, he saw Todd make his way over to the corner of the building and look down at the man. He was pointing a handgun at him but then lifted it up. The man was dead. He looked up and then saw the window where Matt was located. He held his hand out in an "ok" sign. Matt waved in acknowledgment.

He was about to put down the rifle and wipe at his eyes when he saw movement and looked to see Todd fall back away from the building as Derick appeared in Matt's vision. "Oh shit!" Matt yelled. Todd dropped his gun as he grappled with the zombie, and they rolled over onto the lawn. Matt brought up the rifle again and locked the sight on Derick. He pulled the trigger slowly only to hear a click. The rifle was out of ammunition.

He hadn't thought of grabbing any of the magazines from Jay's body, either. Stupid! his mind kept screaming at him as he frantically rubbed his hands over his pockets in a vain attempt to find another magazine for the rifle. Nothing. Finally, he resolved himself to having to abandon the rifle and try to shoot Derick with the handgun. It was a ways away, but he had to try. He wasn't sure what had happened to Keith or David.

He held out the handgun with both hands and sighted, placing the red dot on the front sight between the two white dots on the back sight. He leaned out the window, trying to get a better view of the figures still rolling around on the lawn. It was no good—he couldn't get a clear shot. "Damn it, damn it," he kept saying.

He turned and grabbed the rifle and then ran out of the room and down the stairs. Todd was running out of time. He unlocked the front door and opened it quickly, running out the front of the house to find a couple of ramblers on the sidewalk outside. He brought up his gun and shot one in the head, then ran around the other, knowing that it was too slow to catch him at his speed, which wasn't great, but more than what it could accomplish.

He ran down the street and saw that a few of the other men from his group were doing the same. Suddenly, there was a high-pitched scream, and Matt knew he was too late. He followed the others to the lawn just as someone shot Derick in the head. Matt arrived to see Derick lying there next to Todd, who was clutching his right arm. There was a large wound in his forearm. Matt looked again at Derick and saw that he had shoved his hatchet in his waistband at some point before he was shot.

There was only one thing to do, and it had to be quick. He flung the rifle to the ground and then dropped his pistol, then grabbed the hatchet by its head and pulled it off Derick's still body. He turned, wielding the hatchet and looked at Todd. The man was sitting, rocking back and forth and looking at him, the knowledge of what had to be done in his eyes. He nodded, then laid down in his stomach, holding his arm out away from his body.

Matt knelt next to him and grabbed the man's hand to steady it. He brought the hatchet down at the elbow joint and then waited a moment while Todd screamed and moved, as a couple of men jumped on top of him to steady him. Matt didn't even know who they were at the moment. His focus was on the arm, which was still whole. He brought the hatchet down again, then again. Finally, the arm parted, with just a thick rope of muscle or sinew holding it together. He brought down the hatchet again and felt the hand become still in his own.

He threw the hand and forearm away from him and

the group of men. The stump of Todd's arm was bleeding profusely. He heard David yell, "get a tourniquet on it before he bleeds out!"

Again, Matt felt that sense of mental fugue trying to overtake him. He had just maimed a man for life. There was still no guarantee that it had even worked. Had he been in time? He looked down at the separated limb, seeing the blood ooze out of both the bite wound and the part where he had chopped it apart. He suddenly felt nauseous and leaned away as he gagged. There was nothing except thick saliva, and he wiped his mouth absent-mindedly on his sleeve. He looked back over to see that they were still working on Todd's arm. Tears were streaming from the man's closed eyes.

"Matt," he heard. It was David. The man knelt down next to him and placed his hands on both of Matt's shoulders. "Matt, are you okay?"

Matt looked at him. "No."

"You did great, Matt," David said. "You saved him."

"Did I?"

"We'll watch him, but I think you were in time," David said. "Were you the one who shot the guy with the rifle, too?"

Matt nodded dumbly. He didn't know what to say.

David suddenly embraced him. "You've done enough today, Matty. Let's get you home."

"Todd," Matt whispered.

"What?"

"I want to go back with Todd," Matt said, speaking above a whisper now.

"Yes, you're both going back," David said.

"And you," Matt said.

David released him from the hug and looked at him. "What?"

"You need to come back home, too," Matt said. "You're

our leader now. We can't do this without you. Don't...don't try to attack the store."

"Matt..." the other man began.

"No!" Matt said. "Send the others. You come home."

David looked around at the other men. Some were still working on Todd's arm, and some had taken up defensive positions around them, knowing that the noise would be drawing other zombies, and possibly the rest of the other group of men. "Don't worry, Matty," he said. "Keith has gone ahead with most of our group. They're probably already at the store."

Matt nodded. He finally let the tears fall that had been threatening to overwhelm him. David hugged him again, and this time Matt returned the embrace. He cried for a few minutes—great sobs—for Jay and for the life they were now forced to live. He cried for his family and for all the families that had been torn apart or had to hurriedly pack their bags to flee. He hoped that the young girl and her parents were still alive somewhere, and still together.

He vowed then that he would get Todd back to his family, and this thought brought his tears to an end. He pulled back from David and wiped his face with his hands, then wiped them on his shirt.

He was ready to live.

III.

Matt woke up in his bedroom, feeling better than he had the night before. They had brought Todd back to his house and he'd talked to Nora and Henry about how to care for the wound and to make sure and check in with the medical staff to make certain there were no signs of infection. As he was leaving, Nora had given him a quick, unexpected kiss on his cheek.

"Thank you for saving him," she said, smiling. All he could do was smile back, unable to think of anything coherent to say to her. Maybe he would stop by and see how they were doing before his shift in the lookout tower. The thought made him smile. Then he remembered that Jay wouldn't be there at the end of his shift and the smile quickly went away.

He didn't cry, which was good—he'd done enough crying the night before when he'd finally gotten home and climbed into bed. He decided he would feel better after a shower. He'd been so exhausted when he got home that he hadn't washed the stink of gunpowder off his body. The shower was quick and lukewarm, but he did feel refreshed as he was toweling off. He got dressed and went down to see if there was food.

"Hey, Matt," David said when he saw him. "There's cereal or pop-tarts."

Matt looked in the storage closet and saw that it had been restocked with food. "I take it that Keith was able to get into the store?"

David nodded while taking a sip of coffee. "Yup. The four men that were left gave up pretty easily when they saw they were outnumbered. Keith took their weapons and their truck and let them leave."

"But won't they come back?"

"There was enough killing yesterday," David said. "And we don't have a jail. We don't have the resources to feed them, either. Best to just let them go with a warning never to come back." Matt nodded. He wouldn't have wanted to kill them, either.

"Oh, and another thing," David said. He pointed over to a small table that had a few boxes stacked on it. "We found ammunition for your gun. Did you know your gun is empty?"

Matt nodded, remembering killing the rambler with his last shot. He wouldn't have been able to kill Derick even if he'd wanted to, unless he bashed his head in with the rifle.

He ate a bowl of corn flecks with a little honey on them without talking. He still had a lot to process from the day before. "Morning, Matty," a voice said behind him. He turned to see Sheila stretching her arms over her head and yawning.

"Good morning," he replied.

Suddenly he felt her arms around his chest from behind. "I am so sorry about Jay," she said. He patted her arm, wondering if he'd woken up in the Twilight Zone.

"Thank you. I'm going to miss him."

"Me too," she said, letting him go.

He looked to David, who smiled and shrugged. He knew that their relationship was rocky at best. His shrug said, "enjoy it while it lasts."

Matt smiled back at him and nodded. "I'm going to check on Todd and his family. Make sure everything is okay."

"That's a good idea," David said. "Sheila is going to make enough dinner tonight to share with them."

"I don't think they're going to be able to make dinners for a while, unless the girl is a cook," Sheila said.

"I'll let them know," Matt said, standing up. He walked over to the table to reload his handgun.

"Rinse your dish," Sheila said, absentmindedly as she read from one of the trashy romance books that she'd found at the library.

Matt did as he was told and then left the house. It was a warmer day than it had been the day before, and he was glad that the sun was shining as he walked down the sidewalk, nodding and smiling and the people he saw. Maybe things would work themselves out after all.

He decided that there was no time like the present for him to visit Todd, Nora, and Henry and make sure they got their share of supplies from the store. He walked up the stairs to their front door and knocked softly. Even now he was aware of how noise carried, and he didn't feel like dealing with any zombies that morning.

There was no answer, so he knocked a little louder. Still nothing. He tried the doorknob and found that it was locked. He pulled out his key ring that had keys to all of the houses and unlocked it, pushing open the door. "Hello? Todd? Nora? It's Matt."

There was no answer and now he began to worry. He stepped into the house and closed the door behind him. He turned just in time to see the movement out of the corner of his eye. He barely had time to pull out his pistol when he saw Todd running at him.

Thoughts flashed in Matt's mind. They hadn't been quick enough. The wound had been left too long. Todd was a zerker. Then he pointed and pulled the trigger. The sound in the small living room was deafening. A large hole appeared in Todd's cheek, just below his left eye. He dropped to the ground.

Matt kept his pistol trained on the body, but there was no movement. He looked around but couldn't see anything else. "Nora?! Henry?!" No response that he could detect over the ringing in his ears. He walked to the kitchen, which he found empty. He turned back and saw Nora running down the stairs and felt his heart break within his chest. He raised the pistol and shot but saw that it only creased her temple. The force turned her head for a moment, but then she turned back to look at him and hissed. He pointed again and shot her just as she was poised to jump at him.

This time, the top of her head exploded backward as the bullet entered just below her hairline. She dropped down, and he fell to his knees, sobbing. For a moment, he closed his eyes but then opened them again when he remembered

Henry. There was still one more to deal with. He stood up and walked slowly towards the stairs.

"Henry?" He yelled up the stairs. He waited a moment then began to ascend the stairway; his pistol pointed out before him.

He reached the top of the stairs without incident, then turned left. The bedroom door was closed. "Henry?"

"I'm...I'm here," he heard the boy say. He tried the knob but found it locked. He stepped back and put his pistol on the floor, then hit the door with his shoulder and all his weight behind it. He was rewarded with the sound of splintering wood as the lock broke through the wood of the door. He hit it again, and the door swung open, banging on the wall behind it.

He retrieved his pistol and walked slowly into the room. Henry was in the corner next to the nightstand. He was crying and holding his arm protectively to his chest. Matt could tell it was a bite before he even saw it. Henry held out his arm to show him, crying harder now.

"Oh, Henry," Matt said. He walked over and knelt down before the younger boy. Henry held out his other arm and Matt hugged him, feeling how hot the boy was. The change was coming on quickly. "Henry, I'm so sorry."

Henry nodded. "You killed them?"

Matt nodded.

"And now...you'll kill me?"

Matt sat back. There was no reason to lie to him. "Yes. You're dying, and once that happens..."

"I'll be like them."

"Yes."

"Do it. Now. I don't want to be one of those things, not even for a minute."

"Henry, I..."

"Do it!" Henry screamed at him, crying again. "Please. Please Matt."

Matt looked down at the floor, feeling his own tears beginning again. After a moment, he nodded. "Do you want anything before...?"

Henry shook his head. "Just do it. Quickly. Please."

"Close your eyes," Matt said. Henry did so. His sobs were lessening now. Matt leaned forward and kissed him on the forehead. Then he aimed and fired before he could have second thoughts. He dropped his gun and covered his eyes.

Nothing.

Nothing was going to be alright.

Nothing was going to work itself out.

He thought of using the gun on himself, but the temptation passed quickly. He knew he wouldn't be able to do it. He was a survivor, if nothing else. He picked up the gun and placed it in its holster, then slowly stood. He walked down the stairs to where Nora lay. He knelt and held her hand—something he'd never been able to do when she was alive.

"I'm sorry, Nora," he whispered. He gently placed her hand on the ground and stood, then walked out of the house forever.

The End

Revenge

"Come here, you little bitch!"

"Mama don't. Please!"

It was the same thing every night around here. That crazy woman was beating on her daughter again. It got so a man couldn't even think straight for all the yelling that went on. Now don't think I didn't feel for the girl. That wasn't true at all. Do you think me a heartless monster? No, I tried to help her. When the child welfare people came, they found a perfect little angel with her 'Virgin Mary' mother.

Of course, now the woman knew who called them, and I got a lot of nasty stares, and even nastier letters complaining how I parked my car or played my music too loud; etcetera, etcetera. What a mess.

Anyway, the reason the girl was in trouble, (if there ever even was a reason anymore for her to get beat), was because they'd had company earlier. The woman had to be civil to her daughter for three full hours, and it probably drove her nuttier than she already was, which is saying something.

Oh, and the daughter played it for all it was worth, too. I should know, the walls are paper thin around here. That little girl, Sara was her name, would act up or do something wrong, and all her mother could do was say, "Oh Sara, please behave," or, "Munchkin, don't do that." It had me laughing so hard I almost couldn't hear them sometimes. But now the girl was paying the price.

I think, though, that she was willing, for the short amount of time that she had a 'normal' mother. Even if she could still see the hate in the woman's eyes.

"You little tramp!"

She was willing, as long as she survived her punishment.

That's when I got an idea. There must be some other way to help Sara. The police and everybody else's hands were tied because they wouldn't have any proof until it was too late. The girl would end up dead and everyone would wring their hands and lament that nothing could be done.

I, on the other hand, have been known to...dabble in the occult from time to time. It's helped me to survive for as long as I have. How long is that, you ask?

Long enough. We'll just leave it at that.

The next day, I headed down to my favorite library. This particular one was not what you would call a public meeting place. Only a few people even know of its existence and location. All of those hardworking fathers, devoted housewives, and beautiful children would be shocked to find out there was an occult shop and library located in the cellar of their Catholic church. I think the priest, Father Dave, would have a heart attack if he knew.

Ol' Dave is getting on in years, but the library has been there longer than he's been alive. Don't ask me how I know, that's not important right now. So, after waking to the sound of police sirens, and hoping they weren't headed for the apartment below mine, I headed out.

(By the way, the sirens were heading to a trailer park across town. I learned later that it was for a domestic squabble. Some drunk father beating his wife and son. Made the local paper.)

It sure was a mighty pretty day. On days like that, I never drive, so it took me until about noon or so to walk to the small church on the corner of Main and Elm streets, with a stop at the ice cream shop for lunch, of course. I do have a sweet tooth, I must admit.

I arrived at the almost horizontal cellar doors of the church, and making sure no one was looking, I used a coded knock. There are no windows from the other stores or houses facing the church, so the only way I could have been seen was by a fellow pedestrian out walking their pooch, which never seemed to happen. It's funny how that worked out over the years. Proper prior planning, as they say in the military.

My knocks were answered by a slow rising of one of the doors. The small black crack between them became a larger one, and a low, raspy voice said, "May I help you, sir?" I answered, "Lords of Darkness, Lords of Light, if another enters, I shall not fight." Not only was it a simple pledge that if a "worker" from another side pays a visit there will be no trouble, but it was also a code that, yes, you knew what you were getting into by entering, and you were entering of your own free will.

The door was opened just enough for me to enter, and I did so without fear. I have been coming here for a long time.

The owner of the raspy voice was a small, fat man with wild locks of hair. "Hello, master," he said. Not that anyone really is his master, but he's very polite to all his guests. "Do you know what you seek?"

"Yes, I think so," I said, smiling. I smile every time I'm down here. I love the smell of old books and parchments. I could spend all day ruffling through old tomes and manuscripts. But I was on a very important mission this day, and I wanted to get going.

I nodded to the small man and walked through the maze of corridors created by bookshelves, until I arrived at the section marked simply, "Revenge." There were books on how to get back at anyone for anything there, but I was looking for something special. I passed over the doll section, voodoo and otherwise. Dolls are nice, but I don't think the child would have the heart to use one. I mean, it was after all her mother.

I passed over the curses and the hexes, also. A good curse would be great for the woman, but I was afraid she'd take it out on the child, and Sara had been through enough.

I finally found what I was looking for between a pox and a grimoire. It was a very old, yellowed book. The title on it had been worn off probably before I was born, but anyone who was able could feel the immense power resting within it.

Now you may be thinking I'm talking about the Necronomicon, but that book really doesn't exist, except in movies. The book I pulled off the shelf and held before me was not covered in human skin, and it wasn't good or evil. It was just a magical tool like any other.

I wiped the dust off the top and felt a small jolt move up my hand, wrist, and arm. Yes, the power was here, not quite asleep. I took my find over to one of the tables set up for visitor use and found that it was already occupied by someone.

The man looked up just as I came within his personal space.

"What?" He asked.

"What do you mean?" I answered.

"What do you want?"

"I want to sit down and read. Just like you." I could tell now that he worked for the 'other' side. But that didn't give him the right to hog the table space.

"Oh. Knock yourself out." He got up and walked away with a sneer on his face.

What a delightful fellow. And dressed all in white, too. I do so hate hypocrisy.

I sat and placed the book in front of me on the table. It's really too bad the owner of this place doesn't allow one to check out the things one finds here. I would much rather be doing my research at home, and it would cut down on the confrontations like the one I had just experienced.

Well, we all have our little problems. Now to set about solving Sara's.

Conclusively.

I opened the book to the table of contents and perused the page looking for just the thing to stifle a witch like the one I had living below me.

Let's see; revenge for being cheated on, revenge for killing a member of the family, revenge for rape; I continued on down the page.

Nothing.

The only thing close to what I was looking for was 'revenge for being beaten up by a drug lord for working his turf.' I flipped to that page anyway and started reading.

"On completion of this spell, the party of the first shall be possessed by an outside party to gain revenge on the party of the second. This action will only last for the remainder of the day, or the time it takes to complete the mission, whichever comes first, whereupon the party of the first shall be freed from the outside party with no knowledge or memory of any acts perpetrated by the outside party."

That sounded interesting enough. Maybe this was just the ticket to teaching the lady in question a good lesson. I read the spell involved, taking notes in my head on the more difficult words used. When I was finished, I stood and returned the book to its place on the shelf and bid the 'librarian' good day as he raised the cellar doors once more to allow me to leave.

That day was probably the second loveliest I've seen in a long, long time. The sun was shining, the birds were singing, and the wind blew softly through the long, summer grass. And I finally had the problem of my conscious solved. Not that I 'switched' sides or anything, but it does feel good once in a while to help someone in trouble, like little Sara.

When I arrived home, I was just in time to hear round three.

"Mama, don't."

"You spilled your juice all over the floor, you little shit, now get in there!"

"Mama, please don't put me in here, it scares me."

"Shut up. I don't want to hear one more word out of you until I decide you've been punished enough."

I heard the door close, knowing that Sara had just been placed in the small broom closet downstairs. This wasn't the first time it had happened, and for far lesser offenses than Sara spilling her juice.

Well, now that it was quiet, I decided to take a nap and get ready for that night. I knew that I probably wouldn't get much sleep later, and I do love a good nap on a warm summer day.

After my nap, I listened for any disturbance downstairs. Nothing. Sara must have still been in the closet. Good a time as any to start, I decided. The sooner you start, the sooner you're finished, I always say. I sat on the floor cross-legged and closed my eyes. It's very important that one gets in the right frame of mind for these sorts of things.

It not only assures the spell's ability to work, it also assures the user won't get a migraine from the strain. I started chanting with my eyes still closed, going over the words in my head, as their meanings changed from the language of magic to the human language. I've heard that most bi-lingual people translate their second language the same way.

I could feel the power begin to flow about me, the hair on my body tingling and standing on end, and a taste like metal in my mouth. Finally, I opened my eyes and called forth the spirit that would help Sara gain revenge on her mother. Still chanting, and inserting Sara's name in the appropriate places, I picked the knife up off the floor, watching the light shine on the small blade.

This was the part I've always hated. I brought the knife blade across my forearm and felt the burning sensation of magic as it cut the skin open. I watched the red liquid fall to the magical symbol, carved so long ago into the wooden floor. It hissed and spattered as it hit, turning to a red steam that billowed before me. The last thing I saw before I passed out was the pitch-black eyes that formed in the cloud before me.

◊

The being stayed there for a moment, watching the now still form of the human that had called it forth from infinity. "I...live." was its first thought, and it savored the feeling. It slowly headed down, through the floorboards, its presence killing the spiders and other creatures living there.

Finally, it saw the sleeping form of a little girl, lying on a pile of boxes inside a closed closet. If it was smarter, it could have understood that these boxes contained only worthless mementos. A picture of Sara on her first birthday, her parents around her, smiling; a pretty rock that she had found for her mother when the divorce was over; more pictures.

Now just meaningless junk.

It stopped before the girl, watching her breathe softly.

It watched her eyes move under her eyelids, one a shade of sickly yellow and purple. In between one breath and the next, it entered her frame.

The door opened some little time later. "You can come out now. It's time for dinner." Her mother did not check to see if she had been heard.

The being that was Sara slowly rose and looked around her. The colors, the sensations, all of this was new to it.

"Do you hear me young lady? Dinner's ready."

It stood on its legs, looking at its hands. Raising them to its face to feel the skin, soft beneath its fingers.

"Sara?"

It touched the skin around its eye and felt its first sensation of pain. "Sara doesn't live here anymore," it said quietly, smiling.

◊

I hoisted the young girl to my shoulder as we all sang the closing hymn. It was the most beautiful day I could remember. The sun shone through the stained-glass windows, and we all sang, smiling. Our hearts full of joy.

My newly adopted daughter, Sara's, voice was in my ear saying, "I love you, daddy."

We were all ready for the grade school carnival after the service. Sara had a booth along with her first-grade class. She was a smart girl—straight A student, and loved learning new ideas and concepts, which I was only happy to provide.

A lot had changed in the days following my spell. While some of the repercussions hadn't been quite what I thought they would be, I soon found that it had turned out better than I had expected. The only thing I don't know, is what happened to the spirit I had summoned. But that's really not important now, is it?

The important thing is that Sara is now happy and

healthy, and her future is bright. I gained a daughter I had no idea I wanted. And Father Dave lives on in a peaceful ignorance of what transpires in his church's basement.

◊

Across town, in a run-down trailer park, in a beat-up trailer, a man dressed in a pair of dirty jeans and a grimy t-shirt was angry. "You little bastard. Where'd you hide muh whiskey? Do you hear me? Kenny! Where are you?"

The man felt his hair stand on end, as the answer he received from the darkened room was, "Kenny doesn't live here anymore."

The End?

Malachi

Malachi awoke, his mind filled with muslin and his stomach clenching from lack of food and water to the point that it was painful. He sat up and the room shifted around him. Then he realized it wasn't his mind that was tossing back and forth, it was the room in which he found himself.

The cabin was cramped and filled with all matter of curiosities, from the paintings on the wall to the stuffed dog in the corner, to the small desk with its quill pen and map laid out. There was a mug sitting next to the map, and it again brought to mind his intense thirst.

Light streamed in through cracks in the walls and ceiling, the thin shafts of light highlighting the dust motes softly floating in the room and casting shadows in the corners. He could hear a low whooshing sound coming from outside that made him think of childhood days spent at the lake shore.

When he felt able, he stood on shaky legs and tried to remember how he'd come to this place. There were only shadows and feelings, though, and he soon gave up. He could smell saltwater and hear the cries of gulls outside the room. A ship. He must be aboard a ship, though he'd never set foot on one before. There was no other explanation.

He took a tentative step towards the desk, then another.

He reached for the mug, but the door burst open, flooding the room with sunlight and causing him to throw his arm over his eyes in reaction to the sudden eruption of brightness. He turned to see a young lady standing there, outlined in a halo of light.

When his eyes adjusted, he was finally able to see her face. She was smiling. Her auburn hair flowed over her shoulders and framed a face that was at once exotic and commonplace. Her eyes were green jade set above a snub of a nose covered in freckles. Her lips were full and crimson framing uneven, but clean teeth.

"You're finally awake," she said. "Good. It does no one good for you to be dead to the world this late in the day."

"Who are you? Where am I? Why am I here?" The words poured from him as fast as his mind could produce them.

"You're aboard the Artemio," she answered. "My father's ship. He'll be along shortly to explain all else. Please drink," she said, pointing towards the mug. "I left it there for you."

He wasn't sure he wanted to, but if they had wanted to harm him, they could have done so while he slept instead of waiting to poison him. He grasped the handle of the mug and pulled. It reluctantly came away from the desk and he could see the metallic disk below it. He placed the mug above it again and could feel the pull between the two objects. A magnet. A way to keep the mug attached to the desk during rough seas. He smiled at the unexpected ingenuity.

He brought the mug to his lips and sipped the contents. It was nothing he'd ever tasted before. Both light and fresh on the tongue, but with a fiery aftertaste that warmed his throat. It slaked his thirst for the moment. "What, what is this called?"

"Sea wine," she answered. "Made from fermented berries, lemons, and honey. Though I always thought it should have a more descriptive name. Pirates are such an unimaginative lot. At least it helps us keep our teeth."

He set the mug down quickly, though not on the disk, and it slid to the edge of the desk and fell to the floor, spilling its contents on the thick rug. The rug looked to be made of some exotic animal skin, though its shape was oval.

As he looked up from the mess he'd made, he saw a tall man standing behind the girl. He wore a cocked hat that added to his impressive height. "Eh now, Mary, is our guest awake?"

"Yes, father," she said, moving from the doorway. "I'm afraid he's still a bit addle-pated."

"To be expected," the man said. He took off his hat and wiped his brow with his sleeve. "That rug has been soiled before, to be sure, but the wine will make it smell. Get the twins to come clean it."

"Yes, father."

"I'm sorry," Malachi said. "It was an accident."

"No bother to me," the captain said. "It's Marshall who'll be the one complaining. He's the navigator, and you're standing in his cabin. He's sure to be more disappointed in the wasting of drink than the spots on his rug, though." The captain laughed. "Come, best move outta the way to let the twins through."

Malachi slowly walked to the doorway. The captain was perhaps six inches taller, and wider as well. His hat covered a head of hair that looked to be thinning, but was still long and grey. He had laugh lines and a full beard that matched the color of his hair. He held out his hand. "Captain Bernard."

Malachi wasn't sure if it was the man's first or last name. Not that it mattered. He held out his own hand and they grasped each other's forearms. "Malachi, captain."

"Doctor Malachi?" The captain asked, still holding his

arm. The man's eyes were a faded blue the color of stormy skies.

Malachi squinted up at him. That was right. He was a doctor, wasn't he? "Yes. Doctor."

"I have to say, I was hoping for someone with a little more seasoning when I sent out the party, but it will be good to have you just the same. We haven't had a surgeon in some time, and Richard the carpenter is only good at sawing, if you take my meaning," the captain said, finally releasing his arm.

"You sent out a press gang to kidnap me?"

"Oh, and here they are," Bernard said, motioning to the left of the doorway and ignoring the question.

Malachi was shocked at the appearance of the approaching figure. The twins were joined together from shoulder to hip. They had only two arms, one on the right and the other, the left. They also were both missing an eye, each on the side away from the other's head, so that when they placed their heads together, their eyes were side by side. Both heads were shaved close, with the one on the left wearing a red and white striped cloth over his shorn skull.

"This is Lenny and Denny," the captain said. They both nodded, smiling and displaying their yellow teeth. "Lenny is the one in the cap. It's the only way to tell them apart," Bernard said as an aside.

"But," Malachi began, but thought better of it. Best not make any comments that could impugn the captain's intelligence in the case that it wasn't a joke. "Will they fit in the quarters?" he asked weakly.

"Oh sure," Bernard said. "They're cleaning up in there all the time. Marshall can do a lot of things, but holding his liquor isn't one of them." He laughed again, a full, hearty guffaw.

As the twins passed him, Malachi noted the lump in the

middle of their wide back, under their tunic. He jumped when the lump moved back and forth, and he could see the outline of this other appendage, which was not quite the shape of an arm.

"Let's leave them to their work, and I'll give you a tour of my ship," the captain said amiably. "You've met Mary there, up on the poop" He pointed and Malachi looked behind him to see the girl standing on the deck above the room he'd just vacated, which was at the very back of the ship.

"Penny is at the wheel, as usual," the captain continued. Malachi turned to see the large person holding the steering wheel near them turn and smile. She was taller than both he and the captain, and flashed a gold tooth. "Up in the crow's nest on the main mast is Marshall. Watch where you walk, he hates heights as well."

Malachi's eyes were attempting to take in the full picture as the captain spoke. The ship was larger than he'd imagined and was surrounded by the bluest water he'd ever seen.

"Our bosun, Charles, is there on the main deck," Bernard said, interrupting his thoughts. "He's probably waiting for the twins to return so he can yell at 'em some more." The man he pointed at stood watching them, a sour look on his face and a large bulge in his cheek. As Malachi watched him, he saw the man spit a large, brown ball of tobacco juice on the deck. He assumed the twins would be mopping it up later.

"And there's Christopher up on the forecastle deck," Bernard said, pointing to the front of the ship. "He's missing his legs, but his hands are more'n able to put together barrels and such."

"Where are we?" Malachi asked. He couldn't see any land on either side of the ship, only the endless blue of the ocean.

"We're a ways off the coast," the captain answered. "They'll be expecting us to hug the coastline, but there's no cover there for a hundred leagues. Best to go out to sea and hope they lose interest."

Malachi assumed that "they" referred to some type of naval authority. He was uninformed, though, because he'd never thought he'd need to be anywhere near the sea. His town was quite a way inland. "I don't really care where we are," he told Bernard. "I don't want to be here. I want to go home."

"I'm sorry, son," the captain replied. "There's no going home now. It's too late. Best make the best of it."

"Captain!" a voice called. They both turned to see an older man coming up the steps from below. Malachi could see how he labored to climb. "I told you we needed to stock up on salt and flour."

"We had to leave, Dick, you know that." The captain pointed towards Malachi with his thumb.

The man reached the top of the stairs and then leaned heavily on a staff as he walked towards where they stood. "I also told you it was a bad idea to send a raiding party so far inland. Brought too much attention on us. We wouldn't have had to leave so quickly."

"Malachi," Bernard said, smiling, "may I present Salty Dick, our quartermaster."

"Don't call me that, Bernard, you know I hate that name," the older man replied. "My name is Richard." He held out his arm and Malachi grasped his forearm. The man was stronger than he looked. "I've got boots older than this one, Bernard. Are you sure he's a surgeon and not some jumped-up dentist?"

"Why don't we test him?" Bernard said, smiling. He turned to Malachi. "Dick had a barrel of rum fall on his foot a few weeks ago and hasn't been walking too well ever since."

"Oh no," Richard said. "I'm not to be experimented on.

Why don't you go cure Prickly Paul's gout, or that rash that Penny is always going on about?"

"In due time, I'm sure," Bernard said. "For now, you're here, and so is he." He laughed his grand laugh and turned to head back towards the helm, leaving Malachi and Richard to their business.

"That man," Richard said, shaking his head. "Well, there's nothing for it." He slowly walked to a coiled rope and sat down on it, beginning to take off his shoe as he did so. "If you tell me we need to amputate, I'll give you a right knock on the head with my staff, young man. See if I don't."

◊

The waves lapped lazily against the bow of the ship. Malachi had been standing at the rail for what seemed like hours, but it was difficult to tell due to the unchanging horizon and invariable quality of the light.

'Becalmed' was the word spoken by the captain and his crew. Some said it with a sense of dread, some with an angry growl. With no wind, the ship was at the mercy of the waves, though there was not a whitecap to be seen. He was told by some to pray to the gods of wind and rain, but they were not his gods, so he remained silent.

Malachi had met the rest of the crew after tending to the ornery quartermaster. The man would not be losing his foot, thankfully, but Malachi suspected a break, so the foot could have become lame if not set properly, which he had set to with much cursing from Salty Dick. There had been a steady stream of ailments afterward, from infected cuts and abrasions to Prickly Paul's gout and Penny's rash.

The rash was in a rather delicate location. He had made the mistake of telling the imposing woman that fresh air and sunlight would help to heal it, and now she stood at the helm, naked from the waist down and glaring murderously at anyone who stared for too long, except for Malachi, whom she graced with a wide smile every time he looked her way.

He did what he could for the rest with his limited resources, then made a list of needed items for Richard for when they next made landfall.

Now that the initial rush for his services had subsided, he was alone with his thoughts. He had sometimes dreamed of sailing on a pirate ship, full of adventure and feats of daring and courage. Now that it had happened, all he wanted was to go home.

His emotions were tied in knots, with fear, loneliness, and anger all boiling together in his guts, which still felt like they had been turned inside out. He was unable to eat any food offered and had only taken a few sips of rum from the bottle offered by Christopher the cooper, who pushed himself around on a board with wooden wheels attached to the bottom.

He had tried to nap, but his dreams were filled with darkness and frightening images that he could not recall when he woke, covered in sweat and gasping, as if he had been drowning.

Now he stood watching the unchanging water that surrounded them, heard the dull slap of water on the hull of the ship and wondered if he would spend the rest of his life there.

"First time on a ship?" a voice asked, breaking him out of his solemn reverie.

He turned to see the girl, Mary. "Yes." He amended his thought. She was most likely of the same age as he—a woman, not a girl.

"You haven't vomited yet, so that's a good sign," she said, as she walked to the rail.

"If the wind picks up, that may change."

"Time will pass more quickly if you keep busy," she said.

"You've kidnapped me and now expect me to labor for you for free? Should I be scrubbing the deck? Perhaps mending sails?"

"If you like," she answered. "Captain likes to have his crew trained in other areas. Piracy is a dangerous profession, so it's good to have crew that can fill in if others fall."

"A dangerous profession that you have dragged me into."

"Do you honestly think I chose to be a cabin boy on my father's ship?" she asked, looking at him. "Think I wouldn't rather live on land somewhere with a cozy cabin full of children and a dog? But it's just as easy to die there than here."

He nodded, looking back out at the water. His own mother had died young after giving birth to his younger brother when he was three. Their dog had been a large, gentle mastiff which their father doted on after the loss of his wife. There were times when he seemed to care more for the beast than either of his living sons.

"Be careful," she said, moving away from the railing. "Monty's back."

He looked up, expecting to see a bird, perhaps a parrot, circling for a landing near him. Instead he felt a tug on his left leg.

The octopus was bright red and slowly pulling itself up over the bow. One of its tentacles had wrapped around Malachi's leg. He attempted to step back, but the creature held fast.

"Stand still," she said. "Montgomery is fairly friendly, but he'll give you a bite if you annoy him."

Malachi stopped pulling away as the octopus emerged onto the deck. Its body was the size of a small dog and its tentacles twice as long. One tentacle stayed attached to his calf while two others reached up to inspect him. The creature turned from red to a dull crimson as the tentacles went through Malachi's clothing. It pulled itself up so that it rested on his knee as the tentacles inspected his face and hair. The creature had a faint, clean fishy smell that was not unpleasant.

"He's looking for treats," Mary said, smiling. "Go on you beggar. Go find your bucket."

The octopus lowered itself to the deck and slowly made its way towards the cabins, leaving a trail of water and slime in its wake.

"I think he liked you," she said, watching him go.

"How...how do you know?" The experience had been unexpected, to say the least.

"For one thing, he didn't bite you. For another, he didn't turn white. If he does that, by the way, start praying."

"I'll keep that in mind," Malachi said, wiping his face with a sleeve. He watched as the twins quickly mopped up the path of water, with Charles berating them the entire way if they missed a spot.

"Mary, Malachi, a word," Captain Bernard said. He was standing at the door to his cabin, once he saw they had heard him he turned and disappeared through the doorway.

The captain was sitting at his desk when they entered. It was a moderately large room which also held a cot and a few cabinets for storing clothing. The captain held a piece of parchment in one hand and a quill pen in the other. "Pull up a cushion," he said without looking away from the parchment.

Malachi looked around and finally saw a few large pillows on the floor. They were burlap sacks filled with feathers. He pulled two over next to where the captain sat.

When he and Mary were seated, the captain spoke. "Now as you've had a chance to meet the crew and gather your thoughts, it's time to make this official."

"Do I have a choice?"

"Yes," Bernard answered, smiling. "You can sign the contract and have free roam of the ship and the opportunity to learn from your shipmates about the various exciting tasks aboard this fine vessel. Or you can refuse and be locked in the brig until you're needed."

Malachi looked at Mary. "I see why you were urging me to help the crew earlier."

"I don't want to see you locked up," she said, shrugging.

"Let me read the contract," Malachi said, holding out his hand.

Bernard handed him the parchment and the quill.

Malachi read as far as, "The Party of the First..." before a voice outside screamed, "Ahoy! Ship ahoy!"

The captain rose swiftly and was out the door before Malachi could place the contract on his desk, unsigned. He followed Mary back out onto the main deck.

He could just make out the dark object on the horizon as other members of the crew congregated on the deck to have a look.

"What do you think, Captain?" Gabe asked. The first mate's black skin glistened above his prominent muscles as he raised his hand to shield his eyes.

"Navy galley," Bernard said. "Has to be."

"Galley?" Malachi asked, feeling stupid.

"Sweeps," Paul said. "Slaves rowing in 'er belly."

"Also means they have limited cannon, if any," Mary said at Malachi's elbow. "This won't be a battle of cannons. It'll be hand-to-hand. They're here for you and they don't want to take the chance that you'll be hurt."

"Well, that's good," Malachi said.

"Is it?" she asked. "The rescue part, I mean."

"I..." he began, but couldn't finish his thought. The girl's eyes looked at him imploringly.

"Prepare to be boarded," Bernard called out. At this order, the crew hurried to their duty stations and to retrieve their weapons. The captain turned to Malachi. "I'd order you to stay hidden, but you probably won't. Just try not to die. Death comes aboard that ship, believe me."

Malachi wasn't sure what the other man meant, or how he felt about the true concern he saw in the captain's eyes. Both the man and his daughter looked at him with the same measure of worry. He followed the captain and his daughter up to the poop deck.

He turned his attention to the Navy ship, which was growing inexorably closer by the minute. The crew of the Artemio were still now as they waited for the approaching conflict. The pain in his stomach had increased along with the palpable tension amongst the crew members.

His emotions stormed behind his passive exterior. The ship was coming to rescue him, but he wasn't sure what he wanted anymore. Should he go back to his ordinary life, or stay for the promise of adventure, riches, travel, and possibly, romance?

He looked to where Mary stood against the rail. She was a few years younger than him, at most, but it was difficult to tell. She noticed him looking her way and smiled. It was a good smile, he decided. He quickly looked away, but the smile stayed on his mind as he watched the approaching ship.

"Get those cannons firing!" Bernard yelled as the other ship pulled within range of the guns. It had turned to starboard and slowly moved into a perpendicular line with the Artemio so that the pirate ship couldn't rake it with its main guns. It now approached from the rear.

The Artemio had two smaller swivel cannons mounted

on the poop deck, and Paul the master gunner screamed orders to get them prepped and loaded. The twins ran up kegs of powder from the magazine below decks, and other members of the crew began loading the round shot and wad.

The first shot ripped through the still air with a peal like thunder, and Malachi held his ears at the sudden cacophony. The shot missed, throwing up water near the bow of the encroaching ship. The second shot was closer, but still came up short. While Paul screamed to get the cannons reloaded, Malachi moved to the main deck in hopes of saving his hearing.

He turned to see that Mary had followed him. "Once the ship is closer, they'll switch to grapeshot," she said conversationally.

"How do you stand the noise?" he asked.

She shrugged. "You get used to it, I suppose. We actually don't fire the guns very often. Don't want their ship to sink before we board it and take what we want."

Malachi nodded, then it occurred to him what they were discussing so dispassionately. Being a pirate had always seemed less abrasive when he'd dreamed about it as a child. Now that he was in the thick of the action, he wasn't sure it was right for him.

He staggered suddenly as his stomach clenched in pain. He tasted bile in his throat and stood a moment, bent over, wondering if he was going to be sick. The feeling passed, and he stood up, swallowing the sour taste in his throat.

"Are you feeling alright?" Mary asked, touching his arm. He nodded, but didn't speak. Just then both cannons fired, and they heard the crew members cheer. "Must have hit something," she said, cheerily.

A moment later they were both thrown from their feet by the impact of the naval ship ramming the rear of the

Artemio. Mary quickly rose and drew her falchion. "Stay here!" she yelled at him and ran towards the sound of swords clashing and men screaming.

Malachi waited a moment before following her. He was greeted with a scene of utter chaos. Soldiers dressed in all black were swarming aboard the ship. There were bodies on the poop and quarter decks, some in black, some not. In that instant, he made up his mind.

He ran to the nearest body and saw that it was Marshall, the navigator. He'd been run through, but the look on his face was peaceful, at least. Malachi reached down and grabbed the dead man's falchion, noticing that the blade was in horrible condition, but appeared sharp enough, at least.

He turned to see a short man in black approaching him, his sword held out before him. Malachi had never been in a fight, let alone a sword fight. He backed away slowly as the other man advanced, a smile on his face in seeing how Malachi held his own weapon hesitantly.

Abruptly, the smile was replaced by a look of fear, and a large body rushed past Malachi and swung an enormous cudgel at the man. Again and again the man was able to block or sidestep the attack. Malachi could see, though, that the man's responses were slowing under the powerful force of the blows.

After another blow, the man fell to a knee and the other lifted the club over their head and brought it down with a loud, moist, crushing sound that made Malachi's stomach squirm. The man fell to the deck, and Penny turned to look at him. Thankfully, she had clothed herself for the fight.

"Do you know how to use that bloody thing?" she asked.

"Not really."

She flipped the cudgel around and extended the handle out to him. "Switch. You'll have better control of this, and you won't accidentally cut your leg off."

Malachi nodded and handed over the falchion and in turn grasped the handle of the club. It was heavier than the sword, but not by much. He swung it around a few times using both hands, getting used to the feel.

"Behind you!" Penny yelled.

He turned and was already swinging the cudgel before he saw the other man. He felt the club connect solidly with the man's side and sensed the crunch of bones as the man shrieked in pain and fell, holding his broken ribs. Malachi held the club up over his head to deliver the coup de grace, but stopped in confusion. The man wore the same face as the last attacker.

Penny's falchion came down swiftly, and the familiar face skidded along the deck. "You can't hesitate," she said, then left him standing there with his muddled thoughts. He looked up, for the first time looking closely at the men in black. They all looked identical. It was like the same man, over and over again.

"How...?" he began, before another man came swinging at him and the time for thinking had passed. Malachi parried the blows the best he could but couldn't find enough time to go on the offensive. The cudgel wouldn't hold up long against the iron onslaught. He backed away from the attacker until he felt his heel strike something. He looked down to see a large bucket set next to a pile of rope.

Malachi bent quickly and grasped the handle of the bucket and lifted it, his other hand seizing the bottom. He swung it back and then forward toward the other man. The octopus blossomed in the air like a rubicund flower before quickly turning pearly white. Monty hit the man full in the face and instantly wrapped his tentacles around his head and upper body.

The man couldn't scream as his arms clutched at the slippery beast now attached firmly to his face. Malachi watched in horrified fascination as the blood flowed freely from the man's head as Monty's beak wreaked havoc. The man finally fell to his knees and then backwards to the ground, the octopus riding him the entire way down.

"Thanks, Montgomery," Malachi said softly. He left the man and hungry sea creature and went searching for Mary and her father.

He found them all on the poop deck. The naval seamen had greatly outnumbered the crew of the Artemio, and eventually, numbers won out. The remaining crew, including Mary and Bernard, knelt on the deck, their hands grasping the backs of their heads. Men in black surrounded them, their swords drawn and ready to kill any who made a move to escape.

"No!" Malachi exclaimed, coming to a halt. Everyone turned to look at him, crew and the seamen alike.

"Run, boy," Bernard said before a guard hit him with the pommel of his sword. The captain fell over next to his daughter.

"Father!" Mary said. She cradled her father in her arms. Her tears fell down on his face.

"Don't hurt them," Malachi pleaded to the nearest man in black. "Please. You've come for me. I'll...I'll leave with you if you promise not to hurt them."

"Malachi, no," Mary said. "Please. Come back to us."

"I'm sorry, Mary. I would make a lousy pirate." Two of the men came behind him and pushed him towards where a plank had been extended between the two ships. "Please thank your father when he awakes."

"Godspeed, son," a voice said. Malachi turned his head to see Richard kneeling a few feet away. His forehead was bloody, but he seemed otherwise unhurt. Malachi nodded to the man.

As Malachi took his first few steps on the plank, it occurred to him that his stomach no longer hurt. He stood tall, feeling refreshed now that the persistent agony had disappeared. He felt at peace.

◊

The young nurse shook her head. Her palpitations of the man's wrist felt no pulse. She sighed, resignedly, her green eyes moist with sadness. He had been a very nice old gentleman. A retired family doctor, if she remembered correctly. It was such a shame that the cancer had eaten its way through his internal organs like wildfire.

She looked at the clock mounted on the wall to see the time of death for her records. The face of the clock portrayed an old sailing ship, with a name emblazoned below it. She'd only been working at the hospital for a few months and had never noticed this particular clock or the ship named Artemio that adorned it.

"How's our patient?" a voice asked behind her. It was Dr. Bernard.

"I'm sorry, sir, he's passed on, I'm afraid."

"Ah, at least he's at peace now," the physician said sadly. "Come along, Nurse Mary, the living require your care now."

"Yes, doctor," she replied. She cast one last glance at the man's face before turning away. "Godspeed, Malachi," she said softly.

The End

Book of the Grotesque

The writer, an old man with a mustache that drooped down like a shawl over his upper lip, lived in a house that once belonged to his parents. This house had been a hotel when he was a younger man, but now lay empty, except for the tired old man and me. He had returned from the city only on the death of his father, but had stayed since then, a prisoner to earlier times and earlier memories.

Many were the people that had wanted to visit the old man. He had been the most important figure in town, though still a boy. The writer would see none of them; only I. Strange that a man who had once sought out people for their stories, their memories, would now shun that very thing; holding audience with a man he had at one time barely given notice to.

When he talked, he talked of truths: "Life is made up of a great many truths, yet to put much stock into any one truth, makes it a falsehood," he said. I did not understand this at first, but I am a simple man, and ideas of this sort are hard to comprehend. As time went by, though, I began to notice that the man's old-ness was a facade. Life had withered his body; you could count his ribs if you had a mind to; but it had not touched what lay inside of him. It was a young thing, still there at his center. A thing that had not only saved him from becoming that which he wrote of, but me as well.

I still recall a conversation I had with him, some nights ago, as he was lying in bed, looking out on the frozen landscape; the crystalline whiteness that makes the world into a still photograph. As he laid there, he talked; and as he talked, I listened.

"The world is not the same anymore, and yet it is. Things that were familiar once are now gone; replaced by strange and remarkable objects. You do not understand this yet, do you boy? You, who once slept on a cot by the fire in this very house. You're still young and that is not your fault.

"When I left here, I thought it was forever. I thought I had learned all the truths from this town that I needed to learn. I was a fool. Worse yet, I was a young fool. I could have lived here my whole life and still not have collected all the truths there are. This is because of one simple fact:

"The truth changes. What was once a lie can become a truth, and what was once a truth can become a lie.

"If I had known that then, I might not have left at all; but like I said, I was a young man, ready to experience what I thought were the bigger truths that life had to offer me in the city. The adventure of this was too strong for me to turn away from. You see how it was?"

He stopped to light one of his large brown cigars and I saw his hands shaking; those long-fingered tools, now palsied and deformed with age.

When he began again, he talked of many different people that he had known. Some of them were dead, some, still living grotesques. He told of a man who had died, lonely and drunken. At one time this man had thought himself smart and successful, but the years had decided a different truth, and he was not strong enough of a man to change it.

He told of a woman who spent her life trying to be something she was not. Trying to live up to the prophesized words of a stranger, foretelling her being more than she was capable of being. She was a woman who dared to be loved, yet for all of the wrong reasons. She was a woman that in trying to love everyone, had in fact brought only longing to the hearts of all who knew her.

He talked of a man that everyone in town had loved. They had loved him for an innocence of being and a gentle nature. The only experience that had been able to truly touch this man was the death of his young wife in childbirth; a girl he had fallen in love with while still a youth. When the man was asked how he was at the funeral, he had answered, "I wanted to be hurt, so I could learn. But I never wanted to learn this. Please," he said, crying weakly, "please, I don't want to learn this. Take it back, I don't want to understand."

When the old man told of this, he looked out the window, while as before he had looked me in the eye so as to have my undivided attention. He told of two doctors that he had known, both now dead. One had lived his life with truths hidden away in the pockets of his coat; one had lived life with truths hidden away in the pockets of his mind. One was a philosopher, who thought he was a poet; the other was a fool, who thought himself a philosopher. Neither knew the truths they embraced to be falsehoods, and they died clinging to them as to the very voice of God.

Finally, he talked of a woman that he had left behind all those years ago. As he talked, still looking out the window, he began to cry. It was not the crying of one who has been hurt in some way, but of one who has hurt someone else and is sorry for having done so.

"Why did I not ask her to go with me? I was a boy caught in a dream of manhood; caught in a dream of adventure."

He told of how the girl had moved back to Winesburg from college. She married a gentleman who was a gentle man, against the wishes of her mother.

He paused in his story and looked at me for the first time. "She died, boy. They thought she would be strong enough, but in the end she just...just wasn't." He closed his eyes, softly whimpering, as the image of the pregnant girl passed before his eyes. His tears were as blood on his red bed sheet.

The next night he would not speak to me. He was like a man that had said all there was important to say and would say no more. He laid there in bed thinking his thoughts, while I sat beside him in an old wooden chair thinking mine. He startled me from my reverie by suddenly talking, as one who is in a hurry.

"Boy, I will tell you something now, and I want you to remember it. I do not have much time left. I know that now. I could die anytime, an hour from now, a week from now, you see how it is? Before that, though, I want you to know: the truth is what you make of it. You cannot go about life trapped by one truth or another. That's what I want you to know.

Truths are only truths when you want them to be. Do you understand?" I answered yes, but I didn't, not really. At this he sighed and fell into a deep slumber, as one who is already dead.

I stayed there trying to understand these words that I had been given. It then hit me like a beacon-light passing through my mind; shining on the dangerous cliffs of falsehoods accumulated there over the years of my life. My mind opened to this new way of thinking, and ideas began to parade through my mind's eye. I saw then that I had almost let myself become a grotesque.

While still thinking on this, I heard the old man sigh again, and saw him smile. I watched his body relax slowly, his last breath passing his lips, and he was gone. A great sadness overtook me at this; yet also a great happiness, because as I arranged his hands upon his chest, I knew that the young thing that had been trapped inside of him had finally undertaken a last, never-ending adventure.

And I was about to undertake one of my own.

The End
With Regards to Sherwood Anderson

A Practical Man

John sat on the train with an apple in his pocket and wondered why the world had ended. It had been a nice world, with shiny cars and skyscrapers that gave you vertigo if you went up to the tops, but now it was gone.

John was a practical man, but that didn't mean he wasn't susceptible to bouts of fancy every now and then. Take this current state he now found himself in—he hadn't awoken that morning thinking about the old world. In fact, he hardly thought about it at all nowadays. It was painful and confusing to think about all the people he once knew, and all the places he used to go.

Yet his thoughts kept straying to the apple in his pocket, and he wished he could eat the entire piece of fruit, though it would be foolish. He wasn't sure if apples could grow anymore, what with all the nuclear fallout. It looked like snow outside his rusted old train car, but he knew better. Another man on the train named Daryl had gone out in it, and within hours that man had blistered up badly and began to moan in pain before vomiting to death right here in this passenger car over the course of a few days. The smell had been atrocious.

John had been afraid to touch him at first, but eventually

the smell had become bad enough that he'd had to move the body far enough that he could kick it out the doorway at the end of the car. He sighed, remembering the dead weight of the man, and how he'd been sweaty and tired by the time he could come back and sit in his seat.

It was his favorite seat. He sat in it every day on the way to work, and now he sat in it, slept in it, and ate in it. Oh, that apple! It was the last item left from a lunch packed in anticipation that everything would stay the same in the world. But it didn't, which made him sad.

He had lived alone, a confirmed bachelor. Women just weren't interesting, and men were brutish bores. His cat had liked the couch better than it liked him, and the only time it showed affection was at feeding time. But that's just how cats are, he supposed. And mostly it was the reason he kept it. They were kindred spirits, neither wanting nor needing affection but for a brief pat on the head, or a nudge on the shin before work, as if to say, "I appreciate you being here, human, now leave."

John wondered what time it was. He wondered how many feedings he'd missed, and if his cat, who he had not named, was still alive. Wondered if anyone in his building was alive. It was a serviceable apartment on the second floor. Any higher would have made him feel unsafe. What if there was a fire, and he had to jump from the window to safety? He might break an ankle or leg, but he would survive a drop from that height, he was sure.

He'd wanted the first floor, but surprisingly, the apartments there were much more expensive, and he'd had to weigh his safety and the balance of his bank account. The bank account had won. His act of defiance because of this was keeping an outlawed feline.

He liked the solid weight of the apple in his pocket. It felt like security. He could go a few more hours before the thirst and hunger emanating from his core would be unbearable, and he would have to eat the apple, an act of bodily pleasure and mental pain.

Perhaps one day trees would grow again, when the world was once more suitable for life. John knew, though, that he wouldn't be around to see it. He was, after all, a practical man.

◊

John paced the aisle of his locomotive prison, his hand on the apple in his pocket the entire time. Hunger pains gnawed at his insides, and his mouth and tongue had begun to swell from lack of water. It wasn't this way in any of the books he had read about a nuclear war. No one mentioned you could die all alone on a train car while the world burned outside.

He missed Daryl. He hadn't talked to the man much when he was alive but felt a longing for his company now that he was dead. It was a confusing feeling for someone who was always alone. He hadn't even minded that Daryl had gone crazy at the end, thrusting himself into the falling poison outside the train car before realizing his mistake and coming back, having already sealed his own fate.

John sat down in his favorite seat. The pacing wasn't helping to distract his mind or body. Looking out the window, he saw that nothing had changed. He had expected nothing less and wasn't disappointed. Soft flakes of ash drifted lazily outside his window. There was no wind that he could tell. All was peaceful and dead.

He thought of his life before. A mundane job counting parts in a factory. His only responsibilities making sure that each box was counted by the machine and that they each had the same number before being sealed and shipped to who knew where. An empty apartment, except for the anti-social cat and the roaches that it chased at times as they scurried about underfoot. No light for most of the day and only darkness when he arrived home. It was a dismal existence, and he missed it terribly.

His thoughts strayed back to Daryl. He had recognized the man, having ridden on the train together multiple times, though they had never talked until the train had come to a rumbling, permanent stop. Daryl had looked at him right away then, and they had both shrugged in their confusion.

Their car had been sparsely populated, and everyone else had fled. John, being a practical man, had stayed on the train while weighing his options. By the time he had made the decision to leave, it was too late. The city took a direct hit, and it was only by chance that the train had stopped far enough away from its destination that it wasn't incinerated instantly as well.

Daryl had begun to panic almost immediately. He seemed a high-stress person to begin with, but after the first shock wave, he had begun to rant. Sometimes he would rail against the government. Sometimes, it was pleading for redemption from some higher power. Sometimes he just sat and rocked back and forth in his seat and cried silently, tears streaming from tightly closed eyes.

John had been afraid at first that the man might try to harm him in some way, but Daryl had ignored him for the most part. It was odd to watch the other man fall apart, and strangely fascinating. All the while as the other man had gone insane, John had sat and thought about how his world would change. At least the factory was a pile of ash now, he thought with a measure of satisfaction. All the parts were destroyed and would never be used as they were intended. He felt a sense of closure at this, almost a sense of freedom. He would never have to count them again.

He sighed, knowing the feeling was merely an illusion. He was, after all, trapped on a train car from which there was no escape, with only a small apple in his pocket for sustenance as the hours passed by until his inevitable death. Sometimes it was difficult being such a practical man.

The End

Frozen Meat

"What do ya suppose he had in there, Fred?" Barney asked his partner.

"I don't know. But I'm aimin' to find out," Fred replied. The two men had been partners on the force for close to five years now, and they knew each other like they knew themselves. They had survived all the jokes that came with their names. Had put up with many "caveman" pranks by their fellow officers.

Now they had come to this abandoned house to search for answers.

At least they hoped it was abandoned. The man who had owned it had been somewhat of a legend. He had lived in their town for as long as anyone could remember, yet the only sign that he lived there was that the mail was picked up every day from the rusted-out mailbox at the end of his driveway.

That had all changed the Friday before, when the man, old now, had come into the local bar. He was drunk and crying out how he just "couldn't take it anymore." He had left before anyone could stop him, and was found dead a half hour later, seemingly by his own hand.

Now it was up to Fred and Barney to investigate his

house. There had been many stories told about it, about it being haunted, or that a monster lived deep within its broken-down structure. As Fred opened the front door with a violent squeal of the un-oiled hinges, Barney thought about those stories, and hoped that they weren't true. The door opened to an ordinary looking living room, and both men breathed sighs of relief.

"You check upstairs," Fred said, pointing to the winding staircase to the right of them. "I'll check down here."

"Uh, shouldn't we, like, stay together Fred?" Barney asked nervously.

Fred looked at his partner. "What? Don't tell me you're scared? C'mon, it's all a buncha nonsense."

"Yeah. Sure, Fred. You're right." Barney nodded and went slowly up the stairs, his footsteps echoing through the room.

When Barney had made his way upstairs, Fred walked through the room, looking for anything suspicious or even interesting. He saw pictures of the old man, all in younger days, and sometimes with a woman. He came to an open doorway and saw that it led to a combination kitchen and dining room. A half-finished bowl of cornflakes sat on the table. He went and tried to pull the spoon out of the sugary mass, but it was held fast. Dishes were piled everywhere, some dirty, some almost clean.

He walked over to a standup freezer and opened it. Inside were bags of frozen items, along with ice cube trays and a box of baking soda. He picked up a plastic bag and tried to see what was inside. Some kind of meat. Looked like a haunch of something big. It looked familiar to him, but he didn't know why.

Just then Barney came into the kitchen carrying a small red notebook.

"What's that?" Fred asked.

"A notebook."

"I know it's a notebook! What's in it?"

"Well, I deduce from the dates that it's some kinda journal my dear Watson. Old man's, I think."

"Very funny. You're not even a detective yet. What's it say?"

"Don't know. It's in some foreign-type language."

"Let me see it." Fred reached out and took the book. Barney was right, it was in German. Fred's mom had been half German and had taught him to speak and read a little. He began reading silently an entry dated a week before the old man's death.

"Don't know how much longer I can keep this up. Dexter is getting uncontrollable as he gets older. I am getting older also. Why could I have not died with my sweet Helen?"

Fred flipped a few pages to the day before the man's death; the last entry.

"Dexter almost got loose today. He broke an ankle chain and I had to give him a whole piece of... "

Fred turned the pages but there were no other entries. "We're missing something, here," he told his partner. "This talks about someone named Dexter. But where is he? Who is he?"

"Maybe he's in the basement?" Barney said.

"What?"

"The basement. The door's right behind you."

"Why didn't you tell me that before?"

Barney only shrugged.

"C'mon, Einstein. Let's go see if Dexter is down there. If he is, poor guy's probably starvin' by now." Fred opened the door and flipped the light switch. They both walked down the stairs, each one protesting loudly at their weight.

"I swear I'm askin' for a new partner when we get back."

Fred told his partner. Barney smiled. It was Fred's favorite threat.

When they got to the bottom, they saw the large, thick, metal door with the heavy padlock on it. It was unlocked, the lock dangling. They both walked to it and Barney reached out to grasp the lock.

"Wait. Maybe we should just report the house as deserted." Fred said. He remembered what he had read in the old man's journal.

"Now you're not scared, are you?" asked Barney. He hadn't read the book. He swung the door open. They both stared in shocked amazement at what stood there. It looked human. Almost. It was covered in thick, black hair. It stood nearly seven feet tall, and they could see that it was heavily muscled.

It smiled, and Barney got a look at large, yellow teeth and a smell of rotted meat as it grabbed him. Fred saw his friend lose a good portion of his neck, then noticed that the chains that were attached to the thing's ankles were broken. It was loose.

That's when he remembered the frozen meat. "Human!" his mind screamed, as the son of Helen and Gunter, this thing named Dexter, reached for him.

The last thing Fred thought was, "I was right. He is starvin'."

The End

Alone

How does one say goodbye?

New York City has been reduced to rubble, with a few partially standing structures. Cars, some half-melted, litter the area. The streets are cracked and pitted, many with large craters in their surfaces. Fumes float gently from the sewers and craters in the pavement. The temperature is below freezing. The city is dead. The entire civilized world is dead.

There has been a full-out war between all the nuclear capable nations of the world. Walking slowly among the ruins is a superhero. The destruction goes on for as far as the eye can see—even his eyes. His clean costume and immaculate facial features clash with the destruction around him. His superhero name is Sunbolt. He is six feet three inches tall, with dark hair and blue eyes. His costume is pure black with a dark purple cape.

I was away. Saving the universe. Again. It doesn't really matter now who they were, good or bad. It doesn't even matter that I won--again.

Sunbolt remembers being on some far-off planet, fighting an ugly alien race bent on taking over the world of a less ugly (yet still alien) and peaceful race. Scenes like this litter his memories. It wasn't the first time he'd gone off-planet to help an extraterrestrial race.

While I was away, my world was blown apart.

He recalls New York before the bombs fell, and he pictures the people in the streets, all looking up to see the missiles pass overhead; fear showing plainly in their expressions. He despairs at his imagination's ability to picture it so clearly.

They couldn't wait to unleash the atom upon themselves. There was no chance for me to save them.

In Sunbolt's mind comes visions of world leaders from the United States, England, France, China, Russia, India, Pakistan, North Korea, Iran and Iraqi. All are turning keys or pushing the buttons that launch their nation's nuclear payloads.

How egotistical of me to think I could.

Sunbolt is standing before what used to be a large skyscraper. He is looking down at a piece of charred paper that is lying on the ground before his feet. His right hand is running through his thick, dark hair.

I'm proud of my abilities. I've done a lot of good in my lifetime, there's no doubt of that.

The paper scrap is a page from the New York Times. On the page is a picture of Sunbolt flying with a US flag on a pole in his hands. The flag itself is almost out straight along his body from the wind resistance. It's a picture of a hero. He is smiling at the camera, his perfect white teeth plain even in black and white, basking in the attention of a once again grateful nation.

Yet I'm not sure I could have stopped this if I had been here. From the looks of things, every nuclear capable country in the world launched their payloads.

Again, in his mind, Sunbolt pictures the president of the United States is sitting at his desk in the Oval office, his hand over his eyes and a half-full bottle of whiskey on the desk before him. The president of China is sitting at his desk in almost the same position. There is no whiskey on his desk— only a small flag.

I can picture it: talks between the U.S. and China had completely stalled. We accused them of stealing our nuclear secrets, the way the Soviets had so long ago. The Chinese didn't even bother to deny it. Then we 'accidentally' bomb one of their embassies while on a peacekeeping mission in some god-awful third world country. They 'accidentally' shoot down one of our military planes that had strayed off course into Chinese airspace, on its way from Taiwan to Japan.

Meanwhile, relations between India and Pakistan-

The leaders, respectively, of India and Pakistan, speaking before their followers. They are whipping them into a frenzy of hatred.

Iran and Saudi Arabia--

The leaders, respectively, of Iran and Saudi Arabia, speaking before their followers with the same results.

-And North Korea and South Korea reach potboiler status.

The leaders, respectively, of North Korea and South Korea, speaking before their followers.

-Add a petty dispute between England and France--

The leaders, respectively, of England and France, speaking before their followers.

-And the ever-present animosity between Israel and the rest of the middle east.

A meeting. Many bearded men sit on both sides of a table. On the one side is a man wearing a gold necklace with a Star of David on his chest and a yarmulke on his head.

The result is the same, no matter who actually pushed the first button. Within minutes, human civilization was gone, as well as most of the land animals on all of the human-populated continents. Although I can fly at almost the speed of light, even

I couldn't have stopped this.

A large mushroom-shaped cloud appears in his mind.

Sunbolt is walking down a ruined sidewalk in New York City. His destination, if any, looks the same as where he has come from.

So now I walk. Searching, but not knowing what I'm searching for. Survivors? I doubt there are any. Even if there are, the radiation levels and impending nuclear winter will soon take care of them.

◊

Sunbolt has a shocked look on his face as he observes a human figure kneeling over another human figure a short way in front of him. The figures are surrounded by detritus—a half-burned doll, a few pages from newspapers and other papers, a broken watch.

"My God, no. No!" Sunbolt exclaims when he recognizes the person kneeling.

It is Blackfoot—Mike Taylor. His former sidekick, though when they were together he went by the moniker of Kid Tough.

The sight leaves me silent yet screaming within my mind. I can't stop screaming.

Sunbolt's mind flashes back to when they were partners, so many years before. Mike Taylor was in his "Kid Tough" costume. The costume was red spandex with a black cape, which Sunbolt always criticized because Kid Tough couldn't fly. You needed to be able to fly to really show off a good cape, but KT really loved that cape. On his chest were a 'K' and 'T' in black. He was standing next to Sunbolt, posing for a cameraman at a press conference. They were both showing off their bicep muscles for the photo shoot, hamming it up while everyone smiled around them.

When we...parted ways...he changed his name to Blackfoot.

Brian S. Converse

He was, after all, a Native American before anything else. Just as I considered myself American—even if I wasn't born here.

The two heroes were facing away from one another. Kid Tough was walking out the door, while Sunbolt had his arms crossed over his chest. Both men had angry looks on their faces. Whether it was their respective egos or the stresses of being heroes in one of the largest cities on Earth, their partnership ended as so many do, with a parting of ways.

My earth mother told me that the ship that landed in their field looked something like a cast iron skillet. I called myself a "skilletonian" for a while when I found out, but that grew old within a couple of days. My only memory was my father rolling his eyes while reading the paper.

An alien spaceship was hovering near a small farmhouse. It was shaped like an actual saucer—true to type—with bright lights and protrusions coming from its black surfaces. One spotlight was shining directly on the remote farmhouse that belonged to Sunbolt's adopted parents.

Whatever I am, I soon showed inhuman qualities. Super strength, the ability to fly and other powers made me quite popular with the people from town. There were no secret identities then. Everyone knew who I was, and no one cared.

Sunbolt's mind jumps to another memory of when he was about four years old. He was wearing dirty bib overalls, flying above the house, and his parents and other people from town were watching him, some with their mouths open. Some were pointing and the dirty-faced child with the beaming smile.

I also had a long-life span. I was 'dropped off' in 1872 and haven't aged since about the age of 26 or so.

Sunbolt was on one knee between two graves. Both graves had rectangular gray headstones. One read 'Margaret Heath, born 1829 died 1887.' The other one read 'Thomas Heath, born 1825 died 1887. God Have Mercy.' It was autumn, and the wind blew dead brown leaves past the kneeling hero. It was a gloomy day, and all was silent.

Scientists theorized about my existence, but no one was able to penetrate my skin to collect blood or tissue samples. Some speculated that I was a machine made from the densest material mankind had ever encountered. Even the smallest neutrinos and electrons cannot pass through my skin. For all intents and purposes, I'm indestructible.

There were two men dressed in white coats standing before a portable chalkboard, set on wheels. They were on a bare stage before an audience of other scientific-types. Sunbolt was also on stage, standing off to the side and smiling. He was wearing a nice suit and a fedora, as appropriate for the time. The chalkboard was covered with diagrams of the human body (DaVinci's Vitruvian Man among them) and other equations, as the scientists tried to explain their meager findings to their colleagues.

I have never fit into any of mankind's definitions of a life form. I don't need to eat; I obtain my life energy directly from the sun, hence my black costume.

Sunbolt was walking. It was a beautiful sunny day, and he was smiling up at the bright summer sky.

I have never procreated--

Sunbolt was in bed with a beautiful redheaded woman and doing his best not to hurt her fragile form.

--Though I have tried my best. I don't give off any waste products: no dead skin, no trips to the outhouse, no haircuts, no possibility of a child. For all anyone knows, I could be a synthetic being or an abnormality even on my home world.

I'm losing my focus. I was lost in my past, standing here looking at my future.

Sunbolt is brought back to the present while standing on

the ruined sidewalk in New York. Small drifts of ash have collected at the sides of some of the buildings, and once again he loses himself in the past.

Blackfoot is almost as indestructible as me. He told me that in his tribe, he is thought to have been blessed by the gods. I wish it were true. Blackfoot is also different from me in many ways. One of these is that he is, essentially, human. Which means that he needs to sleep, to breath--

He sees the face of Blackfoot. He was a handsome Indigenous man, about 23 years old. He had straight, long black hair and perfect white teeth. His superhero costume was black spandex with red on the arms and chest.

And suddenly the vision is broken by the new reality.

--and to eat.

The face of Blackfoot now. He is suffering from radiation poisoning. His hair has mostly fallen out. His skin is covered with lesions, some pustulating and running. His left eye is now a white, dead thing. His mouth is full. He is eating large mouthfuls of flesh and muscle, as a starving man would when given a banquet.

Blackfoot is kneeling before the body of a black woman clothed in a burned and tattered dress. He has her somewhat charred, bare leg in his hands. He has been taking large bites out of the leg; there are several places with hunks of flesh missing. His costume is tattered, dirty and burned. Sunbolt walks to where Blackfoot is kneeling next to the body of the woman, almost protectively, as if he is guarding his food. He is still holding her leg in his hands as he looks up at his former partner.

"Is it you? Really you?" Blackfoot asks weakly.

"Yes. It's me."

Blackfoot drops the leg to the ground. "Where...where were you? Why didn't you stop this?" He begins to cry from his one good eye.

"I was...away."

Wish I could cry. God I want to cry. But I have no tear ducts. I can't produce the tears necessary for this moment. So, I let Mike cry for both of us.

For all of us.

"You weren't here! It's your fault. Your fault I'm like... this." He looks down at the leg and picks it up once again as if emphasizing his point. His shame.

Sunbolt reaches down and gently places both of his hands on the sides of Blackfoot's head.

"End it. Please. Just end it. I...can't do it myself. I tried...I really tried..." Blackfoot mutters. He drops the leg to the pavement. His feast is over.

"Goodbye, Mike. You were my true friend."

Blackfoot looks up at Sunbolt. He manages a smile. "Thank you."

Sunbolt easily snaps Blackfoot's neck. "Goodbye," he whispers to his former sidekick. He drops the body of Blackfoot to the ground. He turns away, standing still for a moment. He drops to his knees, then raises his hands above his head and screams towards the sky. "Why?!"

He brings both of his fists down on the pavement. The pavement cracks, large rifts opening out from him for a hundred feet all around. A partial building falls down to his left and sends a cloud of ash billowing into the air. Sunbolt is still kneeling, his forehead on the ground, like a devout Muslim, praying towards Mecca.

I know now what I've been searching for. I don't know yet how to go about finding it, but I know I can offer it to those of us still left.

Sunbolt stands and begins walking down another burned-out street, away from the body of Blackfoot and the black woman who was his last meal.

"And so begins my mission of mercy," he says softly as he once again slips into memories.

◊

Sunbolt was a boy, hunting with his father. He was still just Thomas Heath, Jr.; a boy learning about life. His father was sighting down a rifle at a white-tailed deer buck. Sunbolt was about ten and was watching his father as if the man were a god. His father fired the gun. The buck was hurt but not killed. The buck fell to the ground. They could see that it was still alive and struggling to stand—still fighting for life.

"Damn," his father whispered.

"What's wrong, pa?"

"I always hope to kill 'em on the first shot, son."

"Why?"

"'Cause nothing should suffer like this." He aimed and shot the deer again, killing it this time. They both stood and his father placed his hand on Sunbolt's shoulder as they walked to where the deer lay.

"That's called mercy, boy. I had it within my power to end its sufferin', and I did."

"But, why did it have to die?"

His father knelt down next to the carcass and looked up at the boy. He smiled. "Your not havin' to eat was sure a blessin' in saved diapers and baby food, but it sure is a pain in the keester now. You see, we have to eat, me an' your ma. This meat will last us a good six months if we measure it out right." He rubbed his chin reflectively. "You're probably the only person on the entire planet who doesn't need to eat, in fact. For us to eat, we have to kill. It's just a fact o' life. And death, I guess."

His father stood up again and placed his hand back on Sunbolt's shoulder. "Now, how 'bout helpin' the old man by carryin' this buck back t' the house for your ma to clean up proper?"

◊

A villain in black spandex clothing and a black cloak fastened to his shoulders with white skulls clasps. The hood from the cloak is pulled down to about the level of his nose. His eyes are lost in shadow. He is sitting upon a large chair made to look like a throne, though it is just as burned and ragged as everything else now. His costume is somewhat tattered, but he looks healthy. This is not the case of the men, women, and children kneeling before him. As well as displaying signs of severe radiation poisoning, all of them are filthy and extremely malnourished.

I found Captain Death living up to his name in the remains of Soho. He always did have a god complex.

Captain Death's is smiling maniacally as he watches Sunbolt approach down the street. "Who fails to kneel before death? Kneel, unbeliever!"

He's smiling as if this is a joke. And maybe it is for him. He always loved being melodramatic as well.

Sunbolt stops a few feet away and they face each other across the kneeling forms of Captain Death's followers. "Shut up, Murray."

Captain Death uncovers his bald, white head. "Oh, come on! What's the use of all this if you can't enjoy it a little? Chill out, SB. You always were a stick in the mud.

"There's no use explaining why this is so wrong. You chill out, you son of a bitch."

Sunbolt blows super-cold air, freezing Captain Death and his followers solid. Captain Death is still smiling, even as he cracks and falls apart. Sunbolt looks at his work dispassionately for a moment, then effortlessly takes off, his cape billowing out behind him.

WASHINGTON, D.C.

Doc Liberty.

A superhero is lying on the ground, sick and dying. The ruins of the White House in the background. The hero is a large black man wearing a red, white and blue spandex costume. Sunbolt lands next to the man and breaks the man's neck with a simple twisting motion.

In his mind is a picture of how Doc Liberty looked in the bloom of health, the way he will never look again. He has his arms crossed in a "c'mon sucker, I'm not afraid to kick your unpatriotic ass" pose, though Sunbolt knew he would have never said that in real life. The man had been a surgeon before acquiring his powers and was one of the smartest men Sunbolt had met.

ATLANTA

I'm too late to help Jumping Jack. At least his suffering has ended.

The superhero is already dead. His white mask lies a foot or so away from his head. His staff is broken and lying beside him. He is a white male with very short, dark hair. He still has the remains of his left hand in his mouth. His right hand and arm have been eaten down to the bone. He is lying in the middle of the street on his back, his legs crushed below a few tons of debris from a falling building. Sunbolt envisions him as he was—leaping with the help of his staff around the bad guys as he fought to capture them humanely—he was never a killer.

MIAMI

The Motley Marauder.

A beach shore. There are dead people and animals littering the sand, some are half in the water and some floating in the water as the tide comes in. There is debris everywhere. On the shore is a woman dressed in purple, green, red and gold motley. She is dying, her luxurious long blonde hair spilling around her head.

Sunbolt flies over and burns her to charcoal with his heat vision. Again, there is a faded picture in his mind of the hero as she was before the war. She is smiling and showing why she was Miss Universe before becoming a superhero. She was achingly beautiful.

◊

"My name is Jim. Before the war, my name was...well, I guess it doesn't matter what it was. Those days are obviously behind me now, and I'm not sure if that's for better or worse."

Jim sits on a log next to a homemade shelter, speaking softly into a small recorder, the type with small cassette tapes and powered by batteries. He is wearing clean jeans and a white T-shirt. He has blonde hair and green eyes and a blonde beard and mustache, though both are beginning to turn grey. Before him, over a fire, a cat is spitted and cooking. We can see the remains of the Hollywood sign on the hill behind him, with only the 'H,'Y' and one of the 'O's still standing.

Sunbolt lands next to the man's canvas shelter.

"Hello, Tom," Jim says.

"Hello, Jim. How are you?"

"Wondered when you'd show up, honestly. Still fighting the good fight?"

"No. I'm...on a mission of mercy."

"Good. Heroes and villains became obsolete when the bombs came down. Only reason I became a so-called super villain in the first place was because I hate the hypocrisy that goes along with being a "good guy." I couldn't go around doing good deeds when I knew they'd end up doing this sooner or later." He lifts his arms and looks around at the destruction. "What's the point, you know?"

Sunbolt sits next to him.

Jim lifts the spitted cat out to him. "Cat?"

"No thank you. I...can't stay long."

Jim nods and takes a bite himself of the proffered feline, then speaks with a mouthful of cat meat. "If I didn't know better, Tommy, I would think you've come to kill me out of some misguided attempt to put me out of my misery. If that were the case, I'd have to fight you. I aim to die on my own terms, not someone else's. I'm not some helpless kid in need of looking after, you know. And you're not God. You don't have a right to choose how I'm going to live or die."

Jim points to himself with the spitted cat. "I'm not hurting anyone here, and I don't plan on hurting anyone." He looks down at the cat. "Except maybe the occasional house pet." He looks back up at Sunbolt. "But then, you didn't come here to kill me, did you?"

They look at each other for a moment in silence.

"No, I guess I didn't."

Sunbolt stands up. "Thank you, Jim. And good luck."

"Luck has nothing to do with survival," Jim answers while swallowing part of the contents of his mouth.

"No. I guess it doesn't at that. Goodbye, Jim."

"Bye, Tom." He extends his hand out to his former arch nemesis.

They shake hands, and Sunbolt flies away.

Jim chews the remaining cat meat in his mouth, then looks down at the cat. He picks up the tape recorder. "Not much of a last meal, is it, Sparky?"

The cat's name tag is still around its neck. It has the word 'Sparky' engraved on it.

◊

Yes. This is what I've been searching for. A finish. An end. Only here can I find closure. I can finally be at peace.

An abandoned missile silo in Nebraska. The field is full of wheat, blowing lazily in the breeze. The sun is shining brightly. There is a red barn with a wheat silo next to it. Sunbolt stands next to the silo. In the background is a large farmhouse. Both structures have been untouched by bombs. Sunbolt picks up the silo and throws it a few hundred feet to his right. Beneath it there is a hole in the earth. He floats down the hole and lands on the nose of a nuclear missile.

The US government knew that a certain number of its nuclear missiles would fail to launch. Their contingency plan, of course, was to create more weapons, to have backups ready and waiting if the first wave didn't launch. Due to my...association... with the government in the 50's and 60's, I know of many of the backup sites.

Due to...irreconcilable differences...with the president, I brought my association to an end in 1974 with the Watergate scandal—especially after he was pardoned.

Sunbolt was in the oval office. He was sitting down and had President Nixon lying face down over his knees while he spanked the president, though he didn't use his full strength, of course. Nixon's secret service bodyguards are pointing guns, but some of them are trying hard not to laugh at this spectacle.

Back at the silo. Sunbolt is sitting on the top of the nuclear warhead.

My earth parents were catholic, and so I was raised with a Catholic's beliefs. This ended at my father's funeral.

Sunbolt was with his mother at the funeral. It was in a clearing near their small town. There was a small cemetery in the distance, surrounded by a tall metal fence. His mother was dressed in black, with a black hat and a veil over the top half of her face. She was crying. Sunbolt was sixteen and taller than his mother by about a foot and a half by then.

There were few people present. The priest was an old man with thick, black spectacles.

My father had come to a crisis, not only in his faith, but in his health.

The priest droned on as he gave the eulogy. "...the body of this man to the ground, and his soul unto you, oh Lord. Take pity on him, this lost lamb who has strayed from your path. We pray this in the name of the Father, the Son, and the Holy Ghost. Amen.

Sunbolt's memory is of his father working in the field, hoeing a line of vegetables. He fell next to the hoe and held his head in his hands.

He suffered a stroke when I was fifteen. It left him crippled.

His father in a wheelchair. He was watching Sunbolt and his mother work in the field where he had been working before the stroke. Tears streamed down his face.

He spent his days watching others do what he was now incapable of doing.

His father was in the wheelchair with his hunting rifle across his lap. The same rifle he had used to kill the deer. He was praying.

When he killed himself, it was a release, not only for him, but for the rest of us as well.

Back at the burial site. Sunbolt and his mom were the only people left. They stood side by side, looking down at the square headstone and the fresh dirt covering the casket.

Because of this, the town fathers declared that he could not be buried in the cemetery, or with a cross for a headstone. The catholic faith decrees that to commit suicide is to damn your soul to hell forever. Redemption cannot be found. His act of mercy towards himself was a cardinal sin.

His mother turned to him, looking up into his eyes. "You remember this, Thomas. Remember what they did t' him here."

She walked away from him. He watched her go, feeling the rage slowly build within at the men who had disrespected his father.

My mother died in her sleep a week later. Some say it was a broken heart. She was buried next to her husband, outside of the cemetery. It was what she would have wanted.

Back to Sunbolt, sitting on the warhead.

I don't know if I have a soul. If I have one, and I do this, I don't know if my soul will go to heaven or hell. But I know that I have someone waiting for me either way.

He floats up, now facing the missile. He pulls back his fist.

God forgive me.

He punches the missile. There is a large mushroom cloud. The scene goes white.

And he wakes up.

Sunbolt is lying on the ground, covered with his cape. He is rolled up, knees to his chest, and on his side.

I wake from the dream shuddering, though I cannot feel the cold. Longing, fear, relief and disappointment all course through me. It all seemed so real.

So real.

◊

Sunbolt is walking along a sidewalk, gray flakes of snow are falling all around him.

I feel myself growing weaker as the days get colder. The snow started to fall two days ago. Great gray flakes bringing renewed radioactive death. Though I am not human, psychologically I believe myself one. I am so incredibly lonely. I have been since going to Detroit on my quest to end the suffering of my friends... and enemies...

DETROIT

Henry Dark, also known as Dr. Metal, was a scientific genius, and the only person I knew who would be truly prepared for a nuclear war.

Dr. Metal's headquarters/bunker in Detroit. It is filled with technology that is still working. Computers and other equipment keep track of radiation levels around the world, temperatures, human survivors and other grade-able levels of information.

He was also a widower who had become a recluse after the death of his wife. She died at the hands of Dr. Metal's archrival, the Scarlet Wolf.

A woman was being held by rough looking thugs. They held her before a super villain with a mask that looked like the face of a red wolf. He gave the signal to end her life as he smiled behind the mask.

"Henry? Henry, are you here?"

The headquarters is dark, with lights blinking on and off on numerous panels, and the computers' monitor screens softly glowing, emitting little light. Sunbolt is walking through the darkness. He steps into a patch of light thrown off from a nightlight plugged into the wall.

A bolt of energy comes out of the darkness ahead of him. It hits Sunbolt in the chest and he falls to his knees.

Henry is smart. He knows that one of my limitations is that I see not much better than an average human being. I can't see in the dark. I don't know what he hits me with, but it hurts like nothing I've ever felt before. Maybe it was the darkness, sapping my strength day after day, or maybe he'd finally created a weapon that could hurt or even kill me.

Dr. Metal walks out of the darkness. He is in his suit of armor. It is blue and silver, and it glows softly in the light. He is holding a gun-like weapon, though it is nothing like most modern firearms.

"You don't think I know why you've come? I've been watching your activities around the country, Sunbolt."

Sunbolt half-rises. "Henry..."

Dr. Metal shoots him again. Sunbolt falls to the floor on his back. Sunbolt is on the ground, with Dr. Metal standing about ten feet away, still holding the gun pointed towards Sunbolt.

"Shut up. Your blathering idealism has always bugged the hell out of me. You fail to see the opportunity that presents itself here. To actually study the effects of a nuclear winter, with the entire world as my laboratory. I have enough clean water and supplies to last the rest of my life, Sunbolt. This headquarters is both radiation and EMP proof."

Sunbolt begins to stand again.

"Did you think I just happened to leave that door unlocked?" He shoots Sunbolt again, and the hero falls to the floor in a heap. "Don't get up. A few more jolts and you'll be dead."

Sunbolt slowly gets to his knees and looks at Henry. "You have all of this technology but refuse to use it to help people. You've changed so much since Vivian died, Henry."

"Don't you dare even utter her name, Tom. Don't you dare. She was everything to me, and they killed her for it. Killed her because she was my wife! Don't you dare get self-righteous with me, when you have no clue how one human can feel for another. You don't even know what you are, and I don't know how this weapon works."

Sunbolt looks up at the man, perplexed by what he's just said.

"I've never told you about the visitor I had, have I?"

Dr. Metal stood in a barren field near the outskirts of Detroit. Before him and lifting into the air was the same type of ship that dropped off Sunbolt when he was a baby.

"They told me that this was a failsafe. A way to stop you, in case you ever became a danger to society. Your people. Your own people don't trust you, Sunbolt."

Sunbolt slumps to the ground, defeated, both mentally and physically.

"You've become something far worse to me than a danger to society, Sunbolt. You've become an impediment. A detriment to scientific inquiry. I won't have it!" Dr. Metal raises the weapon and aims it at Sunbolt for one last death blow. "Time to die, old friend."

I thought it was the end. This big quest, this search that I had embarked on. This is what I had wanted since coming home to ruin. And the knowledge sat like a freezing knife in my stomach: I realized in that moment that I didn't want to die.

A bolt of energy splits the darkness, hitting Dr. Metal, and cutting through the weapon and his arm. The arm and gun drop to the ground. The gun has been cut in half. Dr. Metal's face is full of shock, both from the loss of his arm and the sudden, unexpected attack. "What...what...?"

Another bolt cuts through Dr. Metal's midsection, exiting his back with a spray of blood and organ tissue. Dr. Metal takes off his helmet and face mask. Henry is fifty and has dark hair with quite a bit of gray. He has blood coming from his mouth. He is staring at Sunbolt. "Tom?"

Sunbolt looks sad. He has guessed what is happening. "I'm sorry, it has to end this way for you, Henry. I didn't know he would come, too."

Another bolt comes, cutting off Dr. Metal's head. The headless body falls to the ground.

A figure stands in the darkness. It is Jim, now dressed as a supervillain in a crimson and blue spandex costume with a black cape. He has a rifle that looks like something out of a science fiction comic book. "I knew you'd end up here,

Tom. We're even now. You didn't kill me when you had the chance. I didn't allow him to kill you." He drops the rifle and picks up the pieces of the other weapon. "Interesting," he says softly.

He stands back up and looks at Sunbolt. "Don't come looking for me, Tom. You won't find me again. And if you do..." he hefts the pieces of alien technology. "You may not survive."

He walks closer and stands over Sunbolt. "There is something I need to tell you, Tom. We are architects of a new world, you and me. There must be a balance. Do you understand? A balance."

The last sight that Sunbolt sees is Jim's face bent over his.

Yes, Jim. I understand. Thank you.

Darkness.

◊

Sunbolt is walking once more. He is making a snowball with the filthy snow that surrounds him.

Can redemption be had for a race that has killed itself?

We see a burned sign that reads 'Peep Shows--$1.00.'

Does humanity deserve a second chance? The questions move through my mind like lazy butterflies, fluttering in and out of my consciousness.

Sunbolt throws a dirty snowball through the sign, smashing it.

Would it be better to let the earth recover on its own, to allow it to heal over the period of a few million years, just a blink in its lifespan?

He imagines a society of humanoid cockroaches. They have grand structures built from chitin. Some stand and talk, antennae to antennae, others bustle about their business, flying and walking about the structures. Their bridges and towers and skyscrapers straddle the sky.

Who knows what form of life could evolve to take our place as rulers of this small planet on the edge of a small galaxy?

Sunbolt is sitting cross-legged on the top of a wrecked car. He is in the middle of New York. Everything around him is covered in fluffy gray snow. It is still falling from the sky. He opens his eyes. "I am ready."

He takes off flying, straight up into the atmosphere.

Behind Sunbolt on the ground, we see Jim, leaning against snow-covered rubble and watching Sunbolt slowly fly up into the sky. His breath drifts lazily from his mouth into the cold. He is holding his small tape recorder and begins to speak softly into it again. "Many men have dreamed of becoming a god, and many have failed. But what about the man who creates a god? There must be a balance between good and evil. What this means for me is obvious, if not natural. Good luck, Tommy."

◊

Sunbolt moves past all the clouds and debris that has been blown into the sky by the nuclear blasts. He finally breaks through into sunshine.

I feel the energy seep into me, a warm caress of power running up and down my body. But I need more for what I must do. Much more.

Sunbolt flies straight towards the sun, feeling its energy course through his body more and more until he enters its outer layer.

He comes out of the sun, glowing brightly in the darkness of space. He flies to the moon and stands next to the American flag planted there. He breaks the flagpole. He burns the flag with his heat vision.

*No more United States. No more nations at all. If humans are to survive, they can't have such barriers again. There must *be a clean slate.*

He flies to Earth's polar ice cap at the North Pole. He melts all the remaining ice with his heat vision. He flies to the South Pole and does the same thing, melting all of the ice from the land. He flies out a few thousand miles from the Earth's atmosphere and notes the added sea levels.

There's only one way I can think of to cleanse the land of the radiation. I visited Dr. Metal to try and convince him to help, but that had ended in another death before he even heard me out.

He points himself straight at the Earth and begins flying toward it at a high speed. He flies through the earth's atmosphere, the friction making him glow even more than he already is. There is fire along the length of his body. He plows into the Pacific Ocean. This creates a huge tidal wave. The tsunami covers the west coast of North America and part of South America. He continues by doing the same in the Atlantic. The Indian. The Mediterranean. The Arctic. The Gulf of Mexico. Each time, a large tidal wave covers a portion of land and then slowly recedes.

I can't reach all of the land that has been irradiated, but this is enough, for now.

Sunbolt is flying. He is no longer glowing, but he still feels more powerful than he ever had before.

Almost done. Only one thing left to do.

He spins around in the atmosphere, faster and faster, until he has collected a large funnel of debris and clouds. He spins, throwing this mass of clouds out of the Earth's atmosphere, away from the planet that it has kept shrouded in nuclear winter. He stops spinning. He smiles, closing his eyes and spreading his arms. The sun is shining on his body and face. He is radiant. "Let there be light!"

A small village in Australia. Aboriginal people come out of their homes, blinking and smiling at the sunshine now pouring down from the sky once again. The same thing in an African village, with people coming out of their wooden dwellings. The same thing in Northern Canada with an Inuit village, with people gathered around their homes. The same with a tribe in the deepest part of the Amazon. There are pockets of humanity still left.

Sunbolt is looking at the Earth. From a distance, it looks almost normal. It's a new beginning for the world. He has a lot of work still to do, but it is a start.

He was no longer alone.

The End

Omoro

Omoro Non woke up in the hospital, wondering where she was and what had happened. She had no clear idea what day it was or why she was hooked up to the various medical machines that surrounded her bed.

When the doctor came in to check on her condition, she was alarmed to see that he wasn't human. His oblong shaped, drab orange head turned one way, then the other, when he saw that she was awake. He pressed a button on the wall and spoke in his language, in a voice that sounded like pebbles in a garbage disposal.

Two others of his kind entered the room and one of them approached her with a hypodermic needle. Omoro couldn't move, though she struggled in her mind as the needle entered her arm. Then everything returned to black.

◊

Omoro woke from her nightmare to find herself in an unfamiliar house. The bed she was in was clean, with pressed sheets and a light wool blanket. The sun shone through a large window, lighting up half of the room in gold and casting the other half in deep shadow. She didn't notice the man sitting in the shadows until he spoke.

"What is your name?" he asked quietly.

Omoro squinted her eyes, only able to make out a silhouette in the darkness. "Omoro," she replied. "What is this place?"

"Your house," came the reply.

"Who are you?" she asked, alarmed that she seemingly could not remember anything.

"Your husband," the man replied, though she could hear no reproach in his voice to the fact that she had asked who he was, when she should have known.

"I don't understand," she said.

"I know," he said, standing and walking into the light. He was tall and broad-shouldered; dressed in the same simple spun clothing as she was. His black hair was cropped close, and his skin was almost as dark. Brown eyes, broad nose, and full lips. He was very handsome—and a complete stranger.

"I am Thomas," he said in his deep, pleasant voice. "I don't expect you to remember me after your recent ordeal. At least you remember your own name, which is a good sign. Please know that you are safe here." He smiled, his teeth bright in contrast to his darkly lit face. "Feel free to rest if you need to, or if you're hungry, there's food in the kitchen."

Omoro was about to decline, but then realized that she was famished, almost sick with hunger. She threw back the covers and then slowly stepped down from the bed. She stood for a moment, looking around the bedroom, hoping to remember something about her life there, but she could not.

The furnishings were plain but clean. The wooden bed and end tables were made of cheap wood, as was the rocking chair in the corner of the room where Thomas had sat earlier. The rug on the floor was thin and worn through in some spots; showing the wood floor beneath.

She looked up to see that Thomas was studying her, a hungry expression on his face, though it was not the need for food in his eyes. When he saw her looking at him, his expression changed quickly back to the welcoming smile that he had affected earlier; but she had seen.

She had seen and was not sure she felt comfortable in his presence anymore. This was supposed to be her husband, but she had no recollection of him, and it scared her to think that she would have to share his bed. She smiled the best she could and followed him into the kitchen. She needed to eat.

◊

Omoro sat in the kitchen and ate her small meal of fruit and bread. She looked around the room, and again, could find no memories of it. She looked at Thomas as he sipped from a cup of coffee. "What time is it? What day is it?" It occurred to her then that the room had no windows, which seemed strange.

"It is late," he said. "One thirty AM."

"And you're drinking coffee?"

"I stay up late," he answered. "I've never had much use for sleep, as you will hopefully remember soon." He smiled again at her. "You've always scolded me for my sleeping habits, even when we first met."

"How long ago was that?" she asked him.

He looked up at the ceiling as if in deep thought, then looked back at her. "Going on twelve years now. We've been married for six."

"Took you that long to ask?"

He laughed for the first time, a rich, mellow sound. "Extenuating circumstances, to be sure. We were both in school, and we agreed to wait until after we had both graduated."

She sat and thought for a moment. It all made sense, but she still had a hole in her memory. "What happened to me?"

"Are you sure you want..."

"Yes, tell me," she demanded.

"There was an accident at your workplace," he said, putting down his cup to focus solely on her face. "Thank goodness you were wearing your hardhat and other protective equipment."

"Hardhat? Am I performing construction somewhere?"

"No, you're an architect, and you were inspecting progress on a building that you helped to design."

"I'm an architect?"

"Yes, a highly talented one, from what I've been told. Despite your safety attire, you were struck in the head by a falling metal beam and taken to the hospital. You were in an induced coma for some time while your brain healed. Unfortunately, it seems that you may have suffered some memory loss. Hopefully only temporary."

"Some? I don't remember anything. Any of this," she looked around the room, then back at him. "Or you."

"As I said, the doctors are hopeful that your memories will return given time."

She stood and took her plate and bowl to the sink. It was all so frustrating. The man's story sounded reasonable, but it still felt wrong to her. She took her time rinsing her dishes while she thought. Finally, she turned and faced him again. "I'm feeling like I need to get some rest, despite what sounds like an abundance of it lately."

"That's understandable," he said. "The doctors said you would be tired for the foreseeable future."

"I would appreciate it if I could have the bedroom to myself," she said, judging his reaction to her words. His face remained impassive, with no sign of emotion.

"That, too, is understandable," he said after a moment. "There's just one other issue that hasn't been addressed yet."

"And that is?"

"The baby," he said.

"What?"

"You are two months pregnant, Omoro," he said. "We were all afraid that you would lose the baby after you were injured, but thank heavens, the baby survived."

She sat down at the table again, feeling weak in her legs. Baby? She looked down at her abdomen but could see little sign of it. "Are you sure?"

"Yes, quite," he said. "You had examinations each day while you were asleep to check on the baby's condition."

"Do we have any other children?"

"No," he said. "This will be our first. We've tried for a long time, and we were both beginning to lose hope, I think, when you became pregnant. That is another reason why you may feel a bit weak for a while."

"I...I have to go lie down," she said, standing and walking slowly towards the doorway and hallway beyond. She could remember how to get back to the bedroom, at least. She didn't look back to see if he followed, but she didn't hear his chair scrape on the floor, so she assumed that he hadn't.

◊

Omoro woke up with her thoughts already racing. There were so many questions, and she didn't want to talk to her husband about them. She wanted real answers, and for some reason, didn't trust him to provide them. She still had no memory of him or the house or anything else except her name. And even that was questionable, as far as she was concerned.

She wanted to get out of the house. Perhaps a walk would bring back memories—and it would be an excuse to get away from Thomas. She walked quietly into the hallway and was heading towards the front door when she heard a voice behind her.

"Where are you going, Omoro?" Thomas asked.

"I'm going to take a walk," she answered without turning. "I'm sure the fresh air will be good for the baby." She didn't wait to hear his answer but walked forward and opened the door.

It was a bright, sunny day. She paused a moment to let her eyes adjust, then stepped out onto a small front stoop made of what looked like poured concrete. She looked around and the houses near her own, noticing that there was very little variation in them, and that they were laid out in precise, orderly rows.

She could see other people walking a few blocks away, and watched them for a while. Everything seemed normal, but then it occurred to her that she saw no forms of transportation. No vehicles were visible, although there were roads. She wondered if it was because most people were at work somewhere? Was the community so walkable that there was no need for personal transportation?

The door behind her opened and she turned to see Thomas standing in the doorway. "It's a beautiful day," he said, smiling.

"Yes," she said. "What time is it?"

"Just before noon, you slept in."

She nodded. "Do we own a vehicle?"

"Of course," he replied. "Is there somewhere you want to go? I could drive you."

"No, I was just curious. I think I will walk for a little way."

"Don't get lost," he said. "If your memory hasn't returned, it could be difficult to find your way back here."

She nodded again. He was right. With all the houses looking so similar, it would be easy to lose her way. She looked at their house for some signage or numbers that would allow her to differentiate, but didn't see anything. She would have to remember her route and then retrace her steps. She smiled at him and then turned and began to walk to her left. It seemed as good a place to go as any other.

She walked for a few minutes, looking around and the other houses and the trees and thought about what was bothering her. Then she realized that it was quiet. She couldn't hear any vehicles or people or animals or even the sound of buzzing insects. It was as if she were deaf, except she could hear herself if she spoke and could hear her own footfalls.

She made it to the end of the street and looked about, but all she could see from her vantage point was more rows of houses, as if the community never ended. The ground was flat, so there were no better places to go to get a better look around. She turned left again and began to walk. If she made a circle, it would be easier to find her way back.

It was more of the same, and she grew bored as she walked. She decided that she would walk until something changed. There had to be an end to the street. After walking for a while longer, she began to regret not planning her journey better. She was without food or water, and no protection from the sun that shined warmly overhead. She had just been so eager to get out of the house to think that she was now regretting her decision to leave at all.

Omoro turned to go back the way she came instead of trying to complete her circle. She began to walk, though now she had forgotten the street where she had turned. She hurried her footsteps and tried to calm her beating heart with deep breaths. Was this the street? Or the next? She stopped and looked down to her right but couldn't see anything that would tell her. She went on to the next street. More of the same view.

She looked around in disgust—with herself, with the

place, and with the man who claimed to be her husband—
and decided that the best thing to do would be to sit under
a nearby tree and get out the sun so she could think. She
walked from the sidewalk into a yard that was neat and
mowed, just like every other yard, and sat down under the
tree. She looked at the leaves and bark of the tree, but didn't
recognize the species.

The shade helped her to feel cooler, for which she was
grateful. So, now what? she thought. Did she want to return
to the house she had awakened in? Was there a choice? She
became aware of her stomach beginning to complain about a
lack of sustenance. She supposed she would have to go home,
if only to not starve. She also felt like she could drink a gallon
of cool water, if offered.

She looked at the houses that surrounded her and
wondered if they were all empty, and wondered if they were
locked. If she entered an empty house, maybe she could
get a glass of water. If she tried to enter an occupied house,
she might get shot. Now why had that even entered her
mind? Why would she assume that trespassing would mean
possible execution? It didn't make sense, unless she had a
memory in her subconscious of it happening to someone.
But she couldn't pull it up in her mind.

Frustrated, she finally stood up and brushed off the back
of her pants. She looked at the house nearest to where she
stood and looked for any signs of it being occupied. She
slowly walked toward it, ready to run if needed. When she
reached the front door, she saw that it was made of some type
of artificial substance. She assumed that all the houses were
the same. She slowly brought her right hand up and knocked
gently on the door. The sound seemed to echo around her,
and she looked around swiftly to see if anyone had come out
of their house to watch the crazy young black woman.

She stood for a moment waiting and then raised her hand again and knocked a little more forcefully. Again, she looked around but saw no one. She was about to try the knob to see if it turned when the door abruptly opened. A woman stood there, looking back at her with wide eyes. She was a little older than Omoro, but looked like they could practically be sisters.

"What do you want?" she asked without any pretense of welcome.

"I'm sorry to bother you," Omoro replied, "but I seem to have got lost while on a walk."

"A walk?" the woman asked skeptically.

"Yes, I just wanted a little fresh air and got turned around somehow. I'm...new here."

"Bet you are," the woman said, smirking for a moment at her. "Well, come in." She stepped back a step and held the door.

"Thank you," Omoro said and stepped across the threshold. She looked around while the other woman closed the door and noticed that the interior was also similar to where she had woken up.

"Water?"

"Oh, yes please," Omoro replied. "It's a hot day."

The woman made a noise of acknowledgment, but didn't speak again until she handed a glass of water to Omoro. Omoro drank it, conscious not to drink too fast. She didn't want to vomit it back up, and certainly not in the woman's kitchen.

The woman stood looking at her a moment. "What's your name, hon?"

"Omoro."

She nodded. "I'm Denera."

"Pleased to meet you. Thank you again for the water."

"You said you were new to the area. You have someone looking for you?"

Omoro shrugged. "I just woke up in a house like this one, with a husband I don't remember, in a neighborhood I have no memory of," she said. She could feel tears coming to her eyes. When she finally admitted it out loud, she felt alone and lost.

"Oh, honey, you really are new here," Denera said. She took the empty glass from Omoro and placed it on the counter, then turned back and embraced her.

Omoro felt the tears run down her cheeks as she returned the embrace.

"There now, you let it out," Denera said, rubbing her back lightly. "'Cause you're not going to like what I have to say."

Omoro backed up at these words and wiped her face. There had been no threat in the other woman's voice, but her words set her body into alert.

"Now don't worry," Denera said. "You're not in any danger here. I just want you to know that you need to go back to your own house soon. Before dark. There's a curfew."

"A curfew?" Omoro asked. "Why?"

The woman shrugged. "Just the way it is here, I guess. Been that way ever since I can remember."

"Who enforces it? Are there police?"

"I suppose you can call them that. Look, I've probably said too much already."

"Oh, I'm sorry, I don't want you to get into any trouble," Omoro said.

"Don't worry about it," Denera said. "But like I said, you're not going to like what I have to tell you. You need to find your husband as soon as possible and go back to your house."

Omoro looked at her for a moment and then nodded. "Thank you again for the water and conversation. I was beginning to think I was the only one here."

"Oh, there are others. Many others, but people tend to keep to themselves around here."

"I understand," Omoro said.

"You may not now, but you will," Denera said, though not without a small smile on her face. Omoro couldn't decide whether she liked the smile or not.

"You be careful now," Denera said as Omoro stepped out onto the small porch in front of her door.

"Thank you, I will," Omoro replied as the door was closing. She turned and began walking slowly towards the street, then motion caught her eye, and she looked to see her husband walking down the sidewalk towards her.

◊

"I was worried about you," Thomas said, as they walked back to their house.

"I was lost," Omoro replied, shrugging. "All of the houses look the same here."

"True, but I told you that before you left."

"Maybe next time you can draw me a map," Omoro said, trying not to sound too sarcastic, but failing, even in her own ears.

"Omoro, what's wrong? You sound upset."

"What's wrong? What's wrong is that I don't understand any of this. I don't remember this place, and I especially don't remember you."

"In time..."

"No, not in time," she said angrily. "I've waited long enough for things to begin making sense, and they're not. I want answers, Thomas. Either from you, or I'll find my own."

"Watch your voice," Thomas said, looking around.

"Why? Why should I? There's no one around. Everyone is hiding in their houses." She spun around, looking for signs of another living creature, and found none. "What are you worried about?"

"Let's get back to the house and then we can talk," he said, still looking around and not at her.

"What is wrong with you?" she asked him.

"You don't know..."

"Exactly! I don't know, because no one will tell me."

"Please..."

Suddenly he turned his head. She heard it too. A humming. It was becoming louder.

She looked around and finally saw what was making the noise. It was some type of small drone flying towards them from around the side of one of the houses. It was oval and mostly black, with gold accents that also flashed periodically.

"Get down!" Thomas whispered to her as he fell to his knees.

"What?"

He reached for her hand and pulled her down to the sidewalk. Her knees hit the concrete with a painful thump. "Son of a ..." she began, before she heard a loud voice coming from the drone.

"Citizen Thomas," it said as the drone stopped and floated fifteen feet from where they both knelt.

"Yes," Thomas answered, his eyes averted.

"Citizen Thomas, is there a problem?"

"No, no problem. My wife...she's new and she is just... upset and confused since she woke up."

"Citizen Omoro," the voice said. "Public disturbance is forbidden. Further disturbance will lead to penalties."

"What?" she asked. "What the hell does that mean?"

"Be quiet," Thomas said. "Just tell them you understand,

and it won't happen again."

"Citizen Omoro, do you understand the stated and implied consequences of any further actions on your part to disturb the peace?"

"Y-yes, I understand. I won't happen again."

"Thank you for your attention to this matter." The drone rose swiftly and then went speedily out of sight behind a row of houses.

"What the fuck was that?" she asked, beginning to stand. Her knees felt bruised, and her heart was still beating rapidly from the encounter.

"Authority drone," Thomas said, beginning to stand as well.

"More like an authoritarian drone," she said, half joking. Thomas didn't smile.

"You must understand," he said. "We hardly ever see them anymore. Everyone has learned not to attract them."

"You've learned to be slaves?"

"We've learned to be good citizens."

"Sounds like the same thing."

"Omoro..."

"I know," she said, brushing pebbles from her hands. "Don't disturb the peace."

◊

It had been a few days since the encounter with the drone, and Omoro was feeling restless, and bored. She hadn't left the house since that day, and there didn't seem to be anything left to occupy her time. She'd read a few books, played some card games with Thomas, and waited for her memories to return. They had not.

Finally, she couldn't take the confines of her house any longer and she made up her mind to venture outside once more. She opened the front door and stood a moment, half-expecting another drone to show up and tell her to get back inside. When one didn't, she stepped outside the door and stood on the small porch for a moment, looking around.

Nothing had changed—not that she thought it would. She descended the few steps to the sidewalk and then began to walk again. She found she thought better when she was moving. She counted the number of streets she passed, not turning from her path, so she knew that all she needed to do was turn around and count the same number of streets back.

She thought about her present situation. She had no doubt that Thomas was telling the truth when he said that she was new there. She doubted that she'd been there any length of time and had her memory erased. Whatever had erased her memory had done so to delete anything that had happened to her before she arrived. The question was why was she there? Thomas seemed to think she was there exclusively for him to have as his wife, which also meant that he expected to have at least a few children at some point. She still couldn't believe that she was pregnant, because her body didn't feel pregnant. She'd never been pregnant before, but she thought she would somehow feel different if she was.

Were they multiplying for some as yet unseen powers hiding behind the drones? Increasing their numbers like cattle? Injecting new blood occasionally, to expand the genetic code? It seemed they hadn't erased all her memory if she could still ruminate over such concepts. Or else they had meant to but had somehow failed. It was a great deal to contemplate.

It had puzzled her at first as to why the other woman had looked so much like her. It would make sense if whoever was in charge had the need to bring in new specimens to their zoo so that the cases of inbreeding were reduced. That would lead to the belief that there were relatively limited numbers of people here at any given time. But did all the people share similar genetic traits? Were there similar towns elsewhere that had people with different genetic traits? A white town similar to her black one?

She noticed that she had gone the opposite way than her earlier journey. She'd gone ten blocks now, and nothing had changed. Were there no places to gather? No stores to buy food or gather items needed for the house? If there were, they were further away than she could see. She would have to ask Thomas where he bought groceries. The refrigerator was stocked, so she hadn't thought about buying more until now.

She had just reached the sidewalk on the other side of the street when she heard a door open nearby. She looked to see a man who looked like he could be Thomas' father standing on his porch. He stood there a moment, making sure she saw him, before gesturing for her to come closer. He didn't wait to see what she did—only turned and went back inside his house.

She thought for a moment, wondering if she should accept his invitation. She might be new, but that didn't mean she shouldn't be careful of entering a strange man's house. Something told her that she would not have received the invitation if Thomas had been with her.

Finally, she made up her mind and swiftly walked to the stone steps of the porch before looking around, walking up them, opening the door and stepping inside. She closed the door behind her while her eyes adjusted to the dimly lit interior of the home. The man was sitting in a comfortable-looking armchair in the living room area. He had a beer in both of his hands and extended one out to her without speaking.

She stepped forward and took the proffered drink. He

smiled and motioned for her to have a seat. She looked around and decided to sit on the edge of the couch, which looked like it was a matching set to the chair. Still without speaking, he opened his beer and had a long drink.

"Beer isn't going to drink itself," he said once he had swallowed the beverage. His voice had a similar timbre to Thomas but seemed warmer. She smiled and twisted off the cap. The beer was cold, and she was reminded that she had been walking for over an hour in the sun. It was quite refreshing, if a little hoppy for her taste.

"Thank you," she said.

"No problem," he said. "I appreciate you taking a moment to talk to an old man."

"You don't seem that old," she said.

He smiled slyly, but it was the kind of smile that said, "I agree with you," rather than, "I'm hiding something." He took another drink then spoke again. "No, but around here, I'm ancient. Just wondering how long it will be before they come for me—especially since losing my Noreen a few months ago."

"I'm sorry to hear that," she said almost automatically.

"Thank you," he said. "But I didn't invite you here to garner your sympathy." He leaned forward. "I expect that you're new here."

"Yes, how did you know that?"

"Don't see many people, especially unaccompanied women, walking down the street in broad daylight. It's a little strange."

"Is it?"

He smiled. "You'd be surprised. Anyhow, I guess I was curious as to what your intentions are."

She felt her guard go up at this statement. She must have shown her reticence, because he leaned back in his chair again and took a sip.

"I'm sorry, I didn't mean to disturb you," he said. "You must be feeling like the new kid at school around here."

"Yes, I am," she admitted. "I can't get anyone to answer my questions, either."

"That's not a surprise," he said. "People around here have learned to...curb their curiosity when it comes to what happens outside their homes. It's a shame, really. I can remember when I was younger having get togethers with other families. Something must have happened, because suddenly when there were too many people gathered together, the drones would show up and tell everyone to disburse."

Omoro took another drink while she thought about what he had said. Maybe it was the fear of organizing, which would make sense. Whoever was in power would not be there much longer if all of the people they ruled over stood up together in defiance. "What did you mean earlier that you were surprised they hadn't come to get you yet?"

"I'm a bit past my prime," he said, smiling mischievously. "For breeding, that is. And since I no longer have a partner, all I'm doing now is taking up space. I've seen it happen before."

"Seen what?"

"One day someone is living in a house nearby, and the next day the house is empty."

"You've never seen who does it? Who comes for people?"

"No, unfortunately. Though I've wondered who they are plenty. Thought about looking into it but decided I would see soon enough when they come for me."

"That's a little depressing, don't you think?'

"Damn right," he said, taking another swig before laughing. "I've never been one to make trouble, but I see now that I should have been. It's good trouble we need around here."

She took another drink and was surprised to find it was the end of her beer. "So, what do you propose we should do?"

He shrugged. "Never been an idea guy, either." He smiled. "But something tells me that you are." He leaned forward. "You might say that I'm a strong follower, though."

She looked at him for a moment before speaking. "Do you think the powers that be would object to three or four people meeting at once? And then each of them met with a few people after that?"

He stood, and she followed suit. "I think that it's worth trying," he said. "Hell, anything is better than waiting around to disappear."

"Good," she said. "I'm Omoro, by the way."

He held out his hand. "Hello Omoro. I'm Desten."

◊

"Isolation is a form of control."

"What?" Denera asked.

"I said, isolation is a form of control," Desten repeated.

"Which is why I invited you over for dinner," Omoro said.

"Which is why my husband is home watching the kids," Denera said, smiling. "I told him that I was going for a walk, and he about swallowed his beer bottle."

Everyone laughed except for Thomas. As of yet, Thomas had not said a word. He sat in his recliner and watched. Omoro wasn't sure what he thought of their improvised dinner party, because his face showed no sign of emotion as the others joked and got to know each other better.

The four of them were gathered in Omoro's house; sitting in the living room with refreshments of their own as Omoro and Desten tried to begin their uprising. Baby steps,

Omoro kept reminding herself.

"But seriously," Denera continued. "I assume that you invited me over here because of the drones. And the isolationism," she said, looking at Desten.

"Yes," Desten said. "Omoro said that she had met you, and that you seemed like someone who would listen to our little spiel."

"Nothing better to do at the moment," Denera said, though she winked to show she was just playing.

"As I told you before," Omoro began, "I'm new here, and I'm a little unsettled by how things are going. This place feels more like a prison camp than a neighborhood."

"You got that right," Desten said. "Things have changed, and not for the better."

"So, what do you propose to do about it?" Denera asked.

"Just this, for now," Omoro said. "Reaching out to others. Forming a community. Ending the isolation that keeps us afraid to leave our houses. But we know we must be...delicate about it."

"Uh huh," Denera said.

"Which is why we're staying small right now. One person visits another's house. One person from that house visits another, and so on until we've built a network of people."

"To what end?"

"To their end," Desten said, motioning vaguely towards the wall. "Those who are keeping us controlled. Those hidden masters behind the drones."

"Have you seen any of them?" Omoro asked.

"No, never have," Denera responded. Even the groceries are delivered by those big, rolling drones. The ones that look like fridges on wheels."

Omoro thought for a moment as the others stayed silent. "They're not treating us like people. More like...livestock.

Growing us. Allowing us, no, urging us to reproduce for them. I wouldn't be surprised to find that they put something in our food to make us more docile." She looked at Thomas. "That's right, isn't it?"

He looked at her, then at the others, before speaking. "I...I don't know what you mean. We're supplied with everything we need to live our lives. We want for nothing."

"Bullshit," Desten said. "No art. No books. Nothing except sports or reality television to keep us entertained. I'm not even sure if they're real people on those shows or some kind of digital reproductions. No travel to see other places. We're captives in a prison without walls."

"Are you sure there are no walls?" Omoro asked. "Has anyone just started walking to see if there's an end to all of this?"

No one answered, as they all thought about her words.

"I'll take that as a no," she said softly.

Thomas stood up and began pacing. "You all are unhappy because you don't understand how good you have it here. You could be starving. Or living on the street. Or both."

"So, you work for them?" Denera asked him.

"What? No!" Thomas said, stopping to look at them, but his expression said otherwise. "I don't know who they are, either. I just think that we shouldn't be rocking the boat, or it could get worse real quick."

"You spineless little sycophant," Desten said bitterly. He looked at Omoro. "It's obvious that if you want this movement to succeed, that you can't count on the men to lead it or even be a significant part of it."

"Excluding you?" Thomas asked. "You're the special one here?"

"No," Desten said. "But I don't have anything to lose, either. I know how that sounds," he said, looking back at

Omoro. "When I was younger and had a wife and family, I could have stood up and said something, but I didn't, and for that I apologize."

Omoro nodded. "That's in the past. Now is the time, and you've stood up with us. We just need everyone else to stand as well."

"What if we gathered everyone and protested?" Denera suggested. "They can't ignore that, right?"

"They can," Desten said. "And even the most peaceful protest would probably be met with violence. Those drones can be deadly."

Thomas was standing in front of the kitchen window looking outside as she spoke. Suddenly, he walked to the door and left the house. Omoro and the others looked at each other for a moment.

"What's he doing?" Denera asked.

"I don't know, but we'd better see," Desten said.

They all stood and followed Thomas out the front door.

Omoro stopped, shocked at what she saw. There was a drone flying low over the neighborhood, and Thomas was attempting to wave it down.

"What the hell?" Desten said loudly.

"He'll tell them," Denera said.

Omoro ignored them. She watched as the man who called himself her husband waved his arms and even jumped up and down a few times as he tried to attract the drone's attention.

"Thomas, stop!" she finally screamed at him.

He looked at her, and she could see the bitter expression on his face. He didn't stop, and soon the drone was heading towards their location.

"Thomas!" she yelled again and stepped off the porch.

"No! It's too late now," Desten said, grabbing her arm

gently. "Don't go out there."

She turned and looked at him and saw the resignation in his face. They would be killed or captured and possibly tortured. The movement was barely in its infancy, and it had been brought down already. She felt tears come to her eyes, but nodded to him and stepped back up on the porch as she watched the drone settle above Thomas.

"You must listen to me," Thomas yelled up at the mechanical sentry.

"Citizen Thomas, you are causing a disturbance. Cease your activities at once."

"No, listen, I have something important to tell you!"

"Citizen Thomas,, you will receive no more warnings. You are exhibiting an unfavorable pattern of behavior."

"But this is important," Thomas said, though he lowered his arms. "You must listen."

A single ray of red light shot out from the front of the drone. It easily burned through Thomas' chest cavity and then deep into the ground behind him. He dropped without a sound.

"Get inside!" Denera hissed at Omoro and Desten.

They all quickly went inside the house and closed the door. Omoro sat heavily on the floor of the entryway, crying. She wasn't upset so much about the loss of the man named Thomas, but she realized now the incredible odds they were facing. She wasn't sure she was strong enough.

Desten was surreptitiously looking out the kitchen window. "It's still there. Just hovering."

"Probably reporting this to someone," Denera said quietly. She kneeled before Omoro, then reached out and grasped Omoro's hand in hers. "I don't know if what we do will make any difference." She squeezed Omoro's hand between both of hers. "But I'm willing to take the chance.

I'm willing to fight."

Omoro wiped her eyes with her free hand, then smiled up at the other woman. This woman who could be her sister. "Thank you. I'm...I am too."

"You know where I stand," Desten said, walking the few steps over to them. "I'll follow wherever you lead, Omoro."

"So will I," Denera said.

"Help me up," Omoro said. She reached out to Desten, and he and Denera both pulled her to her feet. She hugged Denera and felt the other woman reciprocate. Then she turned to Desten and hugged him as well. Then she backed up and looked at them both. "We have a lot of work to do."

The End

Escape

A Sand Warrior Story

He knelt in a darkened room. At the top of the wall, near the ceiling, was a small vent letting in sunlight from the outside. The beams fell through the vent at a down-turned angle but didn't illuminate much within the room. Dust clouds swirled in the beams of light. A scraping sound repeated over and over. The tall man was hunched over towards the floor with something in his hands.

His name was David, before. He'd been a doctor, working in a profession where he could both distinguish himself and help others. That had been before. Now, he was kept in a small cell with little light and even less to do. So, he kept himself busy.

He stopped scraping long enough to look up and work out the kinks in his neck. The door to the room was closed, locked, and intimidating in its solidness. There was a small slot near the floor for food and water to be passed through, though most times he was shuffled out to the communal eating area of the prison.

He had the number 243 tattooed on his forehead, just above his cybernetic left eye. His clothes were nondescript and bland, not only because of the lighting, but because that's the way all the clothing given to the humans looked there. He wore a shirt and long pants. His feet were covered with pull on moccasin-like shoes that offered little protection from the sand and pebbles in the prison yard.

David was tall and muscular, though thin. He'd kept himself in good shape before, and now, exercise was something to pass the time. The small piece of tubular metal in his hands scraped back and forth across the floor as his thoughts floated somewhere else. The edge was slowly becoming sharp enough to cut easily. He'd found it in the yard when he'd first arrived at the prison. It had been a metal straw, but now it was becoming a weapon. He wasn't entirely sure what he would use it for, but that could come later. For now, it proved a way to pass the time.

"Time for running! All prisoners ready in ten minutes!" the loudspeaker blared above his head. It was a rough voice—mechanical and grating due to the translation device his captors used.

He turned his head to the side while he listened to the voice of the alien jailer while it made announcements over the loudspeaker. The speaker was set into the wall above his head—high enough so that it couldn't be reached easily. His metallic eye gleamed in the dim light, as did the metal tube clutched in his hand.

"Time for running! All prisoners ready in ten minutes!" the loudspeaker blared.

David lifted his mattress and hid the tube under it. He faced the doorway, waiting for the large door to slide to the side. The door to David's room opened all the way and he left and began walking down a long, dingy hallway with many doors. Other prisoners walked the same way in front of him as well as behind him, all of them with numbers on their heads and the same bland clothing. Most have shaved heads, though some still had hair. All the cell doors were open now, with prisoners still coming out of many of them.

A small man with a thatch of white hair on his head, large ears and an even larger nose began walking next to David. His name was Mop, and his number was 459. Behind him was a tall and very skinny black man with the number 871 on his forehead. Mop was maybe sixty-five years old, if David had to guess. The black man, Pope, was about the same age and his curly black hair was graying around his temples. He was wearing thick-lens glasses that made his eyes look very large.

"How's it goin' David? What's new?" Mop asked in his quirky way of speaking.

"Mop. Pope. Staying out of trouble?" David asked.

Mop smiled up at David. "Aw, y'know me. 'M too small to cause a row. An' Pope's too stupid."

A large shape loomed up behind Pope. The shape belonged to Cord. Cord was a massive man, not as tall as David, but pushing 450 pounds easily. He had a long black ponytail, a substantial gut, and sweated profusely through his clothes, even in cool weather. He was about 36 years old. The number on his forehead was 113. He pushed Pope from behind. "Watch out you shits! Get the fuck in line!"

Cord kept a sadistic smile on his face as he walked down the lineup of prisoners heading for the exercise yard. The small metal badge on his chest gleamed in the low light. It was a badge given to him by their captors, to show the other prisoners that he was working for them. Some were like that. David figured he was too fat to exercise, and way too fat to slip out of this place unnoticed, so he'd better make do as a turncoat guard.

Cord was standing (and sweating) over an older man

who was sitting on the floor, holding one of his legs with both hands. His number was 230. "You little piece of filth!" Cord yelled. "What the hell do you think this is, a summer camp, Jonesy! Get up!"

The elderly man's gaunt and sallow face was screwed up in pain and he was almost crying. "I...I can't sir. My leg...oh my leg. Please help me..."

Cord's face still showed his sneering smile, even uglier now that he was focused on a victim. He was holding a whistle in front of his mouth. His cheeks had bloomed into two blotchy red flowers, with his jowls hanging from his ham-like face. "What'd I tell you, slug!? Huh? What'd I tell you yesterday!?"

Jonesy looked terrified. "But you...you, I mean, but..."

"Shut up! That's it for you! Oh yes, it is!" Cord blew the whistle, its sound shrieking through the air of the mostly silent prison. His cheeks inflated to huge proportions and turned red with the effort.

Now the elderly man was crying in fear. He was reaching out towards Cord, begging him to stop. "No! No please. I'll be good. Please Cord. I'll be good!"

Terrelian guards ran up to where Cord was standing over the elderly prisoner, pointing at him and smiling.

That fat bastard, David thought. He beat Jonesy the day before simply because he knew he could. Injured his leg knowing it would impede him from doing his duties.

The guards were dragging the kicking and screaming prisoner away from Cord. "No, I'll be good. I'll be good, I promise!" Jonesy was now almost shrieking with his effort to plead for his life.

The exercise yard was the courtyard of a large brick structure that may have once been a school but was now a prison. The alien piggies were walking the railings, holding their weapons at the ready. All the prisoners—all males—were running around a large oval track for their forced exercise session. A fast-rushing river traveled underneath the main brick building, twisting and turning as it flowed away from the facility.

Two large wooden doors were set into the walls of the courtyard on each side. While the humans were running on the track, the doors on the eastern side opened with a bang. Two human sympathizers were dragging out the beaten and bloody body of Jonesy. Behind the procession of humans was a large Terrelian warrior. Behind him was Cord. As the Terrelian spoke, Cord translated his words into English. "This human has not followed the directives of the masters. We are the masters. We must be obeyed. Because of his lack of obedience, he is hereby sentenced to death."

The Terrelian pulled out his pistol and unceremoniously shot Jonesy in the back of the head. The men dragged the body to an open trapdoor in the ground next to the northern wall, leaving a bloody trail as they went. They dropped the body through the open trapdoor. Jonesy's body fell into the water below with a splash as the trap door banged shut above it.

David was running along with the other prisoners in a single-file line. In front of him was Pope, and in front of Pope was Mop.

"'S a shame about Jonesy. Prolly fer the best, though," Mop said, struggling to breathe.

Pope sniffed loudly at this.

Mop continued without acknowledging it. "God knows there's times...when I'd rather take the plunge than t' stay here another day. Then I see it done like that...and 'm not so sure."

There were tears running down Pope's cheeks. David's

face had an intense look of hatred that he made no effort to hide—both for the Terrelians and for Cord. Jonesy deserved better than that, he thought. We all do.

He decided then that it was time to do something about it.

◊

David sat in his room, the metal straw-turned-weapon in his hand. One edge was now razor sharp. He lifted it slowly and placed the dull end in his mouth and breathed through it. He nodded, satisfied. Then he thought about what needed to be done. He would need some help pulling it off, but if he did, he would be free of the prison, and of Cord.

He felt like his entire life had led up to this. His medical education, his time in the military, and his hatred for the alien invaders who had taken over his world. His thoughts turned to plans within plans and for a while he was still and silent as he contemplated his future.

◊

Breakfast in the cafeteria. The prisoners sat eating their porridge—a simple meal that barely provided nutrients to their listless bodies. Sometimes David wondered why the Terrelians didn't just line them up along a wall and shoot them all. Why keep up the pretense of having prisoners if all they were destined for was a quick death and the inevitable plunge? There had to be a reason they were being kept alive, but he couldn't think of why.

He surreptitiously watched one of the Terrelian guards. The species, or at least what he'd seen of them, were tall and broad-shouldered, hefty with muscle. Two small green eyes in the middle of their faces above large snouts and large teeth that tended to protrude of their mouths at odd angles. Dark complexions with hair in random tufts on their faces.

The guard caught his eye, and he lowered his gaze. No

need to invite trouble with one of the guards if he could help it. Prisoners had been killed for making eye contact too long. Now trustees, on the other hand—those humans who had thrown in their lot with the aliens—they were a different story. Most kept away at their own tables in the cafeteria. They were shunned by most of their fellow prisoners. They were considered by the prisoners to be the foulest of humanity, and Cord was the worst of them.

David once again lifted his gaze and looked over to where Cord sat. The man was eating sausage and eggs. Turncoats were given special privileges, including more nourishment so that they could help to intimidate their fellow prisoners. For the most part, the Terrelians seemed almost uninterested in what their human prisoners did. They left the policing to their trustees, though they looked down on any outright killing by the trustees. They were in charge, and the taking of a life was their providence.

The speakers came to life once more. "Return to your rooms. One hour rest period."

The prisoners all rose quietly. They would get one hour before it was time to run once more. The Terrelians had learned that forcing them to run, even after such a light breakfast, resulted in a courtyard full of vomiting prisoners.

◊

The prisoners were shuffling back to their rooms, exhausted from another day of running. The only point in the running that David could see was to make them use up all of the calories that they got from their food—a way to keep them tired and docile. David was leaning with his back against the doorjamb, his arms crossed before him. This, of course, was just inviting trouble from Cord or another of the guards, and predictably, it caught Cord's attention. "What the hell are you doing?"

Cord was coming at David from a little way down the empty hallway. It was just the two of them in the hallway now, as all of the other prisoners had gone to their cells. David was smiling.

"What, you wanna be next? Want to end like Jonesy? I think you do!" Cord screamed.

"Why don't you shove that whistle up your ass, Cord," David said quietly, but loud enough for the other man to hear. Cord was furious, which left him open to attack from David. While Cord was fuming and sticking his face as close to David's as possible, David shot out a hand, the hard edge of it crushed Cord's windpipe with a satisfying crunch.

"Why you...ack!" Cord fell into David's arms, and then to the floor. David sat on Cord's chest while he struggled to breathe through his broken windpipe. His struggles eventually lessened, and then he was still, his hands falling to the floor beside him. David dragged Cord's body into his room. Mop was sitting on the bed smiling. "We don't have much time, Mop," David said to the older man.

"That's ok. I been sewing a long while now. Won't take but a moment 's all."

David was standing over Cord's body, which was lying on its back. He held the knife that he'd fashioned out of the piece of metal. It was ready to cut now. David had field dressed plenty of animals, and Cord wouldn't be much different. He began to cut as Pope entered the room, arms filled with towels and even a small trash bag that he had found somewhere. He was smiling widely.

David knew that every dead human was dropped into the river pit to wash downstream from the prison. They'd been dumping bodies at a pace of about two per day. When he'd first arrived there, it was by a boat coming up the river. He'd stopped counting the floating, rotting corpses when he reached two hundred.

◊

The Terrelian guards found Cord's body the next morning. They felt sympathy for the human turncoat and had three other trustees drag his massive body over to the trapdoor in the courtyard. They finally managed to drop it into the river below with a loud splash. Both Mop and Pope watched passively as they ran their circuit.

The body of Cord floated down the river, past demolished buildings and lush vegetation on the shoreline. A small metal tube was sticking up from the chest, its end sharpened into a point. The body washed up on the shore of a small, rocky beach on the side of the river. Other bodies had landed there as well, and bones littered the pebbles, some with clothes and hair still apparent on their bleached white skeletons. Most were half-buried by detritus or half in the water. A recent body—Jonesy—was faced down and hideously bloated.

For once the practice of dumping the bodies of prisoners indiscriminately was going to cost the Terrelians dearly. Cord's chest began to undulate with movement below the clothing. It took a long time for David to fashion a knife from the straw. It was worth every minute of struggle, he thought.

Long, black fingers poked out from between Cord's shirt and pants, followed by two arms that extended up, one hand still clutching the metal tube. There was an upside down 'T' cut into the man's stomach, and it had been crudely sewn back together—Mop's handiwork on full display.

The Terrelians wanted to make them into numbers. They wanted to show us humans that a single man is insignificant, David thought as he finally took in a lungful of fresh air. He was sitting up inside Cord's body cavity and covered in blood and offal. But one man, just one, can make a difference in this fight, he thought as he threw the straw to the rocks on the riverside.

David looked up at the sunlight shining down from the sky and smiled, closing his eyes. The water was sparkling and there were lush green trees and birds singing and small animals foraging on the shoreline nearby. Despite the fact that he was sitting inside another human being's body, the scene was almost peaceful.

One man can set himself apart, he thought as he rolled into the cool water.

The End

Blood Moon

The nights of harvest seem to last forever in my town. On this particular night, the moon rose over the cornfield that stretched to the horizon. The blood moon is what we call it 'round here. That's 'cause it looks so red, like it's filled with the blood of innocents or somethin'.

I was sittin' on the back porch with Lester Moody. I can't say as I like him much, but some company is better than none at all. We were passin' a jug of home-brew between us and fertilizing the corn with our stories when suddenly Lester gets all serious on me. Now that's pretty scary in itself, but the story he told me gave me the willies somethin' fierce.

"You know, Bobby, it was a night like this that my Betty Jean died." He took a swig and kept the bottle in his lap. We were both pretty snockered, so I let him keep it for a while. I figured he needed it more'n I did, seein' as how he'd never talked to anyone about his wife's death. 'Specially me.

We sat there a moment in silence; just listening to the insects singing.

"We was comin' down the old Creech Road. We'd been playin' poker at Jim and Nancy Baker's house that night. Actually won fifty dollars, too." He made a face somewhere between a smile an' a grimace. "Betty Jean was so good that night. So pretty." His voice had gotten quiet. I could see his eyes had gotten moist, and by God, mine weren't exactly dry, neither. I'd grown up with Betty Jean Kelly. Probably woulda married her, too. But that's a long story; better left alone for now.

Lester took another pull on the jug and cleared his throat before startin' again. "Nancy offered to let us stay the night. We'd all been drinkin', an' I'm not sucha good driver, even when I'm sober. But Betty, she'd been givin' me the look all night. Like she was promisin' that we'd celebrate our winnin's when we got home. God, I shoulda put my foot down. Just told 'er that we was stayin' there. But I didn't. We'd only been married a little while, then, and the thrill was still there." He chuckled and smiled, lookin' out at the corn.

"Soon as we got out of sight of their house, Betty started kissin' on me. I swear I almost wrecked us when it came time to turn onto Creech." The bottle now lay forgotten in his grasp. He was lookin' at the corn, but I could tell he didn't see it. He was seein' the old dirt road that ran from County Lake to Main Street. It was the most-used road in town in the summertime. Seemed like everyone went to the lake for a swim.

Lester stayed quiet for a while, lost in his thoughts. It gave me time to do some thinkin' of my own. When was the last time I'd gone to the lake? I'm certain it had been a long time ago. Betty an' me use to go all the time. Just pack a picnic lunch; bologna and cheese sandwiches, her homemade potata salad, and a six-pack of Bud. She would get so tan. Seemed all I ever did was burn. But it was alright, 'cause that night Betty'd rub cream on my achin' shoulders.

I never meant ta hurt her. It was somethin' that just happened. A man gets tired of goin' to the same pump ta get his water, if you know what I mean. So, when Betty's girlfriend, Mary Helen, come aroun' the house when she knew Betty was away visitin', I just couldn't help myself. How was I to know Betty would come back early. She always stayed late to her mother's. She just had to pick this day to get inna squabble with the ol' bat.

I tried to make it up to her, but by the time I'd gotten enough money together to buy her some roses, she had already taken up with Lester Moody; the least-liked man in town. It wasn't that Lester was a bad guy, it was just that he was a loud-mouthed sonuva bitch. Not that anyone would come right our and say somethin' like that to 'im. Most folks 'round here are too decent to be that rude. Course, there are some, like that bully, George Hallister, that did just that. I guess bein' the captain of the football team and the son of the mill owner entitles you to that kind of behavior.

So anyways, when I found out that she'd started seein' Lester, I guess I kinda went a little nuts. Not whole-hog, mind you. Just a little. Must have been, 'cause what I did, well let's just say that I wasn't runnin' on all cylinders. Luckily, Lester broke me out o' this train of thought by talkin' some more. That's one thing about Les, you can always count on 'im to be yappin' when most people knew to shut up. But this time, I could forgive 'im.

"Ya gotta promise me, promise that what's said tonight stays 'tween us, Bobby." I thought of makin' fun of his cloak an' dagger talk, but he was lookin' at me with such pleadin' eyes, I just couldn't.

"I promise, Les. Nobody but us'll know."

"Hope ta die?" He says.

"Hope ta die." I even crossed my chest with my finger. Anythin' to get on with it. He musta remembered the almost empty jug in his hands, 'cause he tipped it up and finished what was inside before startin' his story.

"We was goin' down Creech Road. The car couldn't have been goin' more'n twenty miles an hour. I was tryin' ta keep both hands on the wheel, but Betty's attentions were gettin' mighty persistent.

When I felt her unzip my jeans, I must've gotten too excited, 'cause we ended up in the ditch."

I seem to remember seein' a picture in the paper. In it, Lester's 1974 Escort was half-stuck in that ditch. Lester was sittin' on the fender talkin' to the sheriff, and a medic was patchin' up his shoulder. He already had a white bandage on his forehead.

"Neither one of us was hurt much, although I'd knocked my noggin on the steerin' wheel. We were both laughin' as I helped her out the driver's side door. The ditch was half-filled with water, so I carried her ta the road so she didn't get her feet wet."

He stopped to take a swig of whiskey, then saw that he'd already finished it off. "As I was about ta set her on the ground, we heard some rustlin' in the corn on the other side of the road. Now I'd heard tell that some livestock had been killed over at old man Sykes' place, just down the road from where we were, by either a mountain lion or bear. But they usually run when they get winda us humans."

"I called out, 'who's there?' I says. Betty Jean, she'd had just as much to drink as me. She answers with, 'nobody but us chickens, buck, buck.' Nobody could stay sad around my Betty." We shared a chuckle, remembering the sparkle that was always in her eyes.

"We was just turnin' ta see if we could get the car outta the ditch; Betty was taking off her shoes an' socks. All of a sudden we heard a roar come from the cornfield. I'd never heard anythin' like it. I was standin' calf-deep in water an' I saw it as it charged from the stalks."

He swallowed a coupla times, his throat lookin' like there was somethin' in there tryin' to get out. Finally, I says to 'im, "well, what was it?" Even though I knew the answer already.

Up until that time he had been lookin' at his shoes or out into the field. But now he looked me straight inna eye as he said, "I don't know, Bobby. I've never seen it in no book, an' believe me, I've looked plenty since that night. It was huge. Bigger than a dog, but not as big as a full-grown bear would be. It looked kinda like a wolf, but there was somethin' about it that wasn't quite…right. I can't explain what. It was covered in black hair. And it moved so fast, I was still lookin' when it…it…" He looked down, a tear tricklin' down and droppin' on the jug.

"Oh God, Bobby, it was on 'er before she could even scream. She tried to fight it, but there was no chance. Not against that…thing. When I saw it bite her, it broke the spell that was over me. I yelled and jumped outta the ditch. It was standin' on its hind legs, and it was as tall as she was. I grabbed her and turned to push her away from it. It took a swipe at me and hit me inna shoulder. Knocked me clear inta the ditch again. It was back on all fours, and it started growlin' real low in its throat." He wiped at his wet cheek.

"I thought I was dead for sure, but it just sat there an' an' looked at me. Betty Jean was cryin' softly; she had made it to the car, but couldn't get the door closed. Finally, the thing just turned an' disappeared into the field where it had come out. I staggered to my feet then, my shoulder felt like it was afire. I went to where Betty Jean sat in the doorway of the car. The beast, it had…had bit her on the…the arm. It shouldn't've been too serious, but it must've hit an artery or somethin', 'cause she had been bleedin' badly for a while. I couldn't get my arm to work, an' she was too weak to keep enough pressure on the wound to stop the bleedin'. All I could do was hold her in my arms as she slowly d-died." He covered his eyes with his hands an' sobbed. I reached out an' squeezed his shoulder, the same one that had been injured that night, long ago.

The news of Betty Jean's death had rocked our small town. 'Specially since it happened so brutally. The day of her funeral, there wasn't a dry eye in the assembly as Preacher John gave his eulogy.

I made up my mind, then, that Les deserved the truth before he died. I started tellin' my story, an' as I did, he stopped cryin' so as to listen better.

"When you an' Betty got married, I was almost plumb crazy with jealousy, even though I knew it was my own fault for losin' her. You remember at your wedding reception, that strange man that came through town, tryin' to sell homemade elixirs an' such?"

Lester nodded.

"Well, everyone just made fun of 'im, and I did, too. But then somethin' made me stop an' think about it. Maybe he had somethin' that could help me win Betty back. Some kinda aphrodisiac or somethin'. A love potion was sure to do the trick, or so I had thought."

"Like I say, I wasn't thinkin' rational at the time. So, I left when I was sure that he'd made the outskirts of town. I met up with him headin' towards Smithville. When I found 'im, he was sittin' on the hood of the most beat-up lookin' station wagon I'd ever seen. Painted on the side was, 'Josiah McGee, elixirs, tonics and medicines.' Like I said, he was just sittin' on the hood, like he was waitin' for someone. I studied him as I pulled up. He had a head full o' blond hair that looked like he'd spent a great deal of time on it. He was dressed in a dark suit that had gone out of style when I was just a twinkle in daddy's eye.

"I turned off the engine and thought to myself, 'you don't haveta do this, you can start the car an' go back and wish them a good life and then get drunk.' But that wasn't really an option by that time. So, I stepped outta my car and went to talk to 'im.

"'Uh, hello there, Mr. McGee. My name is Bobby. Bobby Jones." I held out my hand for him to shake. He hopped off the hood and shook it three times, up an' down before releasing it.

"A pleasure meeting you, Bobby, and please, call me Josiah." He was smilin' an' showin' all his teeth. That smile almost made me turn an' leave right there, but Betty was all I was thinkin' about.

"What can I do for you today, Bobby? You look like a strong young man, surely there is nothing wrong with you?" It kinda struck me funny that he called me a young man, 'cause he couldn't have been that much older than me, by his looks.

"'Well, Mr. McG...' I began.

"Josiah, please." He was still smilin', an' I was beginning to think his face was stuck like that.

"'Well, uh, Josiah, I was wonderin' if, well, you had somethin' that would help me get my girl back.' I couldn't look at 'im. After a short silence, I looked up to see that his grin had been replaced by a thoughtful look.

"Well, that is a problem, is it not? Especially," he turned to look me in the eye, "when that lovely young lady was just wed this morning." My eyes opened wide at this. How did he know who I was talkin' about?

"It was so obvious at the party, Bobby. And rumors do get around." He was smilin' again, like he was enjoyin' his own private joke. "The question now is not whether I have something that can help you in your predicament; it is whether or not you can pay the price I set."

"I reached into my pocket for my wallet. I wasn't sure how much cash I had on me, though."

"Put your money away, Bobby. All I want for my services is a small...donation from you. It won't hurt...much." That smile again. "And think of how happy you'll be when you hold Betty Jean in your arms once again." He lost his grin. "All you need to do is say one word."

My mind was racin' now. Did she really mean that much to me? Yes, I figured. Yes.

"'Yes.'"

He smiled. "Very well, Bobby. Very well." He reached in through his car window and pulled out a small bottle. It was no bigger 'an a pill bottle. And totally black. He held it out to me and a voice in my head started screamin', "no!" But it was too late, way too late to go back. I reached out an' grabbed it. As I took 'hold of it, I felt a sting in my finger. I looked down to see blood well from where I had cut it on the jagged edge of the top.

"Now, I shall explain to you just what exactly that potion will do for you, Bobby. You see, it is a very special recipe."

And as he explained, I knew I was lost forever.

"The potion," he began, "will allow you to change into your soul animal. What this is depends on the condition of your soul." He smiled at me in what I s'pose was a reassurin' way. It wasn't. "All you need to do is infect the lady in some way. Whatever way you choose, blood must flow."

"As he kept talkin', my mind kept goin' back to those words. Blood must flow. Finally, he stopped talkin'. I was sorta inna daze, 'cause suddenly he was in his station wagon, wavin' and sayin', "good luck, Bobby, and remember, blood must flow."

I just watched as he slowly made his way along the dirt

road, a cloud of dust followin' him like a cape. I looked down at the bottle in my hand. And smiled."

Lester had been quiet this whole time, an' I don't blame him a bit. I looked an' saw that he was grippin' that jug so hard that his knuckles were white. I continued my story.

"The next night I decided to try the stuff. I walked out into the cornfield so as not to be seen and took the bottle outta my pocket. It had grown warm from my body. I slowly turned it this way an' that, lookin' for the sharp piece that had cut me the day before, but I couldn't see it. I unscrewed the cap and took a sniff. Nothing. It coulda been water for all I knew. 'Probably is,' I says to myself. But deep down I knew it wasn't true. There are some things that you just know are true in this world.

The sun rises in the East, the old Coke is better 'an the new, and whatever was in that bottle had no right to even be on the face of the earth. I put it to my lips and drank. It might not of had a smell, but the taste of it almost made me lose my lunch. The thought that I had just poisoned myself went quickly through my mind, but I knew that the only thing that had been poisoned was my eternal soul. Then I thought, "if my soul is lost, what kinda soul animal will I have?" Too late, I realized the truth.

The first pain hit me in the gut. I've only felt pain like that one other time, and that was when Rebecca Cranston had gotten mad at me for pulling her pig tail back on the school playground and kicked me where it hurts the most. She was wearin' her snow boots, too.

"I musta blacked-out then. I don't really know for sure. I came to runnin' through the corn near Virgil Sykes' place. My first thought was not that I was goin' on all fours, or that nothin' was right in my body; all my senses seemed reborn, as if they had been asleep all these years and had just woken up. No, my first thought was that my bladder felt fit to burst. It's funny, when you think about it. Here I was changed into some monster from Hell, and all I could think about at the time was waterin' the corn.

"Afterwards, I trotted over to the barn. That transformation musta took a lot outta me, 'cause I felt like I could eat a horse all by my lonesome, and still have room for pie. Well, you've heard the stories of what I did. I don't want to think about it.

"After that it was justa matter of screwin' up my courage enough to do what I had to do. There was no thinkin' about it anymore. It was justa coincidence that you two crashed your car near where I was headin' towards the lake a coupla days later. I heard you talkin' and laughin' and carryin' on, an' I just...let my anger get the best of me. I only wanted to hurt her, Les, you gotta believe me when I say that. Blood must flow, that's what he said. I'd rather 'ave died myself than to see her die."

I looked at him and his eyes were wide, starin' back.

"When I'd heard that she had...died," the weight of the words were makin' them fall out of my mouth inna rush now, "well, I went all the way 'round the bend. That was why after the funeral I went outta town for a while."

We sat in silence once again. This time, it seemed that the insects had stopped their singin'. Like they were waitin' for somethin' to happen. The hatred that I had kept cooped up inside of me couldn't be bottled-up any longer.

"I'm real sorry about you gettin' mixed-up in this. You shoulda never even dated her, let alone married her. But now that I told you this, I can't let you talk." I could feel the change comin' on me now; could feel the power coursin' through my veins. As the hair came pokin' outta my skin, I heard Les the loudmouth, who nobody liked, who once got beat up by every guy on the football team in the same school year.

Well, I heard him say real quietly, "so it was you, Bobby." He stood slowly an' I saw the jug fall to the wooden porch and shatter. I was down on all fours now, the change strong upon me.

I saw him reach down to his ankle an' pull out the Derringer pistol from the holster he wore there. "You just don't know how much in love we was, do ya? My life ended the same night that her's did, Bobby. But I couldn't kill myself until I found the man that had killed her."

"How could he know it was a man?" I asked myself. Almost like he read my mind, he spoke again.

"Bet your wonderin' how I knew it was a man, aren't you?" He smiled. "Well, about the time you left town, that strange man came through selling elixirs an' such again. This time, I stopped by to chat with him."

With dawning horror, I knew that what was loaded in that gun was more than enough to kill me. Lester chuckled as he said, "you say hi to Mr. McGee for me, Bobby. And tell Betty Jean, I'll be there shortly too." He pulled the trigger.

That's when my world exploded.

The blood moon rode high that night, over the cornfield that stretched to the horizon.

The End

Sucking

The bat flew heavily, gorged on blood in a night not seen since the beginning of the world. The wind screamed through the darkness—a darkness which sucked at the spirit of all those who loved the light. No stars were visible, though no clouds were, either...

Daniel sat with his head in his hands, all hope had faded. Now there was only fear. It was fear that had brought him here, though not fear for himself. It was more a fear of himself.

For a moment the wind was still, and he heard the howl in the distance. The police were on the way, though it was already too late. And besides, they would not have done any good, even if they had arrived on time. His was an act brought upon by an angry god. This was not the god of the Christians or Jews or Muslims, no. This was something far more ancient. And far more evil.

He sat on the stone steps in front of an apartment building where she had lived. He remembered the blood. Its sweet-salt tang, its coppery scent. He leaned over and vomited large gobs of the bitter substance onto the dry grass before him. He also remembered her face. Her pretty face that was now the face of a corpse—yellowed and sunken from the lack of blood pumping through capillaries and veins.

The question now was, what was he supposed to do? He had called the police with the intention of turning himself in. But would the prison bars be able to hold him in when the lust for blood was upon him and he once again became an unthinking monster? Now that he was satiated and able think more clearly, he didn't think they could.

He needed to find a dark place to rest. He would feel better after he rested his body. He was not used to the transformation, having only been turned a few days before. He wasn't sure if it would ever get better, but for now, he needed sanctuary and time to think.

He stood and staggered for a moment before his footing became sure again. The darkness called to him. Called for him to be one with the night. He followed a path that drew him on, unsure of what type of sense he was using, but it wasn't one of sight, taste, or smell. His hearing was filled with the wailing of approaching sirens.

They would find the body, which was good. She deserved to be laid to rest properly. She would not turn. He had shared no blood with her, and had sucked out too much of her own, still unused to the demands of his own hunger.

There was only one place he could think of to go, and he soon found himself standing before his old high school. He had helped the janitor a few times and knew that there was a boiler room below the school grounds that would stay dark, no matter the weather outside or time of day.

He easily broke the bolt of the lock on the front door and slipped inside, smelling the old, familiar smells: chalk, erasers, body odor, someone's lunch inside their locker. It was a Friday, and the school had only been empty for a few hours—little enough time for these odors to dissipate. And it meant that the school would stay empty a day or two, barring the occasional teacher or administrator.

He found the stairway that led to the basement and made his way to the boiler room, which was behind another locked door. No need to break the lock on this one—the janitor had shown him where the keys were located. At the time he'd felt like a prison trustee, but thinking about it now made him wonder if the janitor didn't have some ulterior, and less pleasant motive. Well, let him try something now, he thought, smiling grimly.

The room was dark after he closed and once more locked the door. He could still see—his altered eyesight was much like a cat's—and able to pick up even the most minute particle of light. He looked around for a good place to lie down and noticed a tarp in the corner. He walked to it and saw it was covering some paint cans and other painting paraphernalia. He picked up the tarp and went to the adjacent corner. He wrapped the tarp around himself the best he could, which felt natural for whatever reason, then laid down, and was almost instantly asleep.

◊

If he had hoped for relief when sleep overtook him, he'd been mistaken. His dreams seemed drenched in blood, and he remembered the moment he'd become a creature of the night.

He'd always been a loner all through school. Even in high school, he'd never really had any friends. He also had never felt attracted to anyone of any gender. He'd seen a show that spoke about how it was like going to a buffet and not feeling hungry for anything, which he supposed was a good enough explanation for asexuality.

That had changed when he'd met a girl named Rhonda. He'd been working at a large chain store a few years after graduating, with no prospects and no ambitions. His manager had brought his shift together to introduce new team members, and he'd seen her for the first time. There was something about her that was both exciting and mysterious.

She'd noticed him looking at her and had smiled at him. He'd quickly looked away and had basically stared at his shoes for the rest of the meeting. The next day towards the end of his shift, he was placing bedding items on the top shelf in the Homestyle aisle when a voice spoke behind him.

"Be careful, you wouldn't want to fall."

He turned on the rolling stairway and saw it was her. She was smiling up at him, and he couldn't help but return her smile. "Daniel, right?"

"Yes," he answered, climbing down to the floor.

She held out her hand. "Rhonda." He shook it, and noticed how cool her skin was to the touch. At the time he didn't really think about it—his mother had circulation problems in her extremities as well. It hadn't set off any internal alarms. What had set off alarms was how close she had stood next to him while they chit-chatted about mundane items that he could no longer remember.

"I'd better get to work," she finally said. "I'll see you around."

"Yes," he said. "Are you working the midnight shift most days?" He kicked himself internally, not knowing why he'd asked the question.

She smiled again. "Why yes, I'm definitely a night owl. You?"

"Whenever they schedule me, I guess."

"Enjoy the rest of your night," she said, and turned before he could say anything else, which came as a relief.

On his way out the door after his shift ended, he ran into Allie, who he'd known since the ninth grade. She was a nice enough person, but he kept most people at bay by habit, so he was surprised when she walked up to him and began speaking to him. "Hey, Daniel."

"Hey."

"Done for the night?"

"Yeah."

"Listen, I was going to grab a sandwich from the shop across the street. Want to join me?"

He thought for a moment, unsure of the rush of thoughts and feelings that seemed new to him. "Uh..."

"You don't have to," she said hurriedly. "Just thought you might be hungry too."

"Oh, yeah. Sure. I had planned on finding something to eat." He sounded so lame in his own ears. He hardly spoke with anyone, and this was the second person he'd had to hold a conversation with within a period of a few hours.

"Great," she said. "Let me just stop by my car and drop off this uniform top. He nodded stupidly and followed her to where her Honda was parked. It was still summer, though the nights were beginning to grow chillier. She took off her work shirt and he could see that she was wearing a t-shirt underneath that said, "At least my dog likes me."

"I like your shirt," he said.

"Thanks. I don't own a dog." She laughed at his expression of confusion.

They walked to the sandwich shop, which showed that it was closing soon. Once they received their food, they ate for a moment, not having said much to each other since leaving her car.

"So, what have you been doing since graduation?" she suddenly asked.

"This," he answered, pointing to himself. He still wore his work shirt. He smiled to show that his answer was of the self-deprecating kind.

"I tried college for a year," she said. "Didn't really like it. Guess I was just sick of school."

He nodded. "Yeah, I had a feeling I would feel that way about it, too. Twelve years is plenty."

"Yeah," she said, smiling. She had a nice smile, but he felt no attraction for her. He wondered why Rhonda was different.

"Maybe we could go see a movie or something sometime," she said, breaking his thoughts about the girl he'd just met earlier.

"Oh, um, sure," he said. He didn't even know what was in theaters anymore. Most of the time he stayed home and just played video games when he wasn't working or expected to be at some type of family gathering. He was an only child, and his mom tried to include him in everything.

"Great," she said. "I'll see if there's an interesting matinee on Saturday. By then, they had both finished their sandwiches and both stood up at almost the same time.

"Sounds like fun," he said.

"Okay, I'll talk to you later," she said. "I think we're both working the same days and times this week."

"Okay," he said, smiling. He hoped that she didn't consider this a date. He wasn't sure how to react. She gave him a little wave as they left the shop and he watched her go for a moment, wondering what he was getting himself into. Then he walked to his car, a crappy little Chevy sedan, and drove home. He lived in the walkout basement of his parent's house, which was a two-story monstrosity with multiple empty bedrooms—his parents had wanted more kids, but it had never worked out for them. He paid rent and had to buy his own groceries, but otherwise it was a sweet setup until he could afford his own place.

He went around back and down the hill to his sliding-glass door entrance. He didn't feel like speaking to them at the moment, so he slipped in the door and went straight to his bedroom, feeling unusually tired—probably from the social interaction, which was always draining. He was undressed and under the covers of the bed in no time at all.

◊

The window of his room opened like in a dream. He wasn't sure if he was awake or not, but if he was awake, then it must be a sleep paralysis demon approaching him, because he couldn't move. The creature didn't have an identifiable shape in the darkness of his room, and he only knew it was close by the temperature of the air, which had dropped significantly. Suddenly it was there before him, though he could only see the meager light from his nightlight reflecting in its eyes.

Just as quickly, he felt the pain in his neck as it latched on to him, it's cold lips firmly locked on his throat as something sharp was thrust into his skin. The pain was exquisite, but only lasted a moment, and then all he heard was the soft sucking sound that would haunt his thoughts for the rest of his life. He felt himself falling back into a sleep-like state, when his mouth was filled with a warm, bitter liquid. He instinctively swallowed to keep from choking, still unable to move the rest of his body.

The room went completely dark, and he wasn't aware of anything else until he woke up the next morning. There was very little blood on his pillowcase—less than he thought there should be. As for his neck, he couldn't find any type of injury at all. He was beginning to believe that he'd just had a nasty dream and a bloody nose when the first wave of hunger hit him. It was like nothing he had ever felt before, and he laid there a moment while his stomach clenched, wondering if he was going to vomit.

He dressed in the same clothes as the night before and went upstairs to the main level to look in the refrigerator for something to eat, but nothing sounded good. In fact, he felt a wave of nausea overtake him as he looked at the food. He closed the door and made a half-hearted search of the pantry with the same results.

Suddenly his front jeans pocket vibrated, and he remembered that his cell phone was in it. He swiped the screen and held it up to his ear. "Hello?" His voice sounded weak to his own ears.

"Daniel?"

"Yes."

"Hey, it's Allie."

"Hey Allie," he said, as another hunger pain went through his guts.

"Are you okay?" she asked.

"Yes, fine. Why?"

"It just sounded like you made a weird noise."

"Must have been the connection," he said. "What can I do for you?" He used his best customer service voice to hide what he was feeling.

"Um, I know it's kind of quick, after we made plans last night and everything, but there's a midnight showing of Gladiator tonight. I thought I'd see if you wanted to go after we get off work."

Gladiator? he thought. He'd never seen it—in fact had never been interested in seeing it. Bunch of sweaty men hacking at each other with swords. "I don't know," he said. "I'm not really feeling well. I might have to call in sick to work."

"Oh no!" she said. "Flu?"

"I don't know, honestly. Maybe a stomach bug."

"Oh, those are the worst," she said. "Well, try to keep

hydrated. Drink lots of water, if you're able."

"Yes, I think I'm going to try to get some more sleep."

"Good idea. Sleep is healing."

"That's what they say."

"Yes, well, I hope you feel better soon. Maybe I'll see you at work."

"Yes, maybe," he said. "Bye."

"Bye, Daniel."

He tapped the phone screen to hang it up and then got a glass from the cupboard and filled it with water from the front of the fridge. He took a small sip to see how his stomach reacted. It seemed fine, so he took another, longer drink. No feeling of it coming back up, luckily. He decided not to press his luck and took the glass with him back downstairs. The house would be empty for a few hours, as both his parents worked during the day. Maybe if he slept, he would feel well enough to go into work. He didn't think he had much sick time left, anyway.

◊

He had woken up again a few hours later to find that both of his parents were home. He sat up and waited for his stomach to clench, but it seemed fine now. He looked at the clock and saw that it was almost time to leave for work and decided that he would at least make an appearance. If he got sick there, at least his manager would know that he really was sick and not faking it.

He felt his forehead and then the back of his neck. He didn't seem to have a fever. His skin felt unusually cool, but he'd slept without covers on, and he always seemed to feel cold after waking up from a nap. He slowly got dressed, putting on a clean t-shirt to wear under his uniform shirt. He looked at himself in his bathroom mirror. He was a bit pale, but then, he hadn't spent too much time in the sun lately.

His coworkers laughed about who was the palest gamer in the bunch.

He brushed his teeth and then drank more water straight from the tap. Not as good as the filtered water from the fridge, but not horrible. He stood still, again waiting for his stomach to clench. After a moment when it hadn't, he decided he was okay to go into work. Maybe he would see Rhonda again.

The thought made him smile. Then he remembered that he would also see Allie. It wasn't that he wasn't interested in her as well, he supposed. It was just that Rhonda was much more...mysterious? Was that the correct word? He wondered as he pulled out of the driveway and headed to work.

◊

Daniel was disappointed to find that Rhonda had called in sick to work, claiming a stomach bug—maybe it was the same thing he had. He worked his shift, taking special care to stay hydrated in case he did have the same thing as Rhonda, which would make sense. He could have caught it from her when they were talking.

His shift was just about over when he saw Allie walking towards him. "Hey," he said when she was closer.

"Hey," she responded. "You made it."

"Yes, I felt better after we talked."

"Do you, I mean, are you well enough for the movie?"

He stood for a moment and took a self-assessment. His stomach hadn't bothered him since he left home. He didn't feel like he would faint or throw up, which was good. He also didn't feel like going out, feeling like he should just go home and get more sleep. He looked at Allie and saw the earnest look in her eyes. If he turned her down now, she may never ask again, thinking he was uninterested.

He sighed inwardly. "Yes, I think I feel good enough to go." He forced a smile and saw her return it with one of her own. She did have a nice smile.

"Okay, great," she said. "Um, I guess I'll meet you at the front of the store when our shift ends?"

"Sounds good," he said. Just then he felt a slight twinge in his stomach. He needed to drink some more water and then visit the men's room.

"Great," she repeated, smiling, then turned around. He waited a moment, watching her walk away, wondering why he wasn't more excited about going on a date with a girl— something that hadn't happened in a few years. He turned and headed for the restrooms, which also had a drinking fountain between them.

◊

As he was heading towards the front exit to the store, his phone vibrated in his front pocket. He pulled it out and saw that it was from an unknown number. He was about to ignore it when he saw that it was a local number, and he was curious who it could be—probably junk, but if it was a friend of his mom's they might need help.

"Hello, this is Daniel," he said after swiping the green circle.

"Daniel?" It was a girl's voice.

"Yes? Who is this?"

"It's Rhonda. I'm sorry to call you. I got your number from the employee registry."

Daniel stopped in the cosmetics aisle. "Oh no, that's no problem," he said.

"I was wondering if you could stop by my place after work and bring me some Gatorade or Sprite and maybe some soda crackers. I don't have anyone here that can stop at the store. I promise I'll pay you back."

Daniel's mind was spinning. He had already said yes to Allie. But this was a chance to be a hero to Rhonda. It wasn't like Allie was his girlfriend—they'd never even been out on a real date yet. But he knew she'd be disappointed.

"Daniel, you still there?"

"Oh, yes. I can do that," he heard himself saying. "What flavor of Gatorade do you like?"

"That's great, thank you," she said. "Anything red is fine."

"Red," he repeated. "Okay, text me your address and I'll be there."

"Okay, thank you, Daniel. I appreciate it."

"No problem. See you soon. Bye."

"Bye."

He hung up and felt like raising both hands in victory but saw Allie coming his way once more. He did his best to put a more sober look on his face. "Allie," he said.

"You ready?"

"I'm sorry, something's come up at home and I need to go. I just got off the phone with my mom."

"Oh, okay, hope everything is all right?"

"Yes, I think so, but I have to go."

"Maybe another time?"

"Yes, of course. Definitely."

"Okay, I'll see you later," she said, frowning.

"Yes, bye." He gave her a little wave and then walked quickly to the front door. He'd have to stop at the grocery store instead of buying the items there, so Allie wouldn't get suspicious. He was almost to his car when his phone once again vibrated, and he checked to see that it was a text from Rhonda's number. He opened the car door and sat down in the driver's seat, then typed in her name on his phone to associate it with the number. He smiled as he pushed "save."

◇

Daniel followed his phone's GPS directions after paying for his items at the grocery store. The house was in an area that he'd never been to before. It looked much too upscale for someone who worked at his store. Then he drove a block farther and saw that the nice houses ended, and more moderately priced ones began. He saw his destination was a large apartment complex, which made more sense.

He checked again on her message for her unit number and then grabbed the bag full of items like Sprite, Gatorade, tissues, two different types of crackers, Jello, and a bag of chocolates. He'd made a custom sick kit for her. He hoped she wasn't allergic to anything.

He walked through the main door of the building and down a hallway looking for her unit, which began with a one. He finally found it and knocked softly. He waited a moment and then knocked a little louder. He heard a bolt being unlocked just before the door opened. The apartment was dark except for a small table lamp. Rhonda stood there in a pair of shorts and a white blouse. He could see dark circles under her eyes.

"Hey, sorry, I fell asleep," she said. "Come in."

"That's no problem," he said. "I wasn't waiting long."

"Sorry it's dark, I've had a headache all day, and the bright lights were too much for me."

Damn, he thought. Should have bought her some aspirin or something, too? "Do you want me to put this stuff in your fridge?"

"Yes, please, if you don't mind."

"Sure," he said. He saw that she had sat down on her couch, which was small but looked comfortable. He finished putting the drinks and chocolate in the fridge, then turned to look at her. She was looking at him, though her face was in shadows.

"You want to hang out a little?" she asked.

"Um, okay," he said. He walked over and sat next to her

on the couch, which was smaller than he thought. "Are you feeling any better?"

"Yes, I think the nap did me good," she said, smiling. "So do you do this for all of your coworkers, or am I special?"

Only those I'm attracted to, he thought. He shrugged. "I couldn't let you die of dehydration."

She laughed and he joined. He liked her laugh. "Well, I appreciate it," she said. She bent towards him and kissed him lightly on the cheek. His nostrils flared as he smelled her scent. She wore no perfume, yet her scent mingled notes of some flowery soap, clean hair, and something else he wasn't familiar with. He determined that she had taken a shower recently. After she'd texted him?

He suddenly had a renewed hunger pain hit him and realized that he hadn't drank any water in about an hour. But she was just inches away from him, and her mouth was partially open and so red. He leaned forward a little and felt his lips touch hers, waiting for her to pull away. She didn't. He pressed harder and then felt her tongue touch his, exploring his mouth and then he was lost in the kiss as he closed his eyes.

He opened his eyes, and it was not unlike waking up from a dream. She was still looking at him, yet her eyes were half-closed now and he could see the whites at the bottom. He pulled back hurriedly, letting go of her as she slumped over onto the small couch. It was then that he noticed the blood on his right hand and felt liquid dripping from his mouth. He wiped his mouth and saw that it, too, was covered in bright red blood.

He stood quickly and backed away from the couch. What had happened? He knelt on the floor and put his hand on her arm. There was no response, and he reached for her with his other arm, placing his hand on her other shoulder and gently lifting her upper torso so that she was sitting upright again, though her head lay to the side against her neck and shoulder. Her neck had a wound on it that looked like a row of teeth marks surrounding a kind of bruised hickey.

He dropped her and backed away, unsure what to do.

◊

His eyes opened in the darkness of the small room, and he remembered slowly where he was and what had led him there. He sat up and looked around. He was just about to stand up when he noticed a dark shape in the corner. He couldn't remember if it had been there when he'd laid down. It wasn't the corner with the painting supplies. He looked at it a moment, frozen in his indecision. The form seemed to melt away for a moment and then appear again closer to him and he let out a whimper as he scooted backwards until his back touched the wall.

He recognized the creature from the night before.

It moved slowly towards him, and he couldn't tell if it walked or floated across the floor. Then it was within a foot of him, and he heard himself whimper again.

"Daniel," it said, and the voice was like wet sawdust. He covered his eyes with his hands in an effort to not see it anymore, but he could hear its breathing now as it must have been no more than a foot away from his face. "Daniel," it said again, and this time he heard a woman's voice, and a familiar one. He slowly lowered his hands and looked.

Allie's face was at the same level as his, and she was smiling. He jumped back and hit his head on the wall. The pain was excruciating, and he reached to touch the back of his head.

"Geez, Daniel," she said, standing up. "What's your problem?"

"What?" he asked. "What are you doing here?"

"What do you think?" she said. "You're my thrall, Daniel. I know where you are at all times now."

"Thrall?" he said weakly.

"I created you," she said. "You are mine, Daniel."

Realization crept into his mind. He remembered their call and her telling him to stay hydrated and telling him that sleep was healing and oh God, oh God, the blood. The sucking sounds, the coldness of that kiss. He leaned over and wretched, though nothing came out this time.

"I see you're taking this well," she said.

"Rhonda," he said. "I killed her."

"It's a good thing, too," she answered, sitting down next to him. He could feel her there, though they weren't touching physically. "I would have had to kill her if you hadn't. I'm just glad you didn't accidentally turn her."

He ran both hands through his hair. It was all too much. She continued talking.

"I was born a long time ago, Daniel. My real name is Alexandra. I was named for the city that I was born in. Two hundred years before the birth of Christ." She paused a moment, looking at him. He could feel her gaze upon him, then she looked away once more.

"The light doesn't affect me, as it didn't affect you when you were first transformed. Sunlight killing us is a myth. But our powers are greatly diminished by the sun—solar radiation or something—I've never really looked into it, but the night is when we are most powerful."

"I...I didn't think vampires," he paused as he said the word, wondering if he was caught in a nightmare or if this was real. He looked over at her and saw her smiling at him. "I didn't think they...we...could drink anything other than blood."

"We're able to metabolize water if needed—it at least

keeps us hydrated so we don't shrivel up like a toad. But we need to feed, Daniel. That is true, unfortunately."

"But I saw you eat that sandwich..."

"Did you? Or did you see me nibble at it and throw the rest of it away? And of course, you didn't see me throw it back up near my car. That little trick keeps people from getting suspicious. But, no, we cannot digest solid food."

Daniel's mind reeled with the information—it was almost too much to think about all at once. This girl that he'd gone to high school with claimed she was over two thousand years old. And she claimed to be a vampire. After his experience with Rhonda, he wasn't going to say she wasn't. Or that he wasn't one now, as well.

"I know it's a lot to take in, Daniel," she said after a few minutes of silence. "It was for me when I was changed, too."

"You were changed?"

"You don't think I was born this way, do you? Yes, I was changed. And yes, it was when I was a teenager, which is why I still look like one. And it's why, periodically, I have to move to a new place and pretend to be a teenager and attend school and try to blend in. But it also serves the purpose of immersing me in the societal norms of the time. No better way to learn that to be surrounded by teenagers." She laughed at this. "Without it, I think I'd be lost in time."

"That makes sense," he said. "We don't sparkle..."

"No!" she said, hurriedly, laughing. "No, don't even think about it."

He smiled. "So, now what?"

She looked at him again, her smile disappearing. "I changed you, Daniel, because I am lonely. I'm in need of companionship, and you fit the bill nicely."

"Thank you, I think," he said.

"But I see that it's not going to work out," she said, then

sighed and stood up.

"Wait...what?" he asked weakly.

"You betrayed me, Daniel. You lied to me tonight." She turned to look down at him.

"Wait, no, I..."

"Yes, Daniel, you did. I can't trust you. You proved that to me, and it's really too bad. We could have had years... centuries of fun together."

"No, I'm sorry," he said, beginning to stand up. "I'm sorry. It won't happen again."

"Yes, it will," she said. "People don't change, Daniel. Believe me, I know." She reached down and helped him to his feet. "Don't worry. When they find you down here, there won't be any signs of what you are. What you had briefly become." She slammed him against the wall and the breath went out of his lungs with the force of it. Her hands felt like steel vices on his arms.

"No, please," he said weakly. "I swear, it won't happen..."

"Goodbye, Daniel," she said, before pulling back a hand, the nails long and sharp now, and raking it across his throat so swiftly that he didn't feel any pain until she let him go and he slumped to the floor and saw that his body was covered in a dark liquid that could have only been his own blood. He looked up at her one last time and saw her licking her fingertips.

Then the world went dark.

The bat flew on, its goal once again foiled by the insouciance of men, though this was only a setback, not an end. She thought of any other options, knowing that she had few in that town... Sigh. Okay, let's face it, I just really don't want to go through high school again.

The End

Greystone Manor

The wind blew hard against the walls of Greystone Manor. Even sitting before the fire that burned in the ancient stone fireplace, Eva felt a chill work its way down her body; a living thing, which sucked away any hope of warmth. She pulled her purple shawl tighter around her slight frame. So many winters, she thought, sadly. Look where it has brought me.

She let her gaze move across the room, tracing a familiar painting here, a sheathed sword there. Her eyes rested on the sword for a moment. It had belonged to her father. He was gone now, like almost everyone else.

All that was left to her were her memories, and she wrapped them around herself tighter than her shawl.

◊

"My lady? My Lady?"

She looked around, startled. She had drifted off again. She looked up to see Morton standing before her, his eyes showing his concern for her, as always.

"My Lady, your mother requests your presence. In the east study." He stood up straight, now that he was certain she was awake. The funeral for her father had been long and tiring. Not to mention emotionally draining to all in the household.

It could not have been an accident; she thought for the thousandth time. He was too skilled as a rider.

"My Lady?" She rose to her feet. Morton was a good man, but he would do everything he could to fulfill an order from her parents, especially if it came from her mother. Even if it meant picking Eva up on his elderly back and carrying her himself.

She smiled at the thought, seeing the smile reflected in the full-length mirror next to her bed. Even at sixteen, her smile made her look eleven. She then turned from the aged man and walked toward the spiral stairs. Her shoes whispered against the cold stone steps, carved from the same quarry that gave Greystone its name. Her hand ran along the smooth oak banister, feeling each crack, each irregularity in the aged wood.

She went straight to the east study as she had been instructed and found it empty. It was just like her mother to make her search the house for her. The door to her parent's... no, her mother's room was slightly ajar. She knocked lightly anyway. Her father may not have had held with tradition, but her mother would send her back out into the hall to wait if she did not announce herself properly.

"Who is it?" came her mother's muffled voice.

"It's me, mother. Eva." She hated her name, named as she was after the betrayer of mankind, if the codex was to be believed.

"Enter," was the answer she received. Her mother's voice showed no hint at any emotions lying beneath. Eva pushed the heavy door farther open. Inside, she saw that her mother had already changed from her black mourning dress.

My father has been buried these two hours now, and you have already changed from Widow to Chooser, she thought, disgusted at her mother's lack of devotion and decorum.

Normally, a woman whose husband had died would wait a set time—usually six months for low born to a year or more for high—before Choosing another. In Eva's society, men did not court. They waited...and hoped.

"Eva," her mother said, not turning from her own mirror, "darling, what can I do for you?"

You can mourn for my father, is what she would have liked to have said. But she knew her mother. Knew that this would only lead to more fighting. She was so sick of the fighting.

"Morton said you wished to speak to me," she answered, standing stiffly before the woman.

"Oh. So, I did." Now her mother turned to her. The smile was now a look of weighing, of measuring her daughter as one would a prized possession—or a liability. "You have reached the age of consent," she said simply. Eva could not tell if this was a question or statement of fact, so she did not answer. Her mother nodded to herself, as if answering her own question.

Eva looked around the room, seeing that pictures of her father were already gone—packed away and out of sight. She may be able to hide his presence, she thought, but she cannot take away his memory. "Was there anything else, mother?"

"Yes, you are to prepare yourself for your Viewing."

Eva opened her mouth in shock for a moment before closing it again. She berated herself internally for the lapse—she was sure her mother had seen her visceral reaction, but she could not help that now. A Viewing was rare these days, and Eva knew that her mother had done this purposefully to publicly humiliate her. A Viewing would expose her to the world and leave her vulnerable to powerful men.

She had the right of Choosing, but men would still hold

power in their wish to impress her or attempt to dominate her. A Widow may have rights in her Choosing, but a Maiden was another story altogether. Her family name held power, and men would be attracted to that, as well as the manor itself, which had been her father's stronghold before his death.

Her mother may not be able to marry soon, but this meant that she would use her daughter to gain power in society. Possibly more than she was accustomed to, being the widow of a highborn Lord.

"The Viewing will commence in two weeks," her mother said. "That is all, for now."

"Thank you, mother," Eva said, curtsying and turning to leave.

"Oh, Eva, there is one more thing," her mother's voice purred, stopping Eva from leaving. She didn't turn to look at her mother's face. "Do not think that you can avoid this. It is an old tradition, but to seek to avoid it will only make it... difficult. For you."

"Yes, mother," she said, then left as quickly as propriety allowed.

◊

Eva sat and watched through the window as the rain pelted the ground of the courtyard and the wind swept across the grounds of the manor. Even with a hearty fire in the large stone fireplace, she felt chilled, and not only from the cold.

She missed her father and dreaded seeing her mother. Was this normal? Was this part of mourning the loss of so loved a figure in her life? Was she too hard on her mother for not feeling the same love that Eva herself felt for the dead? She was not sure, but she knew that most women publicly carried a look of mourning better than her mother. Perhaps her mother did not care to show an emotion that she did not feel, as so many others did.

It did not matter, in the end. The truth was that Eva was alone in the manor. She had no friends and no one to talk to except for Morton, who kept his face neutral and his language professional. There was no respite from loneliness to be found there.

She looked at the large clock to see how long she had to her fitting. She was not looking forward to being poked, prodded, and practically crushed into a variety of clothing items. Yet the Viewing was drawing near, and she had to look her best, even with the heightened interest due to her station.

The courtyard was mostly closed to the outside world, with only a few gated entrances in the wall around it, so she was surprised to see a large animal run through the middle of it, obscured partially by statues and trimmed hedges. There was a black flash out of the corner of her eye and when she turned to look, she saw that it was a large dog—no—it was possibly a wolf, and it was looking through the window directly at her.

She stood, transfixed by its green gaze. It showed no fear as it stood there in the rain, and then it turned and just as quickly was gone. She ran to the window and looked out but could see no sign of it. Her breath fogged the window, and she turned back just in time to see Morton walking towards her.

"Are you well, Miss Eva?"

"Yes, of course," she answered, unsure if she was. "Tell me, Morton, do any of the staff own a large black dog?"

Morton frowned as he thought about the question. "Not that I know, My Lady. Why do you ask?"

"No reason," she said, frowning. She wondered if her mind had made up the event. A result of boredom perhaps.

"The seamstress and her assistant are awaiting you in your chambers," Morton said.

"Thank you, Morton," she said, still thinking of the piercing green eyes of the animal.

◇

The day of her Viewing dawned bright and sunny, and she hoped it was a sign of things to come. Morton had already come in to wake her—her mother had fired Eva's personal servant, Kiery, the same day as her father's funeral. A cost-saving measure, she said, although she had chosen to keep her small band of maids, hairdressers, and others. Eva had no idea what services some of them performed for her mother.

She chose to dress in a simple cotton dress. The ceremony would not come until later, so she thought she would spend the time until then in comfort, at least. She ate a quick breakfast in the dining room and then went to sit in the courtyard with a book of poetry that she'd read countless times before.

The black dog with piercing green eyes was in the back of her mind, and she wondered if it would still be around, and if so, would pose any danger to herself if she were to be out there alone. The thought of danger was almost welcome in her morose musings.

Her father had been a hunter and had a plethora of trophies hanging on the walls of his study, as well as a few fully mounted animals that were small enough to fit in the room, such as a leopard, a wolverine, and small red fox that Eva had loved to pet when she was younger. She had not been allowed pets of her own, so the fox, who she had named Cavander, was the closest she could come to one. Her father had never allowed her to touch, let alone shoot, one of his guns.

She would have to fend the dog off with her book of

poetry, she decided, and smiled at the thought. Perhaps it would be easier to be eaten by an animal than go through with the night's ceremony. Her smile was swept away by the thought of the Viewing. Her mother would be all in her element at the ceremony, as all the royalty and other important members of the kingdom had been invited. An invitation had even been sent to the castle, though the king and queen were getting on in years and had not attended a public ceremony in some time. She doubted they would do so for the daughter of a lord whose name was more famous than his holdings.

She felt it had to be coming close to noon when she set down her book and stretched her arms over her head. The sun had risen overhead, but was now obscured by clouds, which promised another afternoon shower. It was still warm enough, however, that she had been comfortable in just her dress, which had short sleeves and a low neckline—it would have been somewhat scandalous to go to town in but was fine for the private courtyard.

She picked up her book and stood, intending to go back to the kitchen and find something for lunch, when she caught a dark object out of the corner of her eye. She turned and saw the dog, which was much larger than she thought when she first saw it outside of the window. The animal appeared calm but alert as it watched her. Suddenly, she was not so eager to flaunt the fact that she was alone with it, without anything but her book to protect herself.

"Run along now," she said as forcefully as she could to it. She made a shooing motion with her hand, which the animal followed as if she were offering it a treat. It stepped forward a few paces and was now within ten feet of her, with only a small fountain between them. Its tongue lolled out of the side of its open mouth, pink and bright against the black hair that covered its body. It almost appeared to be smiling at her.

Eva began to walk slowly towards the manor, keeping her eyes on the ground but towards the animal. Her father had told her that animals did not like to be looked in the eye. She was almost at the door when she looked up and saw that the animal had not moved and felt relief flow through her body. She let out a silent breath. She backed up to the door and felt for the handle. The dog took a few steps forward and then sat.

"Good boy," she said, noticing that the act of sitting had shown her that it was, in fact, a male dog. A thought occurred to her again then—what if it was not a dog? There had not been a wolf sighting near the manor in hundreds of years. Her father had been known to complain that he had been cheated of the opportunity to hunt one of the local wolves, since they had been either driven out or killed long ago.

She had seen drawings of them in books but had to admit that many of those drawings had been of poor quality or stylized so that she probably would not know a wolf if it came to her and sat in her courtyard. She smiled, and the animal's tongue lolled out again as if returning her smile. She realized that she had been standing there too long without going inside the manor and to safety. She turned quickly and opened the door.

Just then she felt a sharp pain in her lower leg and looked down to see the animal's head, which this close, seemed massive. She was about to scream when it disengaged from her leg and ran away swiftly. Again, she marveled at its speed as it loped out of sight. She looked down at her leg then and saw the blood that was running down from punctures in her soft white skin.

The last thing she thought before fainting was maybe she could postpone the ceremony now, at least.

◊

"Wake up, Eva," a voice said as she swam towards a light as if at the bottom of a dimly lit pool of water. "You need to get ready for tonight's ceremony. Wake up."

Eva opened her eyes slowly and saw that the sun was still shining brightly through the window of her room. She was in her own bedroom, she found. And her mother was there at her bedside looking down at her with an expression of exasperation, as if she had just fallen off to sleep at an inopportune time. Suddenly she remembered what had transpired, and she sat up quickly. Her vision dimmed as she did so, and she laid back down.

"Get up, young lady," her mother insisted. "You need to bathe and have your hair arranged and then get dressed for the Viewing."

Eva sat up slower this time and her vision stayed bright. She leaned back against the headboard and uncovered her legs from the thick bed clothes to look at her leg. She saw that her leg had a clean white bandage on it. More than likely Morton's work. "Mother, how did I get in bed?"

"Morton brought you up with help from one of the scullery maids," her mother answered. "He was almost distraught, though it seemed only a few small scratches to your leg. Honestly, Eva, you fainted just inside the doorway. Could you not have closed the door first?"

"But the wolf," Eva said.

"Wolf?" her mother asked, incredulously. "What are you talking about, dear?"

"A wolf bit me," she answered, knowing how outrageous it sounded. "It was a large black beast, and it bit me as I was returning from the courtyard."

"Dear, I think you were daydreaming. Or better yet, were lost in imagination from some book or other. I've told you to be careful what you read."

"But there was a wolf. This is the second time I have seen him out there."

"My dear, there has not been a wolf around these parts since well before you were born. Come now, it is time for your bath. I have had Sandra draw it for you, so you had better hurry before it gets cold."

Eva nodded. Sandra was not a name that she had heard before, but perhaps she was a new hire. She was a bit confused by how congenial her mother was being. She had never come to wake Eva up personally before. Usually, it was Morton or another servant, or her father before he died. She stood and felt how weak her legs were for a moment until she got them under her.

Her mother made shooing motions to her, and she nodded and headed for the large bathroom off her chambers. She opened the door to the bathing room and could instantly smell the foam of the bath, which smelled like lilies and warmth. One of the young maids sat upon the edge of the large iron, clawfoot tub with her hand in the water. She stood as Eva came in.

"Do you need help getting into the bath, m'lady?" she asked, wiping her hand on a small towel.

"No, thank you," Eva responded, smiling reassuringly to her. "I can manage."

"Yes, m'lady," the maid said. "Your mother was quite specific that you were to only get fifteen minutes to bathe before your hair needed to be put up.

"I understand," Eva said. "I am sorry, but what is your name again?"

"Sandra, m'lady," she answered and curtsied.

"Thank you, Sandra. I can manage from here."

"Yes, m'lady," Sandra responded, then curtsied again and

walked to the door, closing it behind her.

Eva sighed. There was no pain in her leg as she bent down to take off the bandage that had been placed on it. When she had, she saw that her mother was correct, and it looked like four small scratches that already appeared to be scabbing over. She wondered if the bath would open them back up but decided that she could worry about that afterwards. If she did not get in now, she would not be finished in her allotted time.

She pulled the simple dress up over her head and off, feeling a chill as her body was exposed to the air. She quickly walked to the tub and tested the water with her toes, and feeling the soothing warmth, stepped into it and sat down amidst the bubbles and smell of flowers. She closed her eyes for a moment and suddenly the green eyes of the wolf were before her once again. She gasped and opened them again, looking around the bathroom as if it might be there beside her. It was not, to her great relief.

She lifted her leg from the pull of the water and looked at her wounds. They had not opened, thankfully. She placed her foot back into the water, where it disappeared once again below the froth of bubbles. In all of the excitement, it had escaped her attention that she was supposed to be bathing before her Viewing ceremony, and she suddenly felt ill in anticipation.

She reached for the bar of soap that sat on a wall rack next to the tub and began to lather up and wash her arms, neck, and then face. When she was done, she placed the soap back on the rack and then immersed herself below the water to rinse. She stayed submerged for a moment, relishing the warmth of the water, before coming back up and pushing her long hair from her face and opening her eyes.

She wasn't alone. She could hear the sound of something

breathing near her. She turned quickly and looked behind her. There was nothing there that she could see. She stood and looked around the floor of the tub on the side that was not against the wall. Still nothing. She could feel the cold prickling against her skin now that she was not surrounded by warm water, and she sat down again.

"Mother?" she asked. "Is someone there?" Silence. Not even the sound of breathing remained. "Hello?" Still, no response was forthcoming. She sighed again, wondering if the excitement of the afternoon had driven her mad. Then she smiled, wondering if madness might not be better than going through with the Viewing. There was nothing for it, she decided.

She reached for one of the large, fluffy towels that were neatly folded on the rack next to the tub and stood up. She quickly wrapped the towel around herself and stepped out of the tub, careful not to slip on the stone tile floor. She grabbed another, smaller towel and began drying her hair. The door to the bathroom opened just as she was finished with her hair and about to towel her body dry. Sandra came in and curtsied again.

"Feeling better, m'lady?"

"Yes, thank you," Eva responded.

"I placed a clean dress here for you to wear while you are having your hair done," she said, picking up the folded linen from another rack.

"Thank you," Eva said. She turned modestly and began drying herself off. She wiped her legs and then stood up straight, holding the towel before her. She turned to see that Sandra was standing close to her, holding the garment. She was taken aback for a moment as she looked into the other woman's eyes, which were a dark brown, almost black. They stood a moment looking into each other's eyes, before Eva blinked and looked down. She also realized at that moment that Sandra was older than she had first thought—maybe ten years older than her.

"Do you need help getting dressed, m'lady," Sandra asked softly.

Eva looked back up at her and nodded. She dropped her towel and held her arms over her head. Sandra stepped closer and held the dress over her head so that Eva could put her hands through the armholes. This brought Sandra even closer to her, and for a moment they were only inches apart from each other.

Eva was surprised to find that the other woman smelled of lilac. She could also smell the scent of the woman's body, which was a headier odor, though not unpleasant. Sandra licked her lips and Eva wondered what they tasted like. She had never before been interested in another person and the feeling startled her. What startled her even more was that she felt herself leaning forward until she felt Sandra's lips on her own. Lightly, at first, then she felt the other woman press forward as well into the kiss and open her mouth.

Eva had not kissed anyone since long before her father died, and then it was the occasional peck on his clean-shaven cheek. This was much different, and she was lost for a moment in the sensation as she tasted Sandra's lips and tongue in a slow, sensual exploration as she closed her eyes. She felt Sandra's hands slide down her arms lightly until they cupped the back of her head. She let go of the dress and it fell down over her head and Sandra's as well.

The other woman laughed quietly and pulled back, allowing the dress to fall further down and cover Eva's body. Eva laughed as well, feeling giddy still from the kiss.

"Your mother will be here any moment, m'lady," Sandra said quietly, then leaned in for another swift kiss, which Eva returned longingly, knowing that she was correct. They were still standing facing each other when they heard the door opening and Sandra quickly stepped back a step. They both looked at her mother as she entered the bathing room.

"Inform the hairdresser that we are coming," she said without looking at the maid, which Eva knew was common for her. She detested looking directly at the staff.

"Yes, m'lady," Sandra said, then curtsied. She looked briefly at Eva and smiled before turning and hurrying out the door.

"Are you ready?" her mother asked her.

"Yes, mother," she answered.

"Then do not dawdle," her mother said and turned to walk out of the room. She did not look back to see if her daughter was following, assuming that she was.

Eva paused a moment, reliving what had just happened. It was like nothing she had done before, and she felt excitement mixed with dread for the ceremony. She looked down and dried her feet on the towel that was now in a heap at her feet.

◊

Her hair was done. Her makeup was set. Her only remaining task was to get dressed. She sat in her room and staired in the looking glass. Her reverie was broken by a knock on her door. "Come," she said.

Sandra entered the room carrying a load of fabric that Eva realized was a dress and all its accoutrements. She smiled at the older woman and stood up. "M'lady," Sandra said, laying out the dress on the bed. "Your mother wants you dressed and standing in the foyer in half an hour."

"That soon?" Eva asked.

"I'm afraid so," Sandra said.

"Can you help me?"

"Of course," Sandra said, turning to look at her. For a moment it seemed to Eva that the woman's eyes were a different shade than what she remembered—it almost looked like they were green, though they had been much darker after Eva's bath. Then the moment passed, and they were once again those dark brown eyes that she knew.

A trick of the light? Perhaps, she thought, but she was still not sure. Yet there was no time to think about it now, she needed to be dressed and ready for her mother's inspection. She shook her head a little to try and clear it.

"Something wrong, m'lady?" Sandra asked. "Are you feeling well?"

"Yes, it is nothing," she responded. She smiled to show that she was well, though she was not entirely sure. She held her arms over her head once more so that Sandra could slip the dress over her head while minding her hair and makeup. This time, she felt no urge to kiss the other woman, and it seemed that Sandra shared her thoughts, because she dressed Eva in an efficient manner and neither spoke again until Eva was standing before her full-length mirror.

"You look very pretty, m'lady," Sandra said. "Good luck at the ceremony."

"Thank you," Eva said, almost automatically. She looked at herself, knowing she now looked much older than her age. All this just for a Viewing, she thought, nonplussed. "Sandra, could you please fetch my shoes for me?"

"Yes, m'lady."

Eva stood another moment looking at herself in the mirror. Her hair was fine. Her makeup was fine. Yet she felt that she looked like a mannequin—a lifeless being set to be paraded about for the enjoyment of others, and she resented her mother immensely for forcing her to do it. Her father would never have dreamed of doing this to her.

The Viewing was a ceremony as old as the kingdom itself. For her to refuse would be scandalous, and her mother would live forever in shame, and more importantly, would hold it over Eva's head for the rest of her life. So it was that Eva steeled herself as she walked from her room to the ballroom of the manor where the ceremony was to take place. She kept her eyes ahead, mostly ignoring the people she passed by.

She nodded to Morton as she walked by. "My lady, you look absolutely beautiful," he said, bowing slightly to her. Normally she would smile and ask him how he was, but in this instance, she wasn't in the mood to speak to anyone.

She walked to the private room just off the ballroom. It was used mostly for private meetings or sometimes storage, though her father had also used it for a trophy room, and the heads of various large animals still adorned the walls, as well as a few weapons that he had acquired over the years. His sword had a prominent place over the fireplace. It was the only weapon he had maintained with earnest, sometimes taking hours to oil and sharpen the blade. He had confided in her once that it helped him to think, and to get away from her mother for a period. For now, it was the room she would wait in until she was formally announced to the assemblage.

She looked out of the window and saw that it was raining yet again. Fitting, she thought. The weather matched her mood.

She was just about to turn away from the glass when she saw a flash of motion and looked to see the black dog running through the expansive grounds. She stepped closer to the glass, her breath fogging up a small circle. Was it a dog or a wolf? She still could not tell, especially since it was so dark and gloomy outside.

"Eva, stop daydreaming," her mother said as she entered the room. "It is almost time for the ceremony to begin. Let us have a look at you."

Eva turned to look back at her mother, noting that she was also wearing a favorite dress that her father had brought back from one of his infrequent trips. "All that time getting prepared, and you still look like you're dying of consumption," her mother said, pinching both of her cheeks to try to add a little color to them. "And remember to smile as you are presented," she added.

Smiling was the last thing she wanted to do, but she gave a half-hearted one to her mother to mollify her. "That is better, my dear. First impressions are so important."

"What are you hoping to gain from this, mother?" she asked.

"What do you mean?"

"What is the point of this ceremony? What are you getting out of it?"

"Eva, you need to be married eventually, this is a good time to introduce you to potential suitors. You know this."

"But what do you get out of it?" she asked adamantly. "Marry me off to some lord so you can keep the manor for yourself? Marry me into an even richer family?"

"Eva, I'm doing this for you, dear."

She looked at her mother for a moment and decided that she wouldn't cry anymore. It was obvious that it would do nothing except spoil her makeup. She was done feeling like a prisoner in her own home. She would go through with the ceremony, then she would leave her mother behind.

There was a knock on the door, and her mother turned to answer it. Eva could hear Morton's deep voice speaking for a moment, though she could not hear the words themselves. Her mother replied with a nod and closed the door. She turned back to Eva. "It is time."

Eva nodded and set herself, both mentally and physically.

She had been practicing her smile for a while, and she turned it on automatically as she followed her mother from the room.

◊

The first thing that struck her was how many people there were in attendance. Not just men, as she had expected, but women and even children stood looking back at her from the ballroom. Many returned her smile, though some did not. She took an inner inventory of those who did not, for future reference. Most of them were older men or women who had no say in any of the proceedings but had been invited due to some type of real or imagined clout that they held within the lands.

But there were a few women her own age who were either simply jealous of her standing or even possibly disappointed in the ceremony being held. It boded poorly for their own futures. A Viewing had not been held in many years, and she supposed that most women had hoped that it was a tradition that had died a slow death.

There was a small stage set up next to the outer wall of the ballroom, and she slowly walked to it, while those around her quietly cleared a path for her as she passed. She walked up the short flight of stairs next to the stage and then walked to the middle of it and took her place, facing the gathered citizens. She stopped smiling, feeling her cheeks beginning to grow sore.

Her mother had followed her to the stage and had also turned to face the people. "Good evening," she said loudly. There was a low drone of replies, most of which were repeating her greeting back to her. "The time has come. A young maiden stands before you, draped in virtue. Adorned in virginity. Awash in the Spirit. Amen."

"Amen," came the reply.

"Who here is called forth to View?" her mother asked, looking about the ballroom.

Eva watched as a line of men walked out from a side door towards the stage. "We are called, Mother," they chanted, at first low, but then rising in volume until they had repeated the words five times. They now stood before the stage.

"Who has called you here this day?" her mother asked.

"The Spirit," they all responded loudly. "The Spirit." They said again.

"The Spirit has called them here today," her mother said, loudly to the assembled. "The Spirit seeks a Union."

"A Union!" the crowd repeated.

"Do you seek a Union?" her mother asked the men.

"We do," they replied in unison.

Her mother turned to her. "My child, do you seek a Union?"

For a moment, Eva couldn't speak. She knew what her reply needed to be, but the words had fled her mind. She saw her mother scowl, and the room seemed to grow even quieter than it had been while everyone waited for her reply. Suddenly the words came back to her, and she smiled and blurted out, "I do."

Her mother nodded, though her face still held the scowl for a moment, promising a conversation for later in the night. Eva's smile felt like a rictus of despair, and she looked around for something that would stop herself from bursting into tears. She caught a glimpse of Morton standing at the back of the assembly. Normally he would be bustling about, taking care that everything that needed to be done was done. But he had stopped and was looking towards the stage. He was frowning, but he nodded encouragement, and she imperceptibly nodded back. Her eyes returned to her mother's back.

"Approach the stage to be seen," her mother said. The men slowly walked up the stairs in single file. Eva could now see them clearly and up close. Most were the sons of local businessmen, or even a few minor barons or dukes. She knew all of them, and she was not sure if that was a relief or not. Then she saw the last man in line. Dark features under dark hair that hung freely down past his collared shirt.

And the greenest eyes she had ever seen. No, that wasn't quite true. She had seen those eyes before, and recently. She recalled seeing the black dog on the grounds and the green of its eyes. It struck her now that the gentleman had the same eyes. Impossible, but there could be no doubt.

The men lined themselves up before her, all of them looking at her. She looked each one in the eyes for a moment. Some could not hold her gaze and looked down at the floor, seemingly embarrassed to be there, while a few looked back with a ravenous look that scared her. The man with the green eyes held her gaze, and she saw neither hunger nor depravity in his eyes.

Her mother's voice broke her concentration, and she blinked rapidly a few times and looked away to where her mother stood. "The Spirit is here upon us," she said.

"The Spirit," the crowd replied. "The Spirit."

"The Spirit chooses the Union," her mother said.

"The Spirit chooses the Union." The crowd repeated the chant for a few minutes, while Eva stood, her face beginning to ache from holding onto the smile that was her only defense.

Finally, the crowd was silenced by her mother holding up her hand. "Let the Viewing begin."

The men turned towards her left and began to slowly circle around her. She stood motionless. She felt a tug on her dress at the back as one of the men seemed overeager. From what she had read, they would normally take one turn around her before anything happened, but she knew that none of the men had ever participated in a Viewing, so norms would no doubt go unheeded. She steeled herself further.

Another tug, this time on her sleeve, and she felt the fabric separate, as it was made to do. Her arm was bare. Another tug at her back, and she knew that part of the dress train was now gone. She held her eyes high over the crowd, not making eye contact with anyone as the tugs and tearing proceeded. There was no other sound, either from the crowd or the men circling around her nor from her mother, who stood by watching her daughter being slowly, roughly undressed.

Eva stifled a whimper as the last shred of the top of her dress was pulled away and she was left only her corset and the wispy remains of the bottom of her dress, which was slowly pulled off.

"What is your name?" one of the men asked her, and she looked at him, a simple-faced young man who was the son of local baron—someone she had known most of her life. Yet that had no bearing on the ceremony. She must answer the questions to the best of her ability.

"Lady Eva Delane," she said loudly. The man reached for her and tore a strip of cloth from her abdomen. The air was cool against her exposed skin.

The questions continued from the men as they came around to her front, as did the tearing of her corset, the fabric ripping at pre-chosen lines, until the last man came around to her front and stood before her. He stepped closer to her, and she looked into his green eyes. "What do you want?" he asked simply.

The question surprised her. All of the others had asked about everything from how much she was worth to how much she weighed, and one man had even asked a math problem about estimating the weight of grain in a ship of a certain size. This question was different, in that it was the only that sought something about her own desires.

"A husband," she replied.

The man shook his head and stepped even nearer. "Do not lie to me," he said quietly. "What do you want?"

She had to think for a moment, and her mind whirled as she tried to come up with an answer that would satisfy him. "I want...I want to be happy."

He stood a moment looking at her, then nodded. "Stand tall and proud," he whispered, as he tore the last bit of cloth that was holding up her corset top and she felt the cloth fall down to the floor of the stage. Her breasts were freed, and they immediately hardened in the coolness of the ballroom, despite the heat coming from the large number of spectators present. She did as he said, knowing that to cover herself would show weakness and she would not give her mother the satisfaction.

She stood naked before all of them, her smile now gone. Who were they to judge her? They were no one of importance to her, she decided. Her mother had held this ceremony to break her and make her want to leave, married or not. She thought a moment of her father and a real smile broke out on her face as she remembered his strength, his kindness and his gentle way. She looked over to her mother to see the scowl had returned to the older woman's face. This made her smile even wider. Her mother had attempted to break her, and she had failed.

Her mother stood scowling a moment more, then turned back to the crowd. "It is time for the Choosing," she said, though her enthusiasm seemed to have waned.

"The Choosing," the crowd chanted for a moment,

though something had changed in their collective demeanor as well. There was no longer a pitiful waif standing on the stage before them. There was a woman.

Her mother turned back to her. "Do you choose any suitor here?" she asked simply.

The men had lined up once again before her, and once again Eva looked each of them in the eyes. Those who had looked away before seemed unsure and hardly held her gaze. Those who had held it with a sense of hunger now seemed unsure and some of them looked away. Finally, she came to the green-eyed man with the dark hair. Once again, he held her gaze for a moment and then dropped his eyes—not in embarrassment, but it seemed, in deference to her.

"I do," she said loudly.

The crowd let out a collective sigh at these words. She could see many of them had broken out with their own smiles, as if this had somehow validated their attending the ceremony in some way. A Viewing did not always commence with a successful Choosing.

"Who amongst those gathered here?" her mother asked her.

Eva slowly looked down the line of men, those petty, eager, pitiful men who had agreed to take part in the Viewing, and she felt her anger swell at their machinations, as well as her mother's. She decided that she would not leave the manor. She would not let her mother win. She was the Lady Eva Delane, and her first act when she came into power would be to ban any future Viewings within her holdings. The idea made her smile yet again and the man in front of her, the one who had asked her the math question, quailed at the power in it.

Finally, she turned to look at the green-eyed man, who was once again looking at her. "I Choose him," she said simply, and held her hand out towards him. He raised his hand to clasp hers as the assembled crowd let out a cheer that echoed off the walls and ceiling of the ballroom. He returned her smile and then winked at her, and she noticed that the eye that stayed open was no longer a bright green, but now a dark brown.

It was a color that she had seen before as well.

Her smile faltered for a moment in surprise, and then the man bowed and then was looking back at her, and his eyes were as green as ever. He shrugged off his coat and offered it to her to put on, and she accepted it, though she had grown accustomed to the chill of the room. She wrapped it around her shoulders and smelled his scent for the first time, a deep, earthy smell that reminded her of walks after a gentle rain, when the soil was drinking in the moisture and its fragrance mixed with that of the flowers growing within it—mostly lilacs.

She turned once again to look at her mother for the last time that night. Her mother's expression was that hated scowl, though it was not trained on her at the moment, but on the man across from her; the man she had Chosen. Yet Eva saw something else as well: was it fear that creased the folds of her mother's face? Her mother looked away before Eva could tell for sure, but she had seen it, if only for a brief moment.

"Eva," a voice said behind her, and she turned to see him smiling at her. She returned the smile.

It was customary for the new Chosen couple to stay while the crowd feasted to their health and virility, but Eva had no intention of staying in the ballroom. "Would you escort me to my chambers so that I can get dressed in some other than your jacket," she asked him. He nodded and held out his hand once again for her to take.

They walked down the stairs to the floor of the ballroom, and once again the crowd created a pathway for them, many of the men and women bowing to her as they did so. She smiled, and this time, it felt more genuine. She had seemingly won some respect from the ceremony. Yet she still felt vulnerable and resentful towards all who had attended.

When they came to the door of the ballroom, Morton bowed to her and she nodded, acknowledging him. "Thank you, Morton," she said as she passed him by, grasping his arm briefly to show that she meant it.

After that, they quickly walked to her room, where she swiftly opened the door and then she was alone with the mysterious man. She realized that she still did not know his name. But then she was in his arms, and his lips were on hers, and her thoughts paused for a moment as they moved slowly towards her bed.

Her thoughts came slowly back to her as he laid her down on the bed. She wanted so much for him to be inside her, but she knew that it had to wait until the wedding and the Consummation afterwards. She was surprised at her own yearnings, but they felt true.

For a woman of her standing, it was both tradition and the law of the land that she must be pure on her wedding day for the wedding to be deemed legitimate. It was another law that she would do away with once she was in power. She closed her eyes and was almost lost again.

His lips were now moving down her throat and his hands were all over her half-naked body and his fingers brought small bursts of ecstasy with their movements. It took all of her will to reach her hands to his and stop him. "Wait," she said, breathlessly. "Wait a moment."

He stopped and then she looked up at him. Only it was no longer him who was looking down at her.

It was Sandra.

Eva gasped in surprise, but then it all began to make sense. She had heard tell of shapeshifters, but to her knowledge she had never met one. "M'lady," Sandra said softly, smiling down at her.

"Sandra," was all she could think of to say.

"I hope you are not too disappointed in me for the deception," Sandra said.

In answer, Eva gently pulled the other woman's head down and kissed her on the lips. When they pulled apart again, they both smiled at each other. "I choose you," Eva said. "That hasn't changed."

"Before you say that," Sandra said. "There is one other secret that you should know."

"What..." Eva began to ask when suddenly there was a large black wolf in her bed. The transition had been almost instantaneous, and she was startled enough to gasp again and sit up with her back to the headboard. The wolf looked at her with its bright green eyes, and then its tongue lolled out of its mouth, and it seemed to smile at her.

"Change back, please," she said, and then Sandra was there again looking at her with sheepish eyes. "Can you... change into anything?"

"With practice, I can change into any living thing that is approximately the same size as me."

"Are you...are you a woman or a man? Or were you a wolf initially?"

"We are not born the same way as you," Sandra answered. "We are born with the possibility for both, or neither. It's our own choice as to how to carry ourselves through life. For the most part, I stay in this guise."

"Wait," Eva said, wrinkling her brow. "You bit me!"

Sandra smiled and Eva could see a blush creep up her

cheeks. "I apologize for that, but I felt I needed to mark you against any other shifters who may be around you."

"Mark me?"

"It is a warning to all others to stay away from you. A protection."

"I had not even met you when the wolf, when you, attacked me."

"I know, but I knew you, and although we had not formally met yet, I felt the need to protect you, whether we ended up meeting or not. Some shifters are not as...morally upstanding as I am."

Eva thought about this for a moment. She could see how the ability to change your appearance could be used for less than noble purposes. Sandra got up from the bed and stood next to it.

"Your mother will be getting worried that you haven't returned soon," she said. "We should get you dressed." She looked down at herself and giggled nervously. "I should be dressed too."

Eva laughed at her joke and was about to get out of the bed when suddenly the door to her chambers burst open. It took her a moment to realize that it was her mother standing in the doorway, and that she had one of her dead husband's pistols in her hand.

"Shapeshifter whore!" her mother screamed and began to fire. Eva screamed and covered her ears at the loud bursts of noise in the confined space. Then she looked over to see the large, bloody holes in Sandra's chest and abdomen. The woman looked at her a moment and then fell to the floor next to the bed.

"No!" Eva screamed.

"Impure temptress," her mother screamed, and Eva looked to where her mother stood and saw she was pointing the pistol at her now. She felt the tears flowing from her eyes and she said nothing, waiting for her mother to shoot.

That was when she saw the sword pierce her mother's side. It was withdrawn and then thrust through her again as her mother screamed and dropped her weapon. Once again, the sword was withdrawn and then pierced her chest as she turned to look at her attacker. The person moved into Eva's view, and she saw that it was Morton, wielding her father's sword.

Her mother fell to the floor and laid there unmoving as Morton stood over her. Eva then remembered Sandra and hurriedly scrambled from the bed where she found the woman lying on the floor, bleeding profusely from her wounds.

"Sandra!" Eva screamed and knelt next to the shifter. She saw that Sandra's eyes were still open and looking at her now, the pain and anguish in them evident. "Sandra," she said again.

"Eva," Sandra said quietly. A small stream of blood accompanied the word and dribbled down the side of her cheek.

"Can you heal it?" Eva asked, cradling the other woman's head in her hands. "Can you fix it?"

Sandra closed her mouth and slowly shook her head. "It does not work that way," she said.

"No, please do not leave me," Eva said, feeling a new wave of tears stream from her eyes. She kissed Sandra on the forehead and then on the mouth, tasting the faint metallic flavor of the woman's blood.

"I'm...sorry," Sandra said, and then she was gone. Her eyes lost expression, and Eva pulled her up and held her close to her, rocking gently for a moment. Then she felt a hand on her shoulder.

"My Lady," Morton said. "I am so sorry I was tardy."

Eva gently laid down Sandra's head on the floor and closed her eyes before turning to look at the butler. "Thank you, Morton. You...you saved my life."

"The shots will draw a crowd, My Lady," he said, helping her to her feet.

"I want...I want this section of the manor closed off," she said. "I do not want anyone here. Let them guess as to what happened. They do not need to know the truth."

"Yes, My Lady," he said, bowing slightly. He turned and left, stepping over the body of the woman whom he had previously served.

Eva slowly walked over to her mother's body and looked down at it. Fittingly, the woman's expression was a scowl, even in death. Eva did not close the eyes of her mother. She felt no need to show her that respect.

She went into her closet and then realized that she had Sandra's blood on her hands, if not her face as well. That seemed fitting, as well. She was marked—and would remain so for the rest of her life.

The End

A Family Story

Come in, come in young man. Do not be afraid. I am your humble servant and wish only to serve you. Why have you come to me today? Fortunes? Palm reading? Ah! You seek knowledge of the past. How exciting!

So, do you have an article or item for me to read? You do! Oh, I...see. How marvelous. A gun. And pointing right at me. How...cute. Please, place it in front of me. There. Now we'll just point it away from me. Much better. Much, much better.

Before we begin, there is a little matter, quite insignificant, really, I assure you, that we should discuss. It's a small concern of mine. So. How will you be paying today? I take cash, Visa, American Express, Discover, Master Card, Diner's Club, checks, money orders, precious jewels, gold bullion...Oh. You have cash! How wonderful! I do love the sound of it rustling in my hand.

Now that that very miniscule item is out of the way, we can get to the business at hand. "Let's get busy!" as the man on television used to say. Oh, you watched him too? I just love it when he...Oh. Um, er, yes. Of course. The gun. So sorry. No distractions. Let's get right down to business.

Be warned! This is not a trivial matter. This is not a parlor trick. Anyway, we are in the living room, so please sit and make yourself comfortable. Ha! Just a little joke, ha. The forces that work through my body are older than time itself. They are nameless energies, yet they are known to only a chosen few. Including me, as it happens. Please, once I've begun, do not, I repeat for you, do not interrupt me at any time. The results could be very, very bad. For both of us.

So. I'd better put this money away where it will be safe. There. Oh, you like that hidden pocket? Yes, I said to my tailor, I said, "John, my friend..." Oh. Sorry. My mind is distracted somewhat still by the spirits from my last session. Shall we begin?

Let us close our eyes. Feel the energy within the room. Feel it trapped by the four walls. Feel it as it dances over, around, and through our bodies. Feel it. Do you feel it? Well, try harder! Close your eyes!

Okay. There. Feel the power, feel the forces. Here we go!

I see a young man, about your age. Only better looking. He has dark hair, like yours. He is, he is, he is buying a gun! From another man! This gun! It is dark. They are in an alleyway. In a large city. Boy, this is getting good. Er, hm, yes. Yes. I see. Get on with it.

I see the young man check the gun for ammunition. Then...Oh my! He shot the other man! The scoundrel! The rogue! Whoops. Almost lost it. There, it's...later on, possibly not the same day, and in a different place. I see another young man and a very lovely young lady. Woo-woo, is she hot! Oh. Of course. Sorry.

The two young people are in what looks like a club; or maybe a bar. They are talking quietly, bowing over their drinks. He is making her laugh. They look very much in love, if you don't mind my saying so. I see people pass by. They all seem to know the young couple. They wave and smile. Ah, young love! Oh, look, they are going to kiss.

Brian S. Converse

Wait!

It is the scoundrel from the alleyway. It looks like he's drunk, and yelling. The young man from the couple is trying to calm him down and keeping between him and the girl. Smart boy. You never know what that cur might do!

The young man is taking that punk outside to get him some fresh air. That's good. Ooh, that jerk hit him from behind! Now the young man is getting up. He hits the scoundrel. A left, a right. Give him an uppercut! Oh. Sorry. I'm getting hot in the collar.

The man is turning to go back inside. Look out! The dark-haired one pulled his gun. This gun. He's...he's shot him! That fink! That piece of camel offal. That rat basta... Wait! Where are you going? What? That piece of trash was your father? And the woman, your mother?

Wait. Did I say...trash? Ha, ha. I was kidding! I meant... uh...that fine upstanding young good-looking man was your father? No! Give that back! I read the article's past. Is it my fault you can't take the truth? Wait. Wait! You've torn my hidden pocket!

Sheesh. I've got to learn to lie better, it seems. Well, the spirits will take care of that man sooner rather than later, I'm sure. Scoundrel, and son of a scoundrel, too.

Oh well. It's almost time for "The Price is Right," anyway. Come on Down!

The End

Tunguska II

The children scurried about like the vermin that they sought. Always underfoot, they were, but thankfully their actions provided many with the food they consumed each day as well as protecting the food staples that were stored there.

"Grandpapa, we caught four!" a small boy child called out, holding up one of the large cockroaches that frequent the home, such as it was.

"Good, good. A feast tonight!" Pavel told him enthusiastically, while his stomach clenched at the thought of eating another meal of insects. He much preferred the large rats that infested the grain silos but were much more difficult to catch and kill. At least in that case, if he closed his eyes, he could still pretend that it was squirrel or even rabbit that he was eating.

He wasn't their real grandfather—his grandchildren were more than likely hunting in a different part of the shelter, but he had earned the honorific as he was now one of the oldest inhabitants there. Someone from "before."

He watched as the children triumphantly carried their catches back to their parents' rooms, knowing that they would be cleaned and then added to the community dishes that would be served at dinnertime.

◊

Pavel was ten years old when the meteor hit. He was no one special, had no great wealth of family, athletic skill or burning intelligence. He lived much as any other child of the time lived in his village. He performed his chores and spent time with his friends getting into all manner of troubles.

Like many of his friends, he dreamed of the future, and wondered if he would ever see America, his people's enemy of old. Theirs was a world he could only imagine; a world that came to an abrupt end one bright spring morning.

They say humanity almost had a chance at redemption: A silver bird burdened with the power of creation and a means of destruction more horrifying than the world had ever known. It was to be their savior, their redeemer, but instead it brought only a prelude of their death. An accident, some said. Sabotage, said others, though who would perform such an unspeakable act, he would dare not even contemplate.

And so, their deaths now assured, he and the other members of his village worked feverishly in hopes that they were wrong, those respected scientific minds with their long white coats and thick black glasses and aromatic pipes.

Four months. Four months is all they were given to prepare for the end. It was not long enough—would never be long enough—but still they planned, and they worked at stockpiling grains and staples and water and other provisions. Their elders worked with the government and tested ways of defeating the cold and lack of sunshine in growing plants that needed very little light and even less water.

The meteor was called Smith-Anush, though some came to refer to it simply as "Smiter" due to the biblical nature of its impending threat to humanity. A monumental failure by their governments and their scientists to detect it while it could have made a difference. Four months was all the time they had to prepare for the worst while their governments hatched a last-ditch effort to thwart the heavens.

Pavel helped his father, as so many other children did, to stockpile the harvests and bring them to that place—a warren of caves and tunnels some fifty feet under the ground near the outskirts of the village. The cave system was millions of years old and purportedly had already survived one screaming rock from the sky before Pavel was born, though it was said that particular meteor had exploded somewhere over the Earth's surface, not impacting upon it.

And so that silver bird had launched, with all of humanity's hopes that it could stop a space rock traveling at seven miles per second. Pavel and his friends and family all watched the launch on their televisions and cheered to see the column of smoke that trailed the ship as it lofted into the clouds.

When it exploded in the atmosphere, there was nothing anyone could say. The mission had failed. There was no time to launch another, and the radiation from the bombs that the ship carried rained down upon the land and sea below. It would foreshadow the near future apocalypse.

Smiter was coming and there was nothing humanity could do about it. Pavel recalled the panic in the streets, even in his small hometown, after the spacecraft explosion. Some people gave up and simply chose to sit in their houses, waiting for the end. Some seemed to lose their last shred of humanity and ran through the streets shooting wildly or taking revenge for any slight both imagined and real. Some simply took their own lives, unwilling to cope with the situation they now found themselves in.

Pavel's father was a practical man and held steady to the belief that they would be able to survive in the caves. When the government men came, they agreed that his father was a valuable person and that he and his family would be allowed to come down to the caves just a week before the impact date.

He still remembered his last view of the sky. It was a blue so beautiful as to stay in his dreams even so many years later. But it was long ago, and he feared that he would not live to see it again.

Smiter struck the Earth like a hammer. They say that it hit somewhere in the middle of what was then called the United States of America. It obliterated thousands of square miles and threw up enough ash and soil into the sky that the sun was obscured, some say permanently, though Pavel's father had shown him scientific studies that showed that the atmosphere would stabilize someday, and the sun would shine once again.

The studies also said that because the meteor was coming from the asteroid belt, it was coming at a slower rate than if it had come from the Oort Cloud because of something called orbital mechanics. This lesser speed would someday be their salvation as a species. Or so they hoped.

The elders of the village and the government representatives who stayed at the site waited for a week while the temperature steadily fell before turning on the heating system in the caves. It was a geothermal system that didn't require sunlight or electricity—a marvel of engineering that kept the caves warm while the outside world was thrown into eternal winter.

◊

Many years later, there were only three thousand people left in the cave system. They'd had no radio contact with any other survivors for a few years, and many didn't want to think too much about that. It's difficult to think that you are all that's left of humanity. Three thousand out of ten billion earthly inhabitants.

And then it happened; a machine within the cave was beginning to falter. Pavel was ten years old when Smiter hit, but after he came into the caves, his education became of utmost importance. They brought him into their learning bubbles. They taught him everything they could about the machines that kept everyone alive.

Besides the heating system, there was the generator that stemmed from the same geothermal source. There was the air purification system that continuously cleaned our air so that they wouldn't suffocate. There were the greenhouses that needed to be constantly maintained so that what little number of seeds they had would grow. There were the animal pens that kept the last of their domesticated animals alive.

The last horse died when Pavel was twenty-one. The last pig, when he was thirty. The last lamb, when he was fifty-three. Animals that were never meant to live underground. The scientists, in all of their wisdom, had seemingly not taken that into account when they were planning. They would have been better to breed groundhogs and rabbits.

Their air purification machine was beginning to break down. No one knew this but a few people, including Pavel. He was the chief engineer, but he had retired a few years back. Let the younger men keep us alive now, he had thought. He believed that he had imparted all the knowledge that he could to ensure that the machines would run smoothly after he was gone, and it turned out that he was wrong.

He told no one in his family. His wife has been dead for over a decade. His children, those who have survived sickness, malnutrition, and disease, had grown and now worked in other areas of the cave system. His grandchildren ranged in ages from young adults to as young as five—his little roach catchers.

What would their future look like? Would they survive long, with their air slowly being poisoned by too much carbon dioxide and their domesticated animals dying? How long would the greenhouses be able to produce living plants when currently the plants were already sickly and sometimes rotting from their roots outward?

Pavel knew what must be done, but he dreaded performing what was needed. He was old. His bones ached and his muscles were seemingly sore from the time he awoke until the time he fell onto his simple mattress for sleep at night. Yet he looked at his grandchildren and all of the other children and he saw the future for them if nothing was done.

There were parts needed to fix the air filtration system, and they didn't have them there in the caves. Someone had to leave the caves on a mission to find new ones. It was Pavel's belief that someone would have to know how the system worked and what was needed to fix it. He would make his plea with the other members of the council and hope that they would allow him to leave the sanctuary to search for new parts.

◊

The council meeting was contentious at best. It always was. Pavel made his thoughts and predictions plain to all of them. If they didn't fix the air filtration system, it would either slowly break down, or possibly just stop working one day with a final gasp. Either way, it would not last more than a few months at most. And when it broke down, so would their air supply. They would die gasping for breath as carbon dioxide levels in the air increased with every exhalation.

While most believed this to be true, there were still some doubters—younger members of the council that perhaps thought that things would keep going the way they were for the rest of their lives. Pavel did his best to dissuade them from that notion in no uncertain terms. They were shouted down by many of the elders of the council. With one hurdle overcome, it was on to the next item on the agenda:

The mission to find parts to fix the machine.

Pavel, of course, raised his hand to volunteer for the mission. He felt that understanding the machine made him the correct candidate for the mission, unfortunate as this was. He'd had understudies, of course, but he wasn't the type of person who would leave the future of his children and grandchildren up to others.

Members of the council argued the points back and forth between themselves, noting that Pavel was no longer young, and that he may not be able to survive outside the shelter long enough to find the parts needed. He knew that some of the younger members saw him as a doddering old fool.

Finally, it was agreed that he would lead the mission but would be accompanied by some younger members of the community for both his own protection and to ensure the success of the mission. He nodded his thanks to them and then left immediately, not interested in anything else they had to say.

◊

Pavel woke in the darkness, unsure as to the time of day. All he knew was that this day was the day that his journey began. It may end in his death if the conditions outside of the shelter were too severe. Yet at least it was a chance to save their futures, if only for a little while.

He dressed quietly so as to not wake any of his grandchildren or their parents. His children had been informed of his mission, some of them reacting thankfully, while others rolled their eyes at him and called him an old fool. Such were the trappings of parenthood. Whether cynical or not, he loved them all, and was willing to sacrifice his own life, if needed, to save them.

He was to meet with his team in a smaller cave near the main entrance to the shelter, and he made his way there after stopping by the food stores pantry (which was affectionately referred to as the vault) and checking his request. They had the required food supplies ready, for which he was grateful. His guess was that word had already begun to spread as to the nature of his mission. Gregor, the head of the pantry, was nothing if not stingy when it came to passing out food and supplies from the stores.

He walked to the entrance of the small cave where they were to meet and again was grateful to see that everyone had come, though he was not familiar with many of them. They had all come, curious about the first foray into the world since the meteor hit.

The sole woman was short but built like a fire hydrant. "I'm Ania," she said, holding her hand out to shake his. He grasped it briefly, smiling at her.

"Thank you so much for coming," he said.

Nikolai was a tall man with long, thin blonde hair. He nodded at Pavel, saying nothing, though his handshake was firm and he didn't shy from looking Pavel in the eyes. Pavel had seen him around and knew that the man barely spoke to anyone. Alek was about the same height as Pavel, and he seemed to have Mongol ancestry. He smiled and shook Pavel's hand, his grip like a vice. The last of the party was Maksim.

"You may call me Maks," he said, nodding to Pavel. He seemed to be the youngest of the volunteers and looked nervous to be there.

"Thank you all for showing up," Pavel told them. He saw that they all carried their own backpacks, and he dropped his own to the floor and opened it, sharing with them the meager rations that he had garnered from the pantry. He saw that Nikolai and Alek carried rifles. Each of the weapons looked to be ancient, and he hoped for their sakes that they still worked.

At last, he pulled out the folded piece of paper—a map he had marked up that showed possible locations of other underground bunkers such as theirs. "I've talked to others who may remember locations we can search," he began. "Others who were either alive when we came to this place, or whose parents would have passed down their knowledge." He knelt on the floor and unfolded and laid the map out on the floor in front of him for them to see.

"As you can see, the closest site is approximately 20 kilometers away to the west, here," he said pointing to a spot on the map. The others had either bent down to see or were kneeling next to the map as well.

"Most of the other points are east," Ania said. "Going west would waste time."

"My thoughts as well," Maks said. "If we head East, there is a line of sites that we could reach more easily."

"The problem is the terrain," Alek said, pointing. "The land begins to elevate here and steadily rises. Many of those sites are in mountainous country."

"It will be breathtakingly cold, either way," Nikolai said.

Pavel nodded. "My father talked of this site," he said, pointing to the one west of their location. "I say that we go and search, and if we find nothing, we head back here to recover and resupply. At least this way we get a sense of what it's like out there."

The others were silent as they thought over his words. Finally, Alek spoke. "You make a good point, my friend. The closest point to the east is almost double the distance. I would hate to have to turn around without having visited at least one site."

Pavel nodded. He looked at the others. "Then I guess it is settled, unless there are any other objections?" He waited a moment, and no one spoke. "Good. Perform a final equipment check and make sure you have everything you need. We'll leave in an hour. Meet at the main entrance then."

◊

Pavel returned to his home—if an eight foot by eight-foot concrete bunker with no windows and only a small partition for a door could be called such. He had an hour to get ready to leave. The others would presumably be saying goodbyes to friends and family. He had already said goodbye in a letter that he placed on his small bunk for his children to find after he was gone. For now, he had an item that he needed to retrieve.

He knelt next to his bunk and reached under it to pull out the metal box that had sat underneath it, unused, for the past forty years, at least. He opened the simple lid and picked up the handgun, its weight reassuring yet menacing in his grip. The Makarov held eight rounds in the magazine and was heavy for its size, but his father had sworn by it, which was good enough for Pavel. His father had taught him to shoot it before the meteor hit to make sure he knew how.

He began to disassemble it for cleaning, noticing that it was still well-oiled with no evidence of rust. His father had served in the army and knew how to maintain his weapons. Cleaning the weapon gave him the opportunity to calm his nerves and think about his mission, which he hoped would be successful. Yet there was still that trepidation in the back of his mind about venturing outside the shelter.

It would be cold. It would be difficult to breathe, since any plant life had more than likely been killed off or gone into deep hibernation long ago. His father had referred to it as "impact winter," which was a fancy way of saying that the meteor had kicked enough debris into the atmosphere to blot out the sunlight and cause a new ice age on the planet's surface.

The going would be difficult and slow. He didn't know what they would find—if there were still any other humans out there left alive, and if so, would they be friendly? He would like to think that they would be happy to see others, but there was a reason he was bringing the gun.

He assembled the pistol and wiped it down before loading the magazine. He closed the chamber with a satisfying clank. He had three full magazines and another full box of rounds, which he loaded into the pistol belt, for a total of fifty-six rounds. He prayed he wouldn't need them. He strapped the gun belt around his waist and placed the gun in the holster. He felt like a western cowboy, and the thought made him smile for a moment.

He knelt and pushed the now empty box back under the bunk, then briefly touched the letter on his pillow. It would be fine, he told himself. It was time to leave.

◊

Everyone but Maks was waiting for him at the rendezvous point. Pavel nodded to the others, then stood and waited patiently for the young man to arrive so they could begin. Finally, he showed up, looking somewhat abashed at his tardiness.

"I'm sorry. My mother...well, she worries."

The others smiled, and Alek put an arm around the man's shoulder. "Be glad you have a good mother waiting for you to return. Don't worry, we'll watch out for you."

It was a good moment, and Pavel was grateful for it. The team needed to bond a little. It might save their lives. "It is time to go," he said, and noted that everyone's smile disappeared at the reminder. Pavel led the way to the outer door, which was thick and made of steel, with a wheel lock on it. A few of the counsel were standing nearby to see them off, and Pavel nodded to them. He had no doubt that they all thought they would never see the party again, and they may have been correct.

Pavel nodded to the young man stationed at the door, who turned the wheel to unlock the door and then pulled it open. A gust of cold air entered the hallway and Pavel walked through the doorway to see a white environment. He walked a few paces forward through half a meter of snow, then turned to make sure his team had followed. He noticed that while the air was bitterly cold, it wasn't much colder than a bad Siberian winter. He also didn't feel short of breath, though his lungs burned from the cold air.

"Are we ready?" he asked, and his voice startled even himself in the still, silent day. Most of the others nodded in response. "Spread out and keep alert," he told them, then turned and began heading west, according to the small compass he held in his hand. The entrance to the shelter had been at the end of a long and winding dirt road. They walked along it, and Pavel saw the forms of cars under snow, some parked haphazardly, as if the occupants had been in a hurry to flee them and seek shelter at the end of the road.

The snow was pristine, there were no tracks, animals or humans, to be found as they trekked along the road. Pavel couldn't help but wonder why it seemed wrong. It should have been colder. And darker. He looked up to see the white clouds overhead, but they were not so thick that they completely blocked out the sun. It was a mystery that he pondered as they walked the entire rest of the day.

◊

They had seen no sign of life as they prepared to stop for

the night. They had made about twenty kilometers so far as they were uninterrupted in their journey. They had stopped briefly for a plain, cold lunch, but had otherwise not stopped moving. Now they searched for an appropriate place to set up camp for the night. There had been few structures along their path. The shelter had been in a sparsely populated area, and its location was kept secret for fear that too many people would head there as the meteor approached.

Maks, who had been sent ahead to scout, came back just as it began to grow dark. "There's a building about two klicks ahead," he said, pointing back the way he had come. "Possibly a barn or warehouse." They all looked at Pavel.

"You saw no one near it?" he asked the man.

"No. No sign that anyone's been there recently."

"We'll make for it and check it out," he said. "But be alert. We don't want any surprises." They all nodded and set off with renewed energy at the prospect of shelter for the night. They had brought a tent large enough for all of them, but it was an emergency measure, at best.

As the building came within site, Pavel directed Maks and Nikolai to make a wide sweep around the structure just to make sure that it was deserted. They stopped one hundred meters from it to observe the area. There was no sign of anyone, and soon Maks and Nikolai came back to report the same. Pavel nodded and began to walk towards the structure. He found a door on the side that was unlocked, and stepped in, waiting a moment to allow his eyes to adjust to the dim light inside.

It looked to be some type of storage unit—a warehouse as Maks had suggested. There were boxes of various sizes and some items that were covered in dust covers. Pavel motioned towards a set of stairs off to the right, and Nikolai went up them to investigate the second story.

Alek pulled the dust cover from an object sitting near the aisle they were walking down. It was a telescope, about three feet long. He waved away the cloud of dust this cause to rise in the still air.

"Make sure we've secured the building before snooping around," Ania admonished him. He nodded to show he understood.

Pavel had reached the far wall and had not seen any sign of life. He turned and nodded to the others. "It appears that we are alone."

There were two doors on the other side, one which was another exit. Pavel approached the other one and opened it, seeing that there was a small office space inside. They all heard a noise and looked to see Nikolai coming down the stairs. He shook his head to show that he had not found anyone, either.

"I want a clear area in the middle of the structure to build a fire. We can use some of the boxes as firewood. Make sure all windows are covered so that the fire is not detectable from the outside. I'll lock the doors, but we'll need to set a watch. I want two people per shift, one on either side of the building. Three-hour shifts should get us through the night sufficiently."

They all nodded their acceptance, then began to explore the space more thoroughly. Pavel turned and checked the door that led to the outside. It was unlocked as well, so he locked the bolt and then went into the office to make sure there were no other doors in there. He found a small restroom on the far side, but nothing that led to the outside. Unsurprisingly, there was no running water, and the toilet was dry as well.

He walked back to the door they had entered and locked that as well, before turning and contemplating the boxes he saw before him. He approached the first stack and opened the box on top, finding neat rows of canned sardines inside. He looked at the expiration date and saw that they had expired some thirty years before. He wasn't about to open one to check—the entire warehouse would smell of rotten fish. He placed the box on the floor and saw that the ones under it were the same.

He checked another stack and found boxes filled with playing cards and other novelties. The cards had the face of a famous actor who had presumably died many years before. Pavel was beginning to get an idea of what the place was—a warehouse for black market items that someone had built in the middle of nowhere to hide it from the authorities of the time.

Pavel and the others had gone through a few stacks of boxes, and they had all found little of practical use. The contraband tended more towards novelties and luxury items from the West that did little to help them on their journey. The most important items were the boxes themselves, which they broke down for kindling and firewood. In short order, they had a small fire in the middle of the concrete floor of the warehouse.

Soon, they could no longer see their breath fogging the air. The smoke collected at the highest area of the ceiling. Pavel climbed the stairs to the second floor and was able to open a small window that allowed some of the smoke to escape. While there, he noticed a few stacks of boxes, and he opened the top box to investigate. There were stacks of cans inside with a picture of a fish on the side. He looked closer and saw that the expiration date was again some thirty years prior. He had no desire to open one of the cans, whether it was caviar or sardines, the smell of rotting fish would permeate the entire building.

He checked another stack and found bottles of vodka. He had never drunk real vodka, and doubted that any of the others had, either. Some within the shelter had attempted to distill liquor over the years, with various levels of success, none of it particularly good.

He knew that if the vodka was still good, he would become a very popular man within the shelter. He smiled at the thought, then replaced the top. This was not their mission, and for any of them to drink it now would only harm their priorities. He walked back down the stairs. He needed to sleep a little until it was time for his watch.

◊

He was suddenly awake. There was a loud noise above the building. He sat up and saw that the others were awake as well. Ania and Maks were standing at either end of the warehouse on their watch, which meant that he had only slept a couple of hours at most.

"What is it?" Alek yelled to be heard.

Pavel shook his head in response. He got out of his sleeping bag, then hurriedly put on his coat and walked to where Ania stood next to the door. "No one else comes out," he told her. "And no one else comes in."

He waited for her to acknowledge what he was saying, then unlocked the door and checked to make sure his pistol was still in the holster at his side before opening the door, stepping through, and closing it behind him again.

The sound was even louder outside, and he held his hands over his ears for a moment. Then the sound began to fade and he looked up to see lights streak across the sky, and he understood what was making the noise. He watched the lights until they went out of sight and the noise was gone. He shook his head to clear it and wipe the remnants of the noise from his ears. He turned and walked back to the door and knocked quietly.

The door opened a crack, and the barrel of a rifle protruded from it. Good, he thought. At least they took his words, and the situation, seriously. "It's Pavel," he said, and the barrel was pulled back as the door opened wider. He quickly walked through, feeling the inviting warmth of the fire.

"Did you discover what it was?" Maks asked him. He had left his post at the other end of the building and Pavel felt anger for a moment, before he realized that he was a young man, and obviously scared. They were all on high alert, so in the end, it did not matter if he wasn't keeping watch.

"Yes," he answered, looking at them all. He walked to the fire, which had burned down to glowing embers. He threw a couple of pieces of kindling on the coals, then turned and looked at them again before speaking. "It was aircraft."

"What?" Nikolai asked. Pavel was surprised that the normally quiet man had asked the question so vehemently.

"Aircraft of some type, though I could not identify them," Pavel clarified.

"How can that be?" Alek asked.

"I don't know, but there could be no mistake. I watched them until they were out of sight. There were four in a diamond formation. I believe they were flying relatively low. Maybe ten thousand feet, which is why they were so loud."

"The question now is, what are we going to do?" Ania asked.

"We go on as planned," Pavel answered. "The presence of the aircraft does not change the fact that we have a mission to accomplish. The fate of our community rests with us."

"We should go back and warn them," Maks said, looking worried, as usual.

"Warn them?" Alek asked. "Are we sure they are not on

our side? Maybe another community was able to survive and fly them looking for other survivors."

Pavel thought for a moment. "True, they could be on our side, but they could also be on the side of a rival who would want to take our resources and kill us. Or they could even be Americans for all we know."

"The shelter is well-hidden, either way," Alek said. "They will be fine."

"But..." Maks began.

"We go on," Pavel said. He sighed. "If you feel that strongly about going back, then go. This is not a dictatorship, nor are you a soldier taking orders. Nor are you my prisoner."

"You would go back alone and unarmed," Ania said. "We cannot spare the weapons."

The young man's face visibly paled at this, as he thought about the implications.

"I am going back to sleep," Pavel announced, trying to sound calm. "Please wake me when it is time for my shift to begin."

He walked to where his sleeping bag was laid out next to the fire and took off his coat and gun belt. He didn't look at the others, but he hoped all of them would still be there when he woke up.

◊

"Pavel, wake up. It's time for your shift."

It felt like he had just closed his eyes, but he was instantly awakened by Maks' voice. He was happy that the young man was the one to wake him. He sat up and tried to stretch the aching out of his muscles from lying on the concrete floor. He didn't think he had moved positions while sleeping, and the sleeping bag didn't offer much in the way of a cushion. He stood and smiled at the young man. "Get some rest."

Maks nodded, though he still looked worried.

Pavel patted the younger man on the arm, then walked to the far end of the room, noticing now the temperature steadily dropped the further away he strayed from the fire. It was the coldest part of the morning. Dawn would only be a few hours away. He made sure that all of the windows were still covered and the door was locked, and then stood for a moment as he thought about the aircraft he had seen.

He had heard jets before, when he was younger. These sounded different. The sound quality was not the same as he remembered. He was also puzzled by the number of them and their formation. It wasn't a single passenger jet or even a small private jet, but a squadron flying together. He made a mental note to himself to keep out of sight as much as possible as they walked and avoid open spaces.

His shift proved to be uneventful. He kept himself awake and somewhat warm by moving around constantly—never sitting down or even leaning against a wall for any length of time. He would periodically look outside, but saw nothing except the sky growing brighter as dawn approached.

Finally, it was time to wake the others. He walked to where the fire had once more burned down to glowing embers. Nikolai had been on duty on the other side of the warehouse, and he nodded at Pavel as he approached the fire.

"Anything interesting?" Pavel asked him.

Nikolai shook his head. "Nothing, thankfully."

Pavel nodded and raised his voice. "Time to wake up, my friends." He bent and softly shook first Ania and then Maks, as Nikolai shook Aleks with a little more vigor, causing the other man to lash out, though not violently. Nikolai smiled, and Pavel could see that the two were becoming friends. Good, he thought. They would need that, if they were all to survive. Especially now with a new wildcard in the mix.

"Wake up, break your fast and then pack," Pavel told

them. "We need to make good time today." Pavel smiled at Maks reassuringly.

◊

They'd all eaten and packed up their belongings. Pavel had made sure that there were no embers left of their fire. He didn't want the shelter to burn down in case they needed it again on their way back.

The bitter cold met them as they left the warehouse, and Pavel pulled his scarf over his face to protect his nose and cheeks from frostbite. He pointed the way after re-checking his map, though he'd looked at it so many times now it was memorized.

It was close to noon when a ray of sun briefly broke through the clouds. They all stood, amazed at the sight. Pavel knew that something was off, now, for sure. There should not be sunlight for a very long time still, if their calculations were correct. The impact of the meteor would have sent so much debris into the atmosphere that it would block the sun for more than the sixty or so years that passed since the incident.

He looked at the others and saw that they were all looking at him for an explanation. He could only shrug and begin walking again. He did not look back to see if they followed. They walked for another few hours, eating lunch as they did so. They didn't hear the sound of aircraft again for a number of hours.

◊

Pavel ducked down and motioned for the others to do so as well. They were in what had been a lightly forested area, but the trees were bare and offered little cover. The sound became louder, and they could tell that the craft were getting closer to their exposed position. Pavel motioned towards the nearest clump of trees, and they all quickly headed towards them.

"Get as close as possible to the trunks," he told them. He stood next to one tree and wrapped his arms around the trunk in an effort to break up his own outline. He hoped that it would offer enough camouflage to be undetected. It would be for nothing if the aircraft were equipped with any type of thermal imaging.

He looked up in time to see the aircraft in the same diamond formation as he'd seen the night before in the dark, only now he could clearly see the vessels. They were not jets. In fact, they did not look like man-made ships at all. They were a dull grey color and shaped almost like a cigar—long and thin, and tapered on each end. He could not tell how they moved, because they didn't seem to have any visible engine exhaust, and no wings.

He watched them on their way until they were gone, then calculated in his head their trajectory, noting that they seemed to be moving along the same path as they had the night before. They would once again fly over their warehouse shelter. He also realized that they were traveling along that same path. He wondered if they walked in a straight line if they would eventually come across where the ships originated.

The thought caused a flash of fear to course through his body. He wasn't sure if he wanted to know where they came from. There were too many variables that simply didn't make sense.

He backed up from the tree trunk and motioned for the others to do so as well. The aircraft were gone long enough that he was fairly certain they had not been seen. The others began speaking at once and he held his hands out to motion for them to stop talking.

"I don't know the answers to your questions," he said.

"I wish that I did. All that I know is that it is likely those vehicles were not made by human beings."

"Could it be the Americans?" Ania asked.

"I do not believe so," Pavel said. "They were struck directly by the meteor."

"What does that mean?" Ania asked, her face screwed up with some emotion between anger and fear.

"It means that we may no longer be alone on this planet," Pavel said. "It may explain why it's not as cold and frozen as it was supposed to be."

"You think they've cleaned up the atmosphere while we were all living underground?" Nikolai asked.

Pavel thought for a moment. "That may very well be what has happened," he said.

"I'll go one step further," Alek said. "What if they sent the meteor to kill us all or drive us into shelters while they took over our planet."

"That's crazy," Maks said. His eyes were wide with fear.

Pavel walked to where the younger man stood. "It is only a theory," he said. "But if it proves to be true, then our people would be able to leave the shelter without fear of the machinery we use breaking down."

"Then our mission is for nothing," Alek said.

"No," Pavel said, turning to them all. "No, it has not changed. We cannot rely on this theory. What if proven untrue? We need to fulfil our mission to ensure that the others, and yourselves, have a future."

"And if the theory is proven true?" Nikolai asked.

"Then we need to make sure that we are safe from them," Pavel said, motioning vaguely up at the sky. "If they did indeed send the meteor to wipe us out, I doubt they would be very happy to see that it failed."

They were all silent for a minute after this, as each

thought of the implications of Pavel's words. "Come," he finally said. "Our mission is still our priority. But we must remain alert and vigilant. We do not want to be caught by surprise. He checked his gun to make sure it was loaded and had a round ready to fire, and this was mirrored by Alek and Nikolai as they did the same.

◊

They walked until it began to grow dark, then began to search for shelter. They were about to give up and resign themselves to sleeping in the tent in the snow when they came across a small cabin nestled in a copse of trees. Pavel pulled out his pistol and motioned for Nikolai to go around the back of the building. He tried the front door and found that it was locked.

He looked in the windows near the door and saw that it was a simple, one room layout, and seemed to be deserted. Suddenly he saw movement inside and pulled his gun up as he moved back. Then he saw that it was Nikolai. The man came the door and unlocked it. "Sorry to startle you," he said when he opened the door. "There was a back window that was open."

They all entered the cabin, with Maks shutting the door behind them and locking it. Pavel knew that the young man was fighting his fear of the situation, and he hoped the man wouldn't break under the pressure of that fear.

Their next surprise was the skeleton they found lying under the bedspread, a pistol still in the man's hand. He had seemingly crawled into bed and ended his life either shortly before the meteor hit, or just after, judging by the amount of dust that covered all of his possessions.

There was no fireplace, but there was a small wood stove. They debated about starting a fire in it. They decided that it might be too risky to have smoke emitting from the chimney, so they laid out their sleeping bags and set the watch shifts.

Pavel was on the first shift, and it gave him an opportunity to think about what they had all talked about earlier in the day after the aircraft went over. If they were some type of extraterrestrial beings in those ships, what did that mean about the future of humanity? What is it they wanted? Surely it wasn't any natural resources such as water, which was plentiful in the universe. Perhaps some minerals or other substances that were scarce?

His musings were interrupted by the now familiar sound of aircraft. He looked out the window into the darkness of the night, expecting to see the lights fly overhead and then out of sight. Instead, he saw them hovering overhead, not too far away. It was a departure from their usual behavior, and it sent a feeling of deep cold down his spine. He turned to warn the others just as the sound of aircraft grew louder and then disappeared. There could be only one reason: they had landed.

"Wake up!" he shouted to them. It was difficult to see in the dimness of the cabin—they had no lights on—but he could see their movements as they woke. He turned back to the window, pulling up his scarf over his nose and mouth so as not to fog up the glass.

"What is it? What is happening?" Alek asked from behind him.

"Keep your voices down," he said in a loud whisper. "I think they may have landed nearby."

Someone cursed in the darkness and then someone was by his side. He turned quickly to see Nikolai armed with his rifle. Pavel nodded to him. "Don't shoot until you are sure what you're shooting at." Nikolai nodded.

They looked outside for a few minutes, seeing nothing. Then, there—a movement. There was hardly any light from the moon, but Pavel definitely saw something move in the near darkness. He looked around and saw that Alek and Ania were stationed at another window. He nodded to them, then waved his hand to get their attention when he noticed that they hadn't seen him. Alek finally waved back. Ania moved quickly to where they stood.

"There is something out there," Pavel told her. "Be alert." She nodded, then moved back next to Alek, who was holding his rifle to his shoulder.

It was then that Pavel noted that he couldn't see Maks anywhere. "Stay here," he whispered to Nikolai. The man nodded without looking at him. He moved slowly and quietly to find the young man. He finally found him in the far corner, sitting with his knees drawn up to his chest.

"Are you alright?" he asked.

Maks nodded, though he did not speak.

"I need every eye looking out the windows," Pavel said.

"No, I can't," Maks said. "I...I don't want to see them. I don't want to see."

"Maks, we're all here with you. Maks, we need you."

The young man looked up at him and sat still a moment. Finally, he nodded his head, and Pavel helped him to his feet.

"I saw it!" Alek yelled from his window.

"What was it?" Ania asked.

"I don't know, it moved too fast," Alek said excitedly.

Suddenly, the window near Nikolai erupted. He turned slowly to look at the others. Pavel could see the wetness on his lips. His fall seemed to be in slow motion, and he hit the floor heavily.

"Nikolai!" Alek yelled. He ran to the other man's side and carefully turned him over. "He's...he's dead."

"Ania, get down!" Pavel yelled as he realized now that Nikolai had been shot through the window. She ducked down just as her own window exploded in, showering her in broken glass.

"Give me his rifle!" she yelled at Alek, who slid the weapon across the floor to her but stayed at Nikolai's side.

Pavel pulled out his pistol and crab-walked over to the window where Nikolai had been standing. He raised his head slightly to look outside but could see nothing. Then a shadowy shape moved in the darkness. He aimed his pistol at it and fired a round. The sound was deafening in the enclosed cabin.

He sat down, not knowing if he'd hit anything and shaking his head from the ringing in his ears. Another shot came through the window in response. Either from the one he'd shot at or from another. If there were four ships, then there were at least four of them outside.

Ania stood and fired the rifle then ducked back down. This was followed by a volley of shots through her window. The shots hardly made any sound in relation to the sound of their own weapons.

Pavel knew what needed to happen. "Maks, come here!" The young man slowly crawled across the floor to where Pavel crouched down. When he was close enough, Pavel spoke in hushed tones. He didn't think whoever was outside could understand their language, but he didn't want to take any chances. "Maks, you have to go back."

"What? No, I can't..."

"Be quiet!" Pavel told him. "Listen to me. You have to go back and warn the others. Tell them what we've seen and what happened here. Tell them it's safe to leave the shelter for short periods, that the air is safe and it's not too cold, but warn them about the others. They have to be ready. Do you understand?"

"Yes, yes," Maks said, though he sounded unsure.

"You must do this," Pavel said. "All of us need you to do this."

"Yes, Pavel," Maks said, now sounding more sure of himself. "What about you?"

"We'll distract them so that you can leave," Pavel said. "Once you do, don't look back. Just run as fast and as far as you can."

"Can't you come with me?"

"No, I'm too old to keep up, and we need to keep their attention on us so that you can escape."

Maks nodded. Pavel couldn't see his face well, but he could picture in his mind how miserable the young man looked. "Wait for me to tell you. Pack up your sleeping bag and the tent and wait at the door."

Maks slid away across the floor to where his supplies were. Pavel raised his head once again to look out and saw a shape from a nightmare standing ten meters outside. The shape was somewhat humanoid, but the number of arms was wrong. It took him a moment to see that there was a set of smaller arms a few centimeters below the main arms.

The larger arms raised, and Pavel realized that the thing was about to shoot again in his direction. He quickly dropped to the floor just as the shot came through the window, then raised up again and shot at it, seeing the impact of his own shot catch the creature in the chest. It fell to the ground.

"I think I got one," he said. This meant they could be hurt or even killed. He raised up again and saw that the creature was still unmoving. "Alek, get to a window. We need to draw their attention away from the door." He didn't look to see if the other man complied, because another shot came through his window from somewhere in the darkness.

A shot rang out and Pavel turned to see Alek firing through the window next to Ania. He glanced over to see

Maks hoist his pack onto his back. "Are you ready?" The young man nodded in response. "Get to the door and unlock it. Be ready to run on my signal."

Ania fired this time. "I think I hit..." A shot came through the window, and she fell backwards.

"Damn it!" Alek yelled, firing off a wild shot.

"Maks, now!" Pavel yelled. He stood and fired a volley of shots through the window. Alek was firing as well in his anger. Pavel turned to see Maks open the door and slip through. The door remained open, but Pavel knew it didn't matter. All that mattered was that the young man get back and warn the others.

Alek was out of ammunition, and he slumped to the floor next to the body of Ania, holding his head in his hands and sobbing. A few shots came in through the window he had just vacated, then the firing stopped. Pavel thought of going to Alek's side to offer support but was afraid of leaving his window unguarded. There was at least one of the aliens left. The word "alien" felt strange in his mind, but there was no other word that fit who was attacking them.

"Alek," he spoke, trying to get the other man's attention. His own ears were still ringing, so he had no doubt that Alek's were as well. He looked around for something small to throw at the man. All he could see was a spent shell casing, so he picked it up and tossed it, hitting Alek in the arm closest to him. The man first looked down at his arm and then over to Pavel. Pavel realized that he could see the man clearer, and turned to the window, seeing that it was getting lighter outside. Dawn was quickly approaching. "Alek, we need to defend the cabin so that Maks can get away. Do you understand?"

Alek waited a moment, clearly processing Pavel's words. Then he nodded his understanding. He crawled forward and grasped the rifle lying next to Ania and checked it for ammunition. He nodded then slowly turned back to the window and raised up enough to look out. Pavel followed suit and stood up slowly to look out. He didn't see anything moving in the murkiness.

He heard a noise behind him just as he remembered that the front door was still open. He turned, knowing that it was already too late. The alien was standing in the doorway, having taken a step inside. It was large—perhaps two meters tall and thickly built. Its head was covered in a mask and helmet, making it impossible to see its face. It was pointing its weapon at Alek, who had also turned. It fired and Alek wheeled around from the impact, though he didn't fall.

Pavel brought up his own gun and fired at the intruder. He hit it in the abdomen, and the thing bent over slightly from the impact. He fired again and heard the gun click. He was out of bullets. He looked down at the gun then over to Alek, who had slowly turned back to look at the creature. He was bleeding profusely from a wound in his side.

"Alek, kill it. Kill it!" Pavel yelled. Alek raised the rifle and fired wildly, missing the creature. Then the rifle fell on an empty chamber as well. Alek and Pavel looked at each other for a moment, then Alek's face screwed up into a snarl. "Run, Pavel!" he screamed as he threw himself at the alien, knocking him to the floor of the cabin.

As the two fought on the floor, Pavel quickly grabbed what gear he could and then fled the cabin. He had two options: to follow Maks and go back to the shelter, or to go on ahead to see if he could find where the aliens were coming from. He decided to go on. If he could, he would at least take notes that could be found by others to know the dangers of what they were facing.

He broke into a light jog, about all he could do at his age, and continued this until he felt that ache in his lungs that told him he had to stop and rest. His legs felt heavy, and his chest was heaving and burning from the cold air. He stopped and rested at the base of a tree, looking back at the way he'd come. He didn't know if Alek would be successful in defeating the creature, but one of them could be following him.

When he felt he could stand again and still breathe, he began to walk. It was still pre-dawn, but it was light enough for him to see clearly. He hadn't seen any movement since leaving the cabin, but he kept alert for it, or the sound of anything moving. But all was still as he crested a large hill. He hoped that it would afford him a better view of the surrounding territory.

What met his eyes was unexpected, in a way, but also confirmation of his worst fears. In the valley below him was laid out a large camp. No, he thought, not just a camp, a base. A large number of the aliens were going about their business, like ants on the march. There were other ships like the ones they had seen and a few that were larger. There were large holes in the ground where they were entering and exiting, and Pavel understood instantly that most of the base was underground.

His legs buckled as he watched them, and he knelt down on the top of the hill, feeling immense despair and hopelessness. An alarm started, and he knew he'd been spotted. But he was tired, and running was not an option. He sat down and waited for them and thought of his family and his new friends that he'd lost. His last thought before they arrived was of Maks. He hoped the young man had made it back to the shelter.

The future rested on him now.

The End

The Office

Doug Burns sighed and closed his laptop. His work for the day wasn't finished, but he needed a break. He looked around his small cubicle, neat for the most part, except for the stack of redlined resumes his supervisor, Clint, had dropped off on his way out to lunch. An hour and a half later, Clint hadn't returned, and Doug hadn't looked at the required changes.

The proposal was due the next day at noon, and they were still changing personnel. It was going to be a late night because 'A Deadline is a Deadline!" as the stickers read that were posted around the office. It was also proudly proclaimed in his email signature and on the front page of the company's intranet.

Doug had worked at the engineering firm on the twentieth floor for a few months now and was already tired of Clint's forced enthusiasm and the company's jolly facade. He was even more tired of Clint's penchant for printing out sections of the proposal to redline with red ink, when he could have just performed it electronically and emailed it.

He stood and grabbed his Officially Branded company mug and headed for the breakroom, only to find that someone had finished the coffee and hadn't put a new bag in the machine to brew, even though there was a sign right there that read, 'It's everybody's kitchen!" and another that read "Fill 'er up when its Empty!"

He was closing the coffeemaker after inserting a new bag of coffee grounds when Tanya and Greg, two of the junior civil engineers, walked in.

"Hey Doogie, how's the proposal coming along?" Greg asked. He had stupid nicknames for everyone it seemed. Except Mr. Rayburn, the company principal and part owner. Doug saw Tanya roll her eyes. Seems she didn't appreciate the nicknames, either.

"Fine," Doug answered. "Due tomorrow."

"We probably won't win it," Greg said, turning to Tanya to explain. "But it's good to keep in touch with the client. Out of sight, out of mind, right Doogie?" He opened the refrigerator as Tanya filled a glass with water from the water cooler.

Doug cringed inwardly, knowing that Greg was probably right, and that he would still be working on the proposal until late in order to hit the deadline. Greg closed the door, a soda in his hand that Doug would bet money that he didn't buy.

"See you later, Doogie," he said, smirking, as he walked out of the breakroom.

"Sorry," Tanya said. "Wish I could help, but we have a meeting with the city and we're going to be swamped with revisions on our final report for the rest of the week."

"It's okay," Doug replied, noticing for the first time how close she was standing to him. "Good luck. I've heard the city people are really nit-picky."

"You too," she answered smiling and turning away. He watched her disappear around the corner, wondering if he was imagining things. He wasn't exactly boyfriend material, he knew. Mid-thirties, a bit overweight from long days sitting in front of a computer and not eating properly, already starting to thin on top. Not to mention a middling job, crappy apartment outside the city, and a barely running 2004 Honda Accord that he had to pay a quarter of his paycheck to park in the building's parking garage.

Now depressed, he pulled the coffee carafe and was pouring some nasty smelling liquid that passed for coffee into his mug when suddenly he found himself on the floor, his left hand burning from spilled liquid. The floor was still shaking, and he covered his head as items rolled off the counter and fell out of the cheap wooden cabinets.

When he felt it was safe, he uncurled and sat up, wiping his sore hand on his shirt and noticing how red it looked from the burn. It was tender, but he didn't think it was burned too badly. He noticed that no alarms were sounding. What in the hell had just happened?

He stood just as Katrina ran past the breakroom, her red emergency cap on. She was the "floor warden," tasked with coordinating with the company safety officer and taking a headcount in case of an evacuation of the building due to things like fire or earthquake, which is what Doug realized had just occurred. She also took her job way too seriously, in Doug's opinion. She enjoyed telling people what to do a little too much.

Doug stood and walked gingerly towards the doorway. His hip and shoulder hurt from when he had fallen. He didn't smell smoke, which was a good thing. He looked around the office area and saw several people lying on the floor still, but they were all beginning to recover. No one seemed to be hurt too badly.

He waited a moment, trying to clear his head and think clearly. More than likely, they would want to evacuate the building. He remembered that they weren't supposed to take the elevators in case the power was interrupted. It was going to be a haul to walk down all those flights of stairs.

"What happened, do you know?" a voice close to him asked. He looked to see Desiree, an estimator walking towards him. She had a small cut on her forehead that was bleeding down the side of her face.

"Earthquake?" Doug said, though it sounded more like a question. "Not sure. We probably should get out of the building. Are you okay to walk?"

"Yeah, I think so," she replied. She touched the side of her face with her hand and then looked at the blood on her fingers for a moment, wide eyed.

"It's a small looking cut," he said, trying to sound reassuring. "Probably won't even leave a scar."

She nodded, though she still looked unsure.

Doug looked around, trying to see if Katrina was in sight. She was supposed to be helping people and doing the reassuring, not him. Others were beginning to congregate near where he and Desiree stood. The volume of their chatter was growing. Everyone had the same question: what had happened?

"I think a plane hit the building," someone said, and the chatter immediately stopped. Doug had visions of 9/11, and he was sure that most of the others did as well.

"Are you sure?" Someone else asked. By this time, most of the people were heading over to look out of the windows to see if they could see anything.

"Come on, people, we need to leave!" a voice rang above the sound of the others. They all turned to look to see Katrina heading back towards them. She had a megaphone in one hand and a walkie talkie in the other. "Move quickly but carefully to the southeast stairwell. Just like the drills."

People reluctantly began filing towards the stairwell

with Doug and Desiree in the lead. Katrina stayed where she was, making sure there were no stragglers. He turned to look at Desiree.

"You going to be able to manage going down all of the stairs? Are you light-headed or anything?" He grasped the door handle and turned it.

"I think I'm okay," she said, smiling at him. "I just need to..."

She never finished her sentence as he pulled open the door and a chihuahua-sized animal jumped at her from the other side, clasping a large, toothy mouth on her left arm. She began screaming a high, earsplitting scream and waving her arm around. People behind them began to scream in terror also.

Doug closed the door and tried to get a better look at the animal, which was difficult since Desiree hadn't stopped waving her arm around. He could see blood running down the arm and spraying the floor as well. Sid, an older mechanical engineer, managed to stop Desiree and grab the animal, which was a sickly brown and yellow color. Doug still couldn't make out its outline or see if it was fur or skin covering it.

Sid had both hands around it now and was trying to pull it off Desiree's arm, without much luck. Every time he pulled, she screamed shrilly. Her face was a mess of makeup, tears, snot, and blood. Finally, the animal came free, leaving a large area of her arm devoid of skin. She sat down abruptly and hugged the injured arm to her chest.

Sid fought with the animal, trying to get it under control. Suddenly it was loose again, and it jumped from his hands to his face, clamping its mouth first on his cheek, then moving down to his neck. "Son of a bitch!" he yelled as he pulled furiously on the creature. Doug rushed over to him and grabbed the creature, which slipped out of his hands. It was some type of skin covering it, and it was slimy. Not only with Desiree and Sid's blood, either. It almost felt like a fish, but it was warm. He looked around for something he could use to either stab the creature or pry it from Sid's neck. He saw a cutting board with a hobby knife on it. The triangular-bladed tool was used to cut down full-bleed color covers for their reports.

He ran to the cutting board and grabbed the hobby knife, then turned to see Sid make one final pull and the creature come away from his neck. Blood began spurting immediately from the severed artery, which began another round of screaming as Sid dropped to his knees, his eyes wide.

The creature, now on the floor, began to run for the cover of one of the cubicles. Doug looked back at Sid, who was now lying on his back as Katrina and others tried to stop his bleeding. He turned back and began to slowly walk towards the cubicles where he'd last seen the animal. Meanwhile the internal dialog in his head was telling him that he'd never even heard of a creature like this before. He grasped the hobby knife tighter as he bent to look under the chair in the newest cubicle. Nothing.

"Where is it?" Doug looked up, seeing that it was Tanya addressing him. He stood up swiftly, feeling lightheaded as he did so.

"Uh, I don't know. It could be anywhere now," he answered, feeling foolish while he brandished the small hobby knife.

She nodded. "We should help Katrina evacuate everyone. I think Sid is dead."

Doug winced. He had liked the old engineer. "We can't carry him down the stairs. We'll have to tell the first responders he's still up here."

"Yes," she said, folding her arms before her. It was the first time he'd seen her appearing anything close to vulnerable.

"Do you know what happened? Someone said we may have been hit by a plane."

"No," she answered. Her eyes strayed to his hand, which was now red and beginning to grow blisters from the hot coffee spill.

"Oh, God, you're hurt," she said. "Why didn't you say something?"

He looked at his hand and realized that it did hurt, now that he thought about it. "Adrenaline, I guess," he mumbled as she grasped his arm to look at the hand closer.

"Let's get the first aid kit," she said, pulling him along after her and heading towards the break room. He swiveled his head around, making sure the creature wasn't hanging from the ceiling or in a corner ready to jump at them. It had disappeared.

"Sit," she told him when they entered the room. He did as he was told and sat at the closest round wooden table, while checking below it just to make sure there was nothing there that would bite him. He watched her pull the white first aid kit off the wall and begin to rummage through its contents.

She came over to the table with a large roll of gauze and a few small packets of ointment. "Hold out your arm," she told him.

Again, he did as he was told. He noticed that there were about a dozen blisters now on the back of his hand. Second degree burn, he knew. She looked at his hand and then again at one of the packets. "Says here not to use on a burn with open blisters. Might be better to just wrap it in gauze until we get downstairs."

"Okay," he mumbled. The hand was really beginning to hurt now.

She gently wrapped a roll of white gauze around his hand, which did nothing to alleviate the pain. "Do you want an aspirin or something?"

"It might help," he said, trying to sound brave. The truth was the pain in his hand was now excruciating. She tore open a single dose package and dumped the contents into his hand. He put them in his mouth and immediately swallowed, though they still left a chalky taste in his mouth. He stood slowly and went to a nearby cupboard to get a glass for water. While he filled the glass in the sink and drank it, he turned to see that she had walked over and was now standing next to him. He smiled at her. "Better," he said.

She smiled uncertainly back at him. Her arms were crossed before her, and he noticed she looked around uncomfortably. "We should get back to the others."

"Wait a moment," he said. He began opening drawers near the sink, looking for a better weapon than the hobby knife. He was rewarded by opening a drawer and seeing several serving implements and a few paring knives and one large chef's knife. He grabbed the large knife by the handle and looked at the blade, which was large but didn't appear to be very sharp. He looked around to see if he could find a sharpener but had no luck. It would have to do.

He turned to see her standing patiently waiting for him. "Sorry," he said, sheepishly. She nodded, though she still looked worried. He felt like hugging her to let her know she was safe but checked his impulse. HR would have a field day with him for that type of unwanted touching, even under these unusual circumstances.

"Do you want to hold this?" he asked her, holding out the hobby knife to her. She looked at it a moment then shook her head. He nodded and put it down on the table.

"What should we do with the body?" she asked. He

looked at her a moment before they both started to laugh. "I'm sorry, that sounded horrible."

He was grateful for the release of tension. "I know what you meant. We'll have to leave him here for now until the police or firemen come up here. He's too heavy to try and carry down the stairs."

She nodded. "I just feel bad leaving him here."

"I know, but we have to be safe, too. You ready?"

She nodded, and he walked towards the stairwell entrance, the knife held out in front of him. "Keep aware of your surroundings," he said. "There may be more of those things."

"What are they, do you think?"

"I don't know. Nothing I've ever seen. But then, I grew up in the city."

"Me, too. Visited the zoo a few times growing up."

He smiled back at her. "The Metro?"

She nodded. "Until it closed down."

"Yeah, that was a bummer."

"Where did you grow up?"

"On Tiburon Street. The apartment complex just south of 99th Street."

"You're kidding," she said. "I grew up north of 99th on Figuero."

"That's funny," he said. "But you were in a different school district." May as well have been in a different world, he thought. North of 99th was a much posher neighborhood than where he'd lived.

By this time, they had walked steadily towards the door to the stairwell without seeing any more of the vicious creature that had killed poor Sid. Suddenly, the door crashed open, and Katrina, Greg, and a few others came rushing through the doorway. Katrina's face was covered in blood, and Greg was holding one of his hands, which was bleeding profusely.

"Close the door!" Greg screamed. The last person came through the door, and Doug noticed that there were fewer people than had headed down.

"Katrina, what happened?" Tanya asked.

Katrina sat down on the floor and leaned against the wall, not answering.

"Those fucking things are everywhere down there," Greg said. "One of those bastards bit my fucking finger off!" He held out his hand before them to show the bloody stump on his left hand where his pointer finger used to reside.

"Oh, God," Tanya said.

"I'll get the first aid kit," Doug said, turning to go. None of the others seemed in a hurry to move, and he had a knife. Hearing no calls of dissent behind him, he hurried back towards the break room. In the back of his mind, he remembered the ribbing he'd received from Greg earlier that morning and tried to suppress the urge to slow down so that the other man would suffer a few more minutes.

He shook his head ruefully. Now wasn't the time to be petty, though he also felt a slight sense of glee that Greg had lost a finger. It wasn't a lethal wound. He was about to walk into the break room when he heard a scuffling sound inside it and froze. He listened for a minute but didn't hear it again. He tightened his grip on the knife and walked slowly through the doorway.

His eyes went to the table, and he noticed that the craft knife was no longer there. Oh great, he thought. Did they have the ability to hold a knife, too? He bent down a little and was relieved when he saw the knife on the floor under the table. His relief was short lived when it occurred to him that something had knocked it off the table. He looked around as he slowly approached the white OSHA first aid kid.

He turned quickly when he heard the scuffling sound coming from somewhere under a table. He held the knife out as he looked around, feeling the counter pressing into his wallet, which was in the back right pocket of his dress pants. He couldn't see any movement. He tried to take a deep breath and steady himself, then he squatted down so he could see the floor under the tables.

The creature moved faster than he thought was possible as he ran at him from under the table to his left. He only had time to hold the knife out, pointing at it. He thought that maybe the creature's momentum would be enough to impale itself on the tip of the kitchen knife, but his heart sank as it easily dodged the blade and jumped up onto his arm. It was heading for his face when he dropped the knife and grabbed it with his right hand.

The creature felt a little slimy in his hand, and he had a difficult time holding onto it. It explained why poor Sid had been unable to keep it from his neck. It squirmed around in his hand, and he felt a moment of intense pain as it bit into the skin between his thumb and forefinger. He almost let it go, but then thought of Sid's fate and held on, knowing it could just as easily do the same to him.

He held it out at arm's length and then picked up the knife with his left hand and brought it around and stabbed it squarely in the middle of its body, hoping that he could hit any type of organ. The knife only penetrated about an inch into it, and the creature let out a blood-curdling scream. He tightened his grip on the knife because it felt like the gauze bandage on his hand was slipping, then brought the knife back and stabbed it again, this time to the right side of the initial wound. He noticed that its blood was thick and a dark blue color.

The creature continued screaming and he brought the

knife up again and stabbed it straight through its mouth into the back of its head. The creature went limp in his grip and he threw it to the floor. He'd seen enough monster movies, so he stomped on it with his right foot again and again until its head had turned into a pulp of blue blood, bone, and a dull grey material that he assumed was its brain.

He looked down at his injured right hand and saw that it was bleeding from several small wounds where its teeth had penetrated his skin. He turned and grabbed the white first aid kit and then ran for the door of the break room, hoping that there weren't any more of the creatures in there chasing him. Soon, he reached the others again and handed the kit to Tanya, who looked at him with worried eyes.

"I'm fine, for now," he said. "Take care of Greg." She nodded, still looking unsure. He looked at the first aid kit and saw that it had both his blood and the creature's blood on it before he sat down heavily on the floor with his back to the wall. He looked around to make sure he couldn't see any more of the creatures, then closed his eyes. The pain in his right hand had lessened since he'd come back into the room with the others.

He looked down at his hand and saw that the wounds were rapidly scabbing over, and that the scabs were dark blue, just like the creature's blood. He closed his eyes and shook his head to clear it and then looked again. Just as he'd already seen, the wounds were all closed now and a dark blue in color.

Just then, he saw Tanya walking back over to him. "How's Greg's hand?"

"Wrapped up," she said. "We managed to stop the bleeding, at least. How is your hand?"

He held out his right hand to her, and she looked at it, confused.

"I know, weird," he said, placing the hand back in his lap. "I killed one of those things in the break room."

"It looks like it bit you."

"It did. Hard." He turned his hand around, looking at it. "I stabbed it a few times with the knife. It was bleeding pretty good, and some of the blood got onto my wounds."

"And did this?"

"I guess," he answered. "It's the only thing I can think of for why it's closed up the wounds."

She crouched down and gently took his hand to look at it closer. The wounds were closed, and he still had blue blood on the hand. "Give me your other hand for a moment."

He complied and held out his left hand. She carefully unwrapped the hand to reveal the ugly red burn on the back of it. It didn't look any better than it had when first wrapped. She took two fingers and rubbed them on his right hand, and then lightly rubbed the blue liquid on the worst of the burn.

"You don't think..." he began to say.

"Thought it was worth a try," she said, shrugging. She let go of the hand and he pulled it back protectively to his chest, holding the elbow with his right hand, which didn't hurt at all now.

"I should go talk to Katrina and see if they've come up with some type of plan," she said, standing up. "I'll come back to check on you soon."

He nodded. He wasn't exactly the type that was going to take over a situation. It wasn't his personality. He'd been an introvert his entire life and that wasn't going to stop now just because they were in a crisis. He'd let someone else take that on. He looked around again to make sure he didn't see any of the creatures sneaking up on them, then when satisfied, leaned his head back against the wall and closed his eyes.

He just wanted to go home; he decided. Feed his

cat, Calliope, and then sit on the couch and binge watch something while not thinking about work or proposals or any of this bullshit. He opened his eyes and looked down at his left hand. He saw that the blisters had turned a lighter shade of blue and were now almost gone. The redness surrounding them was much less angry now, as well. He flexed his fingers on that hand and felt how tight his skin still was from the burn.

He moved his other hand over and rubbed more of the alien blood on the burn wound, covering the entire thing now, then placed both hands in his lap and closed his eyes again.

"Doug? Doug?"

He slowly opened his eyes and realized that he'd fallen asleep. "What?" he asked, looking down at his watch to see that the face was broken and that it had stopped telling time. Must have happened in the scuffle with the creature, he thought.

"Doug, we're going to try and go back down the stairwell again," Katrina said.

That brought him fully awake. "What, are you sure?"

"Those bastards caught us off guard the first time," Greg said. "We're better prepared now, and Tanya said you were able to kill one, unbelievable as that is."

"Yes, I killed one," he said, looking down at the knife lying next to his leg. It was covered in blue blood as well. That reminded him, and he looked at his left hand. The blisters were gone, though there were still blue circles where they used to be raised up. The redness was mostly gone. He stretched his hand and felt little of the tightness he'd felt before from the burn. "Amazing," he said, quietly.

"Well, get up, Rambo," Greg said. "It's not like I can fight them very well with this." He held out his bandaged hand to show Doug and everyone else that he couldn't hold a knife in that hand. He looked disappointed that it didn't elicit the large show of sympathy and commiseration from the group that he'd hoped for.

Doug thought of offering to rub some of the alien blood on Greg's mangled stump but then thought better of it. He probably wouldn't accept it, especially from Doug. He slowly stood up, feeling a kink in his neck from the position he'd fell asleep in, then stretched to get his blood pumping again. He felt cold in the air conditioning of the office. He bent down and picked up the knife off the floor, holding it in his newly healed right hand.

He looked up and saw that Tanya was looking at him. He held out his hand to show her and nodded when he saw that she understood. He thought she had the same expression on her face as he had on his own—wonder, with a bit of 'what the hell' thrown in for good measure.

"Uh, the creatures are very fast, and their bodies are also slippery," Doug said, hoping that everyone could hear him. He wasn't used to speaking to large groups of people. They all turned to look at him, and he felt his face growing red from the attention, but he needed to warn them. "If you're lucky enough to catch one with your hand, you have to hold onto it tightly, or it can twist out of your grip like it did to Sid."

"Does everyone have a weapon of some sort?" Tanya asked. They looked around at one another and Katrina held up a small black box that Doug realized was a taser.

She shrugged. "Personal protection," she said.

"Anyone else?" Tanya asked. No one else said anything. "Knowing they're there and being prepared for them are two different things, Greg," she said.

"We'll have to look through drawers in the cubicles to

see what we can find," Doug suggested.

"We can't split up!" a young woman said, her eyes wide.

"No, we're not splitting up," Tanya said. "We go together from now on." The woman looked a little reassured but still had an expression as if they'd all voted to go their separate ways.

"Those with weapons can stand guard while those without can look through drawers," Katrina said. She looked to Tanya, who nodded. Doug wasn't surprised that Tanya had become the leader of their little band of survivors.

"Okay, we go now," Tanya said. "As a group. People with weapons on the outside."

Doug nodded and then stood back as Greg planted himself squarely in the middle of the group. He kept himself from rolling his eyes, though it was difficult.

The small group slowly made their way to where cubicles were set up, each about four feet tall so that people could see each other while they worked. It was thought that this setup would build teamwork amongst employees, but it usually ended with someone mad that someone else was playing their music too loud or holding a virtual meeting and speaking too loudly into their headset.

Most of the desks had little in the way of effective weapons. Some had a surprising amount of junk food stashed away in them, and Doug saw Greg open a bag of potato chips from the desk he had just rifled. "Have to keep up my strength," he said when he saw Tanya looking at him.

"Oh," said the young lady with the worried expression. Doug thought her name was Beth, but he'd never interacted with her. She held up a Swiss Army knife that she'd found. Technically, weapons of that sort, even with short blades, were not allowed in the building.

"I'm checking this office," Tanya said, pointing to an

office in the corner of the room that belonged to the vice president of the structural engineering group. She looked at Doug and he nodded, beginning to follow her.

"Okay, love birds," Greg said, smiling. Tanya rolled her eyes at him, then opened the office door. Doug put his hand on her arm to stop her from stepping through the door.

"Let me check first," he said, holding up his kitchen knife. She nodded. He didn't think one of the creatures could be in there since the door was closed, but he didn't want to take the chance. He looked around and under the desk and didn't see anything. He nodded to her, and she stepped into the office, which was about ten feet square. She closed the door behind her.

"Let me see your hand," she said as she turned to look at him. He placed the knife on the desk and then held out his left hand for her inspection. "Unbelievable," she said after looking at it. She grabbed his right hand then and looked at the small blue teeth marks, which now were the only indication that he'd been bit.

"I know," he said. "The pain in gone in both hands." He made fists with both hands to show her and then wiggled his fingers. "Almost good as new."

"Why didn't you offer to use it on Greg's hand?" she asked, looking up into his eyes.

He looked away for a moment, then back at her. "I didn't think he would believe it worked. And he probably wouldn't take it from me."

"True," she said. "But now that we know it does work, we should offer."

"Be my guest," he said, trying not to smirk too much. She nodded, then bent and began to look through the drawers of the desk. Mostly paperwork and office supplies met her inspection. She looked in the last drawer, which held files tucked neatly into file folders. She closed it and stood up, placing both hands on her hips.

"Nothing," she said.

"We should catch up with the others," he said, reaching for the door handle.

"Wait," she said. She walked toward him, and he was surprised when she put her arms around him and hugged him before pulling back. "Thank you for being here. I think your calm approach to this has really helped the group deal with this."

"Really?" he asked. "I guess I'm just a quiet person by nature. It helps with proposals," he said, smiling. He was happy when she returned the smile. Had she really just hugged him? You idiot, he thought, realizing that he'd been so surprised that he'd failed to return it.

"Well?" she said, and he realized she was telling him to open the door.

"Oh, right," he said, feeling himself turn red again. He opened the door, standing in front of her to make sure there were no vicious surprises standing just outside of the door.

He saw that the others were at the other end of the room, and that some were in another office in the corner, which belonged to the CEO, when he was in town, which wasn't often. He looked back at Tanya and smiled again, and she began to walk beside him towards the others. "Maybe the police and animal control are below cleaning up any other creatures that are in the building," he said, trying to sound cheery.

"I hope so," she said, sounding unconvinced. "I don't care if they are, as long as we get out of this building safely."

Suddenly there was a high-pitched scream from the others. Doug looked and saw that Beth was attempting to pry one of the creatures away from the side of her head. It seemed to be clamped onto her ear. Doug ran towards her, not thinking about leaving Tanya, but he saw that she was running along with him.

By the time that they arrived with the others, he saw that Katrina had stepped in as well and had the creature around the body with both hands and was pulling. Doug was about to step in and try to stab the creature or possibly slit its throat, when there was a sound like ripping wet cardboard, and Beth's head was spurting blood from a hole where her ear used to be, and Katrina had the creature in hers and she fell back.

Doug caught her in time to stop her from falling completely backwards, then began to stab the kitchen knife at the creature. He stabbed it a few times in the head, and it went limp in her grasp. "Throw it down," he yelled at her. She did as he said, and he stomped on it just to be sure.

Beth was still screaming, holding her head while blood leaked between her fingers and down her arm. Without thinking, Doug reached down and picked up the remains of the creature with his right hand, moved Beth's hands out of the way with his left, then unceremoniously shoved the creature against the hole in her head.

"What the hell are you doing?" Greg yelled.

"Shut up," Tanya said.

"What?" Greg asked, looking confused now.

Doug ignored them and kept a steady pressure against Beth's ear, hoping that it would work. He looked into Beth's scared eyes. "Is it feeling any better?"

"Y-yes," she said. He couldn't tell if she was going into shock or not, but her pupils looked relatively normal, and she had stopped crying. "What is happening?" she whispered.

"I know it's confusing," he said. "I need you to calm down and have a seat."

She nodded and began to sit on the floor. He helped her down, still pressing the creature against the wound until he was finally kneeling next to her. "I'm going to check it now, okay?"

She nodded weakly. He gently pulled the creature from the side of her head and set it on the floor. The wound had the same blue effects that his hands had shown, which he took as a good sign. The bleeding had stopped, at least, which let him see the full extent of damage. She had lost most of the outer cartilage, with only a small strip at the bottom still there. The lobe laid against the side of her head like a piece of chicken fat. The thought made him feel nauseous, and he stopped looking at the wound.

"What the fuck?" Greg said.

"What's wrong?" Beth said shrilly.

"The bleeding has stopped," Doug told her reassuringly. "But you've lost most of the ear."

"No, no," she said, beginning to cry again.

"Stopped?" Greg said. "It looks healed."

Doug stood and looked at the other man for a moment, but didn't say what was on his mind, which would have probably started a fight. He looked to Tanya. "It worked."

She nodded. "We discovered that the blood of the creatures has some type of healing factor in it," she said to everyone. "We were able to mostly heal Doug's hands."

Doug obediently held up his hands to show that they looked almost normal.

"Wait," Greg said. "You knew this, and you didn't try to heal my finger?"

"Honestly, I didn't think you would let me do it," Doug said. "Am I wrong?"

Greg said nothing for a moment. "No," he finally admitted. "But Tanya..."

"Is tired of your shit, Greg," she finished for him. "I doubted you would let anyone help you. You were enjoying being a martyr."

"That's not fair, Tanya," he said.

"But it's true," she said.

"Fuck," he said. "Can we try now?"

Tanya looked at Doug. He nodded and picked up the creature again. Most of the blood on the outer part of its body was coagulating and dry now. He looked to see Tanya unwrapping Greg's hand. The wound was still raw and red. Some of the skin had been ripped away down the back of the hand as well, when the finger was severed.

He must have pulled it away and the skin came with it, Doug thought. He walked to where they stood and pressed the creature against the wound. After a moment, he pulled it away and all three of them leaned in to see. The wound looked the same.

"What the hell?" Greg said. "Why isn't it working?"

Doug and Tanya looked at each other. "Maybe the blood needs to be liquid still?" Doug asked.

She nodded. "Or it needs to be fresh. Freshly squeezed, as it were." He smiled at her joke.

"Well, squeeze that fucker and see if it works," Greg said.

Doug looked at the creature, which was now only a mass of hair and dried blood.

"Here, let me do it," Greg said. He grabbed the creature and squeezed it over his hand, but nothing came out. "Come on you little son of a bitch," he said. Still nothing. "Damn it!" he yelled and threw the body across the room.

"We'll have to find a new one," Tanya said.

"Oh, that's great," Greg said. Tanya began to rewrap the hand. "Forget it," he said, pulling away, just leave it alone."

She looked at Doug, who shrugged and tried not to roll

his eyes. She smiled. He really liked her smile. Stupid incel, he thought about himself, knowing he fit the description. Now is not the time for this, as much as he would like to stay and talk with her in hushed tones, they needed to get out of the building. What happened after that? He certainly didn't know.

"Uh, we should get everyone back together and see what they've found," he said.

"Yes, good idea," she said, becoming business-like once more.

He watched her walk away and begin to wave people over.

"Dude, you don't have a chance," Greg said. Doug was startled. He had forgotten that the other man was still standing next to him.

He looked at Greg and shrugged. "We have to get out of the building first." He walked away, not caring if Greg said anything else. He was tired of the man's shit as well.

When they tallied up the weapons, Doug was disappointed to see that they had not been able to find much. An older man named Jeff had found a metal letter opener that looked like it could be used to stab one of the creatures. Katrina had discovered a pocketknife in an executive's drawer.

"So, we now have two small knives, a letter opener, and a chef's knife," Tanya said, looking around at the faces gathered around her.

"Were there any other knives in the break room?" Greg asked. "Maybe we should go back."

"No," Doug said. "This was the only one."

"It's true," Tanya said. "I was there when he searched all of the drawers and cabinets.

"We have four weapons to protect eight people," Katrina

said.

"Could be worse," Tanya said. "We'll have to keep the unarmed and injured at the center of the group when we go down the stairs. Everyone needs to stay alert."

They all nodded in agreement at Tanya's words and then they slowly moved towards the door that led to the stairwell on that side of the building.

"Doug can go first, since he has the biggest knife," Greg said.

Doug looked at him. "That's fine. Everyone form up behind me. Katrina, can you bring up the rear with your taser?"

She nodded. "If we need to go single file, remember to keep it every other person with a weapon."

Doug nodded. He turned to open the door.

"Wait," Beth said. "I...I don't think I can use this." She held out the Swiss Army knife.

"I'll take it," Greg said, reaching for it.

Tanya stepped in his way. "You can't hold it in your right hand," she said.

"So."

"So, its better if someone has it who can wield it with their dominant hand," she said. She reached out and took the knife from Beth. "You have a problem with that?" she said to Greg. He just looked down at the floor.

"Are we all ready?" Doug asked. He saw nods and then turned back towards the door and opened it. They all smelled a burned odor, but there weren't any creatures waiting for them.

He heard Tanya say "good luck" quietly but didn't turn, in case she wasn't speaking to him. The light bulb must have broken, or the power lost in the stairwell, because Doug saw that it was darker as they descended. He slowly walked down the stairs, looking for signs of movement in the gloom. The group behind him were all quiet, and the only sounds he heard were their footfalls.

Doug kept descending the stairwell as it slowly got darker. They had gone down at least two floors when they came to a body on the floor of the landing. "This is where we were attacked before," he heard Greg say loudly before being shushed by Katrina. He turned back and could see that Tanya was behind him in the darkness. She nodded to him, and he nodded back, then turned and began to walk, slower this time.

There were no signs of the creatures for the next few levels, though it was almost completely dark now. For whatever reason, the lights that were supposed to be on in the stairwell landings were out. Doug wasn't sure if that boded well for the rest of their descent. He was about to turn and ask if Tanya or someone else had their cell phone with them so that they could turn on a light, when suddenly there wasn't anything under the foot he had just put down on the next step.

He had put too much weight on the leg and was falling forward before he could call out a warning. He was in freefall in the darkness and heard a scream nearby. Tanya had fallen as well. Then there was darkness.

◊

"Doug, wake up," he heard. "Wake up." It was whispering, and it was close to his head. He opened his eyes and couldn't see anything. His head was aching as was his body, and he realized that he was lying on his stomach. Then he felt hands on his shoulders, gently shaking him. He turned his head but still couldn't see anything around him.

"I'm awake," he said dully. "Is it dark here?"

"Yes. Pitch black," Tanya said.

"Good, I thought I was blind for a moment," he said. He slowly sat up and rested on hands and butt. "Are you okay?"

"Yes."

He could feel wetness on his face but wasn't sure if it was blood or tears—or both. But he was awake, which was a good sign. "That last step was a doozy."

"Doug, I don't know where we are. What happened to the steps?"

"I don't know. Maybe when the plane crashed into the building, it took out the stairwell on this side."

"That makes sense." He felt her hand on his chest and reached his hand up to hold it reassuringly. "Are you sure you're alright? I was trying to wake you up for a few minutes."

"Might have a concussion," he said. "But I think everything is still working." He suddenly remembered his knife. He got up on his knees and felt around on the floor for it but couldn't find it.

"What's wrong?"

"I think I lost the knife," he told her. "Do you happen to have a cell phone or flashlight?"

"No, sorry," she said. "Oh, wait," she added. He heard her moving in the darkness and waited patiently. Suddenly a small light illuminated a small patch of where they were. She had a little light on her key chain—one of those cheap little tchotchkes that had a little push button on one side and the company logo on the other. At least it was something. His eyes adjusted and he looked at the floor, which looked strange.

"Doug..."

"I see it," he said. He wasn't sure what he was seeing. The floor was black, but it looked almost like it was made of small beads that reflected a prism when she shown the light on it. "What is this?"

"I don't know," she replied.

He stood and helped her to her feet, then he was leaning on her as his vision when grey for a moment. "Uh," he muttered. "That wasn't good."

"Do you need to sit back down?"

"No, no, I'm good," he said. "Just a little lightheaded for a second. Do you see the knife?"

She swung the light back and forth a little. He didn't see it. "No," she said.

"Well, we need to get out of here, either way. Have you heard anything above from the others?"

"No, nothing."

"Strange, I would have expected Greg to be screaming his lungs out."

"I think they're afraid of attracting any of those creatures."

"Good point. I'm surprised we haven't run into any more of them."

"Don't jinx it."

He smiled. Then realized that she couldn't see it. "Alright, lets see if we can find a way out of here."

"How about I'll hold the light, and you hold me," she said. She reached out her arm and lifted his right arm up and then stepped closer so that he could put the arm around her shoulder.

"That was smooth," he said.

"Better than the ol' yawn trick," she said. He could see that she was smiling in the dim light.

He cupped his hand around her shoulder, and they began walking slowly while she shown the tiny light back and forth before them. At first there was no change in what they saw, then they saw some concrete rubble that must have come from the building. Doug was glad they had avoided landing on any of that. Their injuries may have been much worse. He also began to smell a burning odor that began faint, then became heavier.

"Do you smell that?" he asked her.

"Yes, smells like burning tires."

"You're right," he said. It did remind him of burning rubber. They came to a place where the floor, or whatever it was, began to slope. They carefully made their way forward, and then they saw it. There was a large hole up ahead, with the black substance pulled back as though something had burst through it from the other side.

"What the hell is that?" she asked.

"I don't know." He pulled his arm from around her shoulder just in case he needed to fight. He wished he'd kept the small craft knife in his pocket—but then again, he could have woken up a gelding if he had. But he felt vulnerable without something. He looked down and picked up a rough piece of concrete and hefted it in his hand. It wasn't much, but beggars and choosers and all that.

They slowly walked to the edge of the hole and looked in. There seemed to be a hallway with doors at intermittent spacing along it. "What the hell?" Doug said.

"Oh my God," Tanya said. "Is this some type of...ship?"

"It's sure as hell not an airplane," Doug said. He was attempting to sound calm and nonchalant, but his mind was racing, and he felt a bit lightheaded—this time not from the fall.

"So, now what do we do?" Tanya asked. "Do we go on, or do we go in?"

"Go in?" he asked. "In the ship?"

"Maybe there's a way of getting out of it on a lower floor," she said. "I don't think we can get past it another way."

He thought about it for a moment. She had a point. He

didn't see any fires, though the interior had a faint light of its own. "Fine, but I'll take the lead in case we run into any more of those things." He almost said "aliens," but then thought better of it. There was still no proof that this was some type of flying saucer. He handed her the piece of concrete and then lowered himself slowly down into the hallway. Although there was a faint light, there wasn't much he could see looking either way.

He saw that she was lowering herself down and reached up to help her. She landed directly in front of him, and he saw that his arms were around her. They looked at each other a moment, then he backed up self-consciously. "Uh, which way should we go?"

"Your guess is as good as mine," she said.

He nodded and began walking to his right. He noticed that the floor was slightly slanted to the left. The ship had come to rest at an angle. "Can you shine the light ahead?" The corridor was darker here, as if the lights were out in this section.

She shown her light ahead, and they saw that the hallway was coming to an end in approximately ten feet. There was a door at the end. Doug walked toward it and looked for a handle or buttons or some other way of opening the door. He didn't see anything. He held his hands up to either side of the door, then moved them around the border just in case there was a sensor that would open it. It stayed closed.

"Any ideas?" he asked her.

"Maybe there's something on the door itself?"

He moved his hands over the door, which felt slightly bumpy, almost like it was made of the same substance as the hull. Still nothing that he could find, and the door stayed closed. "I feel like a wizard trying to open a dwarf door," he said quietly. He turned to look if she got the reference, but her face was impassive. "Never mind."

She moved her light to the side of the door again and then to the wall of the hallway near it. The light rested on a lighter patch of material that was in a square shape, which he knew meant that it wasn't a natural discoloration. He pressed at it, and the door split apart in the middle and each side slid to form an opening in the middle. He hadn't even felt a crack between the two sides.

He turned to look at Tanya again, and she shrugged. It was up to him to make the decision. He nodded, then turned and went through the doorway. He found himself on a sort of bridge, which was well lit compared to the corridor. There were a few seats with monitor-like devices in front of them. Some of the seats were occupied. Though he couldn't see any movement. There was a large seat in the middle that was also occupied, and he walked a few steps to look at the inhabitant.

It was definitely an alien. "Damn," he whispered as he looked at the being. It was humanoid in shape, having two arms and two legs. It also had a tail and scales. It was dead, as far as he could see, as it slumped in the chair with eyes half open. It wore a sort of metal cap that had a few buttons and knobs on it. He didn't want to touch it to check for a pulse—especially because he didn't know where to check.

He looked back around at Tanya and noticed that she was looking at another of the crew. She looked up and shook her head. It was dead as well. He noticed that this alien also wore a cap like who he assumed was the captain and looked around to see that they all seemed to have one.

He was surprised to see as he looked closer that the alien she was near was not the same species as the captain. That one had black hair covering its head and upper body under a thin top that resembled a t-shirt. He slowly looked around and saw another reptilian-like alien and a third crew member that looked like cross between an armadillo and a badger.

"Mixed crew," he said.

"What?"

"They're not the same types of aliens."

She cupped her elbows in her hands, looking around. "You're right. Maybe it's a pirate ship."

He smiled, but saw she was being serious. "Maybe," he said. She had a point—they could be pirates or smugglers, or this could be a normal crew where they come from.

"Can we get out of here?"

"Yeah, I don't see another door here that could lead somewhere." They headed for the door before he remembered something and turned to look at the captain again. That was it—a sheath at his belt. "Wait a minute," he said not looking at her. He squatted down and reached out it. Just as his hand made contact with the handle protruding from it, a large hand closed over his.

Tanya screamed and he almost soiled his pants. He looked up and saw that the captain was looking down at him. He had a thick liquid coming out of the corner of his mouth. Doug didn't know if it was blood or venom, considering his appearance. The alien said something softly in a light, hissing dialect. Doug stood and backed away, pulling his hand out of the other's weak grip as he did so.

"I'm sorry," he said. "I don't understand you." He stepped closer again. "I don't understand you," he said again, slower, shaking his head. He felt foolish, knowing that he probably didn't make any sense to the captain.

The alien looked at him a moment and then slowly reached out his hand towards Doug. He stopped and moaned, and more of the liquid came out of his mouth. Doug now suspected that it was blood, and that the captain had some internal injuries and bleeding. The captain's other hand went weakly up to the cap on his head. His outstretched hand moved to point at one of the crew members.

The captain reached out again for Doug, and he realized that the alien wanted him to put on one of the caps. He reluctantly walked to where the dead alien was slumped over and slowly pulled the cap from its head. It didn't have any blood or tissue on it, which he was grateful for, and he turned to look back at the captain. He placed the cap on his head, while Tanya gasped a warning. "It's okay," he said, turning to look at her. He looked back at the captain.

"My name is Doug, and this planet is called Earth."

Suddenly he could hear a voice in his head. He instantly knew that it was the captain's voice. "You," he said haltingly. "You...need to understand the...danger you are in." In addition to the voice, he somehow began to see pictures—even whole scenes in his mind, and he closed his eyes to concentrate on them. He could see the ship's crew members loading large cages in the cargo hold of the ship. Inside he could see the small creatures that had attacked them recently.

"Doug?" Tanya asked, sounding worried.

"It's okay," he replied. "He's communicating with me."

"We know that your ship crashed here," Doug said, turning his attention back to the captain.

"Destroy the ship," the captain said. "Our cargo. The Epulions. They...they are loose. You are in danger."

"Epulions?" Doug said. He looked around at Tanya, who shook her head. She couldn't hear the captain's voice. "Are they..."

"They are deadly, though small," the captain said. "But we sought to carry a load of them for their extreme worth."

"Their healing powers?" Doug asked. He was beginning to understand what had happened. A cargo ship full of those little monsters had crashed on Earth. Other pictures appeared in his head, and they began to flash quicker, as if the captain was trying to impart as much knowledge as he could. Finally, Doug couldn't stand it anymore and pulled the cap from his head. He opened his eyes once again and looked at the captain, who nodded in understanding. He placed the cap back on.

"You must kill...kill them all. Do not...let them breed. I...I am sorry." The captain's eyes closed weakly, then slightly opened again. Doug could see that he had stopped breathing. He once again pulled the cap from his head, this time dropping it to the floor of the bridge. He wouldn't be needing it anymore.

He turned to Tanya. "He's dead."

She nodded, holding her arms tightly to her chest, though it wasn't because of the temperature. He felt the same. If those creatures, Epulions? Were to get loose on Earth and breed, no one and nothing would be safe. God, why did he get out of bed this morning?

"Was he talking to you?" Tanya asked.

"Yes, in my head," Doug said. "It's a cargo ship, alright. They were carrying what they call Epulions; those little bastard creatures. Probably smuggling them. He wasn't just speaking in my head. It felt more like...thinking in my head. I saw flashes of memories as well. They were evading the popular spacing lanes, which is why they were way over here near us. One of the containment units in the hold failed, and a few of the creatures escaped. They killed all the crew."

She nodded. "So how do we stop them? And how do we get out of this ship?"

"There was one last thing he showed me in my head," Doug said.

"What was that?"

"The self-destruct sequence."

"Shit."

"Yeah. He wanted me to destroy the ship, with all of them still aboard."

"But the building..." she started to say.

"I have to fly the ship out into space," he said, interrupting her.

"What?!"

"It's the only way," he said. "Or else the self-destruct will take half the city with it. He showed me how." He turned to look at the control panel set before the captain, then turned back to look at her. "You have to make sure that everyone is out of the building. I think it might collapse when I take off."

"Doug, you can't do this," she said.

"I have to," he said. "Do you know what will happen if those things get loose and begin breeding?"

She was silent, contemplating the thought of millions of the creatures overrunning the Earth.

"We don't have much time," he said. "The Epulions could get out at any time."

"Doug, I..." she said, then stepped forward and kissed him on the lips. He returned the kiss, lost in it for a moment.

"Go out the way we came in," he said. "I think the north stairwell is your best bet to get down." It was strange—it still felt like the captain was in his head, and that his thoughts were not all his own. Even his way of speaking to Tanya had changed. Whatever kind of mind meld had happened when he put on the cap, it was still impacting his thoughts. He wondered how long it would last.

She nodded and wiped her eyes.

"I have to warm up the engines," he said, turning towards the control panel. He closed his eyes a moment and thought about what the captain had shown him. There was a particular sequence of buttons to push and knobs to turn.

He pushed a large red button, and they felt a lurch in the ship. He turned back to look at her. "That's the pre-ignition switch. That gives you about sixteen minutes to leave the ship before I begin the ignition sequence. I wish...well, I wish things were different."

"Me too," she said.

"Hurry," he said. "Get the others out if you can but get to safety. If the building collapses, you need to be a few blocks away, if possible."

She nodded again, then turned and left the bridge. He watched her for a moment, then turned and looked at the captain. He needed to get the body out of the chair so he could sit and take control of the ship. He bent and pushed the button that unbuckled the safety belt, and the body slumped down, free now from restraint.

He walked around to the back of the chair and used both hands to push the captain's shoulders and watched dispassionately as the body began to slowly slide out of the chair. He had felt sorry for the captain at first, but the reality was that he had brought these dangerous creatures to Earth because of his own greed.

He sat in the chair, ignoring the blood that had pooled in the bottom. It didn't matter now. All that mattered was getting the ship away from Earth and then destroying it. He hoped that Tanya was able to get out on time, but it was too important that the ship was destroyed. He couldn't wait too long before the ignition sequence needed to begin.

Flashes of the captain's thoughts still popped up in his head as he waited. He understood now that this was the way that the captain and crew spoke to each other while in the spaceship. It was a much more effective form of communication than having the captain bark out orders. The crew could wear the cap everywhere they went and would still be in contact with the bridge.

Suddenly he heard movement behind him—a scuttling noise that could only be one thing. He slowly stood and looked around for something that could be used as a weapon. He heard the sound again and turned to see a quick flash of something moving on the floor to his right. Then he remembered that the captain had a weapon on his belt. He quickly knelt and rolled the captain onto his back.

There it was. He grabbed the handle and pulled it out of the sheath and saw that it was indeed a sharp-looking knife, long and thin and made of some sort of dark metal. It felt good in his hand, and he realized that it wasn't just the fact that it was reassuring to have it, but that it felt comfortable and somehow...right. He realized that it was probably the captain's thoughts again in his head, which was less reassuring.

Just then he caught another glimpse of movement and turned to see an Epulion racing along the floor towards him. He held the knife before him in his right hand and waited for it to get near enough. When it was about two feet from him, it jumped towards him and he slashed at it with the knife, knocking it to the floor, where it began to squirm. He didn't pause to let it recover and brought the knife down at it again and again, stabbing it repeatedly.

Finally, it stopped moving and he rested, sitting back on his feet. His knees were beginning to ache, so he slowly rose to his feet and looked around again for any signs of other aliens. He didn't see anything and thought about trying to close the door to the bridge, when a loud beeping alarm began to sound, and he realized that it meant that pre-ignition had finished, and the ship was ready to go.

He sat back in the captain's chair and closed his eyes; trying to remember the sequence of buttons and knobs he was supposed to use to start the engines of the ship. He slowly remembered now, and almost like slow motion, saw his fingers pressing buttons and flipping switches and turning knobs almost on their own. There were all types of calibrations to be made, and he thought he got everything correct to put the ship in reverse so that it would back out of the building before taking off in a trajectory towards space.

He admitted to himself that he was a little disappointed that there was no type of steering yoke or wheel. All of that was handled by the ship itself once he had laid in the commands to take off from the planet's surface. All he had to do now was sit and wait for it to happen. Then he felt a sharp pain in his neck and realized that one of the creatures had crept up and bit him.

He stood and turned around quickly before realizing that it was still on his neck. He brought up left hand and tried to grab it so he could pull it away and not have to try and stab it while it was still on his neck—he could do more damage to himself than the creature. He felt its slick body and squeezed it as hard as he could in an effort not to lose his grip. The pain was excruciating, and as he pulled the creature away, he saw his own blood spurt out.

In a panic now, he dropped to his knees once more and brought the knife up to stab the Epulion in his other hand. He stabbed it twice in the abdomen, then finally killed it by stabbing it in the face. He felt the knife pierce his hand and screamed in pain. He saw that the creature was bleeding profusely and brought it up so that the blood would fall on his neck. He laid back onto the floor and felt the creature's warm fluids washing over where his neck still blazed in agony.

He felt weak and thought he was close to passing out from loss of blood, when he saw movement again out of the corner of his eye. He didn't think he had the strength to stand, let alone fight another of the creatures. At least the ship should make it out to space, even if he was dead. It would be away from Earth.

That was when he felt a hand on his forehead and opened his eyes. It was Tanya, looking down at him. "Tanya?" he asked, sounding weak as well as stupid in his own ears.

"I'm sorry, Doug, I couldn't leave you," she said. "And I admit, I couldn't find a way off the ship, either." She smiled. He weakly returned it. He was beginning to feel stronger, though he made no attempt to stand.

"The ship...is it moving yet?"

"I think so," she said. "I felt a jarring sensation a few minutes back that might have been it dislodging from the building."

"I hope everyone got out alright," he said.

"Me too," she said. "Now what do we do?"

He closed his eyes and tried to remember how he was supposed to activate the ship's self-destruct sequence. "We have to blow up the ship," he said.

"I was afraid you'd say that," she said. "Good news is that your neck looks like it's healing well. You should be healthy again when we both die in a fiery ball of death."

"That's great," he said, smiling. He opened his eyes and looked at her and saw that she wasn't smiling. He reached up his hand and placed it gently on the side of her face. "I'm sorry, there's really no other way."

"I know," she said. "It's just that...we haven't had much time together. I'm sorry that it took an alien invasion."

He smiled again and began to sit up. A wave of dizziness overtook him, and he laid back again. "How about you come down here," he said. She bent down close to him, and he forced his head to rise far enough for their lips to meet, gently at first, then more passionately, and he put his arm around her and felt her weight on his chest. He knew he should be telling her to watch out for more of the creatures, but he didn't care.

Another alarm went off, and they broke apart. "I think that might be telling us we've left Earth's atmosphere," he said. "Help me get up."

"Are you okay to stand?"

"I guess we'll see," he said. He slowly sat up and felt a little dizzy, but the sensation soon passed, and he nodded. She helped him stand up, and he walked over to the captain's chair once more and sat down heavily. He looked at the flashing light and clicked a switch acknowledging the alarm. He was correct. The ship was now in space, away from the Earth and still moving. "It's time," he said, turning to look at her.

She nodded, though he could see that she was beginning to cry. He closed his eyes again, then opened them to begin the self-destruct sequence. He slowly pushed the buttons, hearing alarms begin to blare in warning of impending doom. He finished the sequence and knew that they only had about ten minutes before the ship exploded.

He closed his eyes. Being a hero sure did suck, he thought. He'd been bitten multiple times as well as stabbed, fell on his head, and now he could add having a broken heart to the list. It wasn't fair. Suddenly one last vision flashed in his mind, and he stood up so fast that another wave of dizziness overcame him for a moment.

"What?" Tanya asked. "What's wrong?"

"Nothing," he said, opening his eyes. "Nothing. Come with me. Hurry!"

He didn't wait to see if she followed but knew she would. He had to move quickly while the vision was still in his mind.

"Doug? What is it?" he heard her ask from behind him as

he ran down the corridor. Where was it? He had a picture of it in his mind. He just had to remember where it was.

They ran down the corridor and then he turned down a corridor to his right and ran a short distance until they came to another double door. He stopped at a panel on the side and punched in a sequence of alien letters and numbers from memory—the memory of a captain who was now dead but had left a final gift in Doug's mind.

"Where are we going?" Tanya asked.

"Home," he said. "We're going home." The doors opened, and they were met with a sight that brought tears to his eyes. It was an escape ship.

"Is that what I think it is?" she asked.

"Yes," he answered before turning and kissing her. "We don't have much time, c'mon."

She nodded and he turned and opened the hatch of the pod. It opened and he stood back to allow her to enter first. She had gone in most of the way when he heard her scream. Just then, he saw movement down the corridor and looked to see several of the creatures running towards them. He turned back to look at Tanya and saw that she wasn't visible in the darkened escape pod. He quickly entered it and shut the hatch to prevent the Epulions from getting in.

He turned and felt his legs lose all strength as he dropped to his knees. In one of the seats was one of the crew members, dead. It looked like it had tried to escape when it knew the ship was overrun but hadn't been quick enough. Some of the creatures had gotten in as well.

Tanya was lying on her back on the floor, her eyes open, but unseeing. One of the creatures was still tearing at her throat. The other was sitting on top of her abdomen, its face buried in a hole it had created there. It sat up and looked at Doug, its head covered in Tanya's blood.

    "No!" Doug screamed but knew he was too late. She was dead. He was too late. He brought out the captain's knife and held it before him but then lowered it. There was no point killing the creatures now. No point in doing anything except sitting and waiting to die. At least he would be taking them all with him, he thought.

The End

The Bear

The bear awoke around dawn. It knew immediately that something was wrong in its environment. Its instincts told its body to prepare for fight or flight. It was not so much a smell or sound—two senses it relied on heavily because of its poor eyesight. It was more a deep feeling in its chest. A feeling of both danger and rage.

It stood slowly, its ears back and a tremor in its muscles in anticipation of running—either towards or away from something, though that something was still vague in its mind.

It stood on its hind legs to better sniff the air. There. Something upwind. Something new. Different. Possibly dangerous. Better to run than to face an opponent it could not overcome with tooth and claw. It dropped to all four paws again and began to run, picking up speed as its body responded to the impetus to run.

It swerved as something large and dark flew overhead—not the source of the peculiar smell. This thing smelled of food, and normally it might stop to open the thing to find the promising food smell, but not today.

The bear felt the growl in its throat as it continued on away from the bad smell, away also from the possible food. Towards another familiar smell as the wind shifted. This also was not a welcome smell, though it was familiar. It topped a rise and saw the intruder standing there on its own hind legs.

The bear paused a moment, then began to charge towards the creature. It wanted, no needed to get away from the other smell and this one was in the way. There was no thinking now, only the rage that this creature would be in its way when it needed to escape.

It ran towards the creature even as it saw the creature turn and run the other way. Too late, now, events were set in motion and nothing would change that. The rage was too great.

The creature reached its large den—one of the confusing dens that smelled like trees but also of so many other unnatural scents as well.

The bear had almost caught up to the creature, but then it was gone and the bear's rage was now at its peak with his frustration.

Then the other smell was all around it. It had not run away fast enough. Had not escaped the smell of unnatural decay. The rage that had begun to dissipate with the other creature now out of sight turned to fear for its own survival.

There were two of them, each with that smell of rot, sickness, blood. Death.

The bear felt the claw-like appendages rake its body. Felt its own claws do the same. It swung its head about, biting deep into the rot. The stench made it want to run again; to flee the abominations. But it was trapped now and losing strength as its blood flowed freely.

Its eyes began to dim even as it felt the two beginning to take chunks out of its own skin with their teeth.

◊

The bear awoke, confused and angry. Its senses seemed to have stopped working right, and it couldn't see well with only one eye left in its head. It stood on shaky legs and felt the hunger pangs deep inside. There was nothing else but hunger now. It turned around to inspect its environment, then charged off in a promising direction. One that smelled of the familiar others that meant food.

The End

Other Works by Brian S. Converse

The Rajani Chronicles I: Stone Soldiers

The Rajani Chronicles II: Resistance

The Rajani Chronicles III: War

The Rajani War I: Outsiders *(coming soon!)*

The Island of Despair *(poetry collection)*

Updates on

www.BrianSConverse.com

www.ingramcontent.com/pod-product-compliance
Lightning Source LLC
Chambersburg PA
CBHW030019200726
48283CB00012B/683